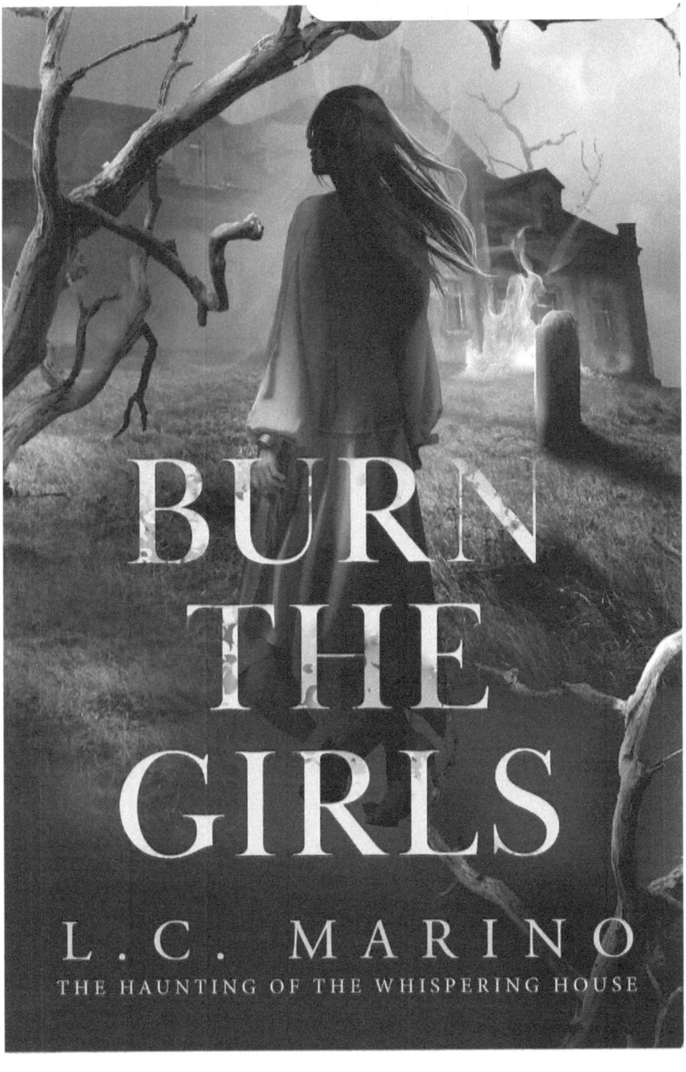

BURN THE GIRLS

L.C. MARINO

THE HAUNTING OF THE WHISPERING HOUSE

BURN THE GIRLS

L.C. MARINO

Paperback ISBN: 978-1-960535-10-8
Hardcover ISBN: 978-1-960535-09-2
eBook ISBN: 978-1-960535-11-5

CONTENTS

DEDICATION

This book is dedicated to my children, Caleb, Gabriel, and Madelyn. I love you beyond comprehension.

PROLOGUE

OCTOBER 3RD, 1966

Dingy incandescent beams radiated from the kitchen table light into Wade Jones's sleep-deprived eyes. Just two months ago, he'd been a proud husband and father. Then, within only weeks of each other, he'd lost both his daughter, Adeline, and his wife, Lydia. Now, Wade was a widower, and a bereaved parent.

The sturdy oak kitchen table that used to be the gathering place for his small family instead supported piles of paper and several partially drained coffee mugs. He sat at the head of the table, reading and signing the closing documents presented to him by the broker sitting to his right.

Delilah, Lydia's cousin, sat opposite him. Wade watched her fidget with a pen in anticipation, her constant movement in concert with the unsettled nerves in his gut. She buzzed with repressed relief while he fought to contain his anxious motor.

Lydia had spent her life loving Delilah more like a sister than a cousin. They'd been inseparable in their youth. Their love had endured their adult years as they started new families and raised children. Now Lydia was gone. This godforsaken house in rural southeastern Virginia was her last refuge. The cemetery beyond the trees in the backyard had become her eternal resting place.

Delilah broke the silence. "We really appreciate this, Wade. I know selling the house must be difficult for you, considering ... well, everything." She cleared her throat. "I guess what I'm trying to say is that this place is special to our family, and we're grateful. It's been in our family for generations. The circumstances are anything but desirable, but it's my honor to carry on our legacy."

Wade scrawled his last signature, slid the pages to the broker, and set the pen down beside his mug without lifting his eyes to meet Delilah's. He lacked the energy to respond meaningfully. Wade had always liked Delilah. Anyone who'd meant so much to Lydia held his respect. Her ex-husband, on the other hand, was a grade-A loser in Wade's opinion. Any man who chose drinking and flirting with bar trash over a life with his wife and daughters didn't deserve such precious gifts. He'd left Delilah and her girls with a mortgage they couldn't afford. The opportunity to help them by turning their family home over to them, brought some light to Wade's own horrible family circumstances. He wanted out of this place and Delilah's family needed a new home.

Wade felt Delilah gently blanket his left hand with hers. She leaned forward, pulling his eyes up to hers.

"Thank you, Wade."

He mustered a slight smile. His lips quivered as he repressed his nervous energy. "I'm grateful for your willingness to take the house. Lydia would have loved to help you and the girls in this way." Wade looked down at the table. "I just can't be here any longer."

Wade turned his gaze beyond the screen door to the backyard. Just past the trees, Adeline and Lydia's graves called to him.

Wade washed the last of the coffee mugs in the kitchen sink, the almost-scalding hot water turning his hands into vibrant red bundles of needles. He hardly noticed, consumed by staring out the window above the sink while he worked, his darting eyes scanning the yard.

Delilah and the closing agent had left soon after signing the papers and completing the sale, leaving Wade alone in the house once again. Weeks prior, Delilah and Wade had negotiated a quick turnover to benefit both parties. He'd spent the past few days packing and moving his things to his new place, fifteen miles away in West Point. Tomorrow morning, he would load his few remaining items into his truck and leave this house for good.

Wade would settle in a small rancher on the edge of West Point. The house was a bit run-down, but it was only five minutes from his work at the paper mill and what remained of his childhood home and family in Urbanna.

He didn't feel great about any of this. He and Lydia had intended to make this their lifelong home. They'd planned to raise Adeline here, then pass the house down to her when they aged out of the place or passed. It's what Lydia's family had done for generations. Those plans died first with Adeline, and then Lydia's passing only weeks later. Now, Wade was alone in a house he had no right to occupy without them. And things were not as they should be.

He turned the water off and dried the last mug with an already-damp dishtowel. His eyes fixed on the empty yard as he worked, his breath shallow and his ears scanning for any sounds in the house beyond the kitchen.

Wade set the mug top-down on a dry towel on the counter and moved from the kitchen to the stairs, hesitating to turn out the kitchen light until the last second.

He paused before climbing.

Head down, listening, he closed his eyes and cleared his mind. Everything that had happened in the house—*everything terrible*—had happened upstairs. A short internal pep talk got him moving again.

One step, then the next, Wade ascended the stairs. With each step, his pulse increased, flushing his body with nervous heat. He kept a steady pace as he climbed, each stair groaning under his weight.

Wade felt someone behind him, right *against* him. He snapped his head around and, as expected, he saw muddy footprints where each of his footfalls had been. It was obvious those footprints were not his, his clean socks leaving no trace of his path in their wake.

Just get to the bedroom, he thought.

As Wade crested the stairs, he picked up his pace, rushing down the hall to the primary bedroom. He kept his eyes locked on the room ahead, refusing to look back.

Breaching the bedroom, Wade swung the door shut behind him, and climbed into the bed. He exhaled into the dark void of the room as he reached for the small lamp on the bedside table and rolled the switch with his fingers.

Its light was sudden and harsh but gave Wade the relief from the dark that he needed. He rolled onto his right side, facing away from the window and the lamp.

Wade closed his eyes and willed his heart rate to slow. *Just one last night. Please let me rest, girls.*

Behind the closed door separating the bedroom from the hall, sounds of footsteps and running water in the hall kept Wade's heart rate captive and elevated.

Please.

A narrow band of pinkish-yellow light interrupted the darkness at the bottom edge of the door, the hall beyond the door awash in color.

Please.

Door hinges sighed in the hall. Water met water in the tub as the pipes in the walls groaned.

Please!

In the yard beyond the window, Wade heard the tree-tops bristling and wild in a sudden gust of wind. The eaves whistled and the roof creaked in the changing pressure.

Lydia's voice slipped through the colliding thoughts in Wade's mind. "Thank you, Wade."

Somehow, he knew Lydia was happy with Delilah and the girls taking the home. He'd honored her family's tradition and Lydia knew, even in death.

"Be good to them," Wade said. "I don't know what else to do, but I know I can't do this anymore." A wellspring of despair rose in him, and his mind drifted to his lost daughter.

He willed Adeline to speak to him, but she never did. He felt her about the house, saw the things she did, but never heard her.

"Adeline, baby, would you talk to me tonight? Daddy misses you so much." Tears poured from his eyes to the pillow on one side of his face, puddling in the nook of his nose on the other.

"I miss you so much, baby," he sobbed. He felt the pull of her grave in the cemetery behind the home. It was an undeniable force, so great it consumed his thoughts day and night. He clung to this land of the living, but he wasn't sure how much longer he could hold on.

If he loosened his grip, he'd suffer the same fate as Lydia.

His dead wife's voice came to him again. "Thank you, Wade."

The world went quiet. The yard and the house stood in an unblemished, deafening silence.

Wade wept until sleep immersed him in a dreamscape of Adeline's brightness and love.

CHAPTER ONE

NOVEMBER 1ST, 1966

Constance stood in the backyard, the fall sun warming the exposed skin of her face and hands. She was tired most afternoons around this time, but that day she felt a bit more sluggish than usual, her post-Halloween fog in full effect. Keeping up with her twelve-year-old sister, Abigail, during the previous night's Halloween trek through Aunt Jenny's neighborhood had taken more out of her than it should have. She knew her age was the furthest thing from the root cause of her exhaustion, but it felt like the adult thing to think. That, and the lie, was sometimes easier to believe than the truth.

Frankly, she hadn't slept well since they'd arrived at their new home several weeks prior. Her mother, Delilah, seemed energized by the fresh start, and Abigail appeared happier than ever. That all checked out to Constance.

She never could find motivation or happiness in the same places as her surrounding family.

Her new school was the worst. She'd spent her childhood and teen years building a small but tight group of friends in her neighborhood and schools. Now, entering her senior year, her mother had ripped her from that familiar place and dropped her into a run-down school of backcountry degenerates.

She was restless and itching to finish high school in the late spring and move on with her life. She wasn't sure she'd survive living on the outskirts of the county until then. Constance longed to be in the city, to fall in with the pulse of the urban shuffle. Here, she found nothing but seasonal allergies, her sister's unbound imagination, and her mother's droning infatuation with honoring a "family legacy."

Speak of the devil.

"Constance, where's your sister? I asked you girls to meet me here at 4 p.m. sharp and I don't see her anywhere in the house."

Constance released a heavy sigh. "How should I know? She's probably playing teatime with her imaginary friend somewhere. You need to find her some real friends; the girl is weird."

Delilah shot her a disapproving look under furrowed brows. "You know I don't like you talking about your sister that way. She looks up to you, you know? It would devastate her to hear you say that."

Constance rolled her eyes, crossed her arms, and kicked her hip out in true teen fashion. She wasn't interested in being lectured. She just wanted to get this trip to the cemetery over with and move on with life. With or without her sister.

Out of the corner of her eye, Constance saw movement where the trees met the yard. The borderland between the shadow of the trees and the brightness of the sunlit yard hid the young girl hiding behind the great maple.

Delilah had turned back into the house, calling Abigail's name with next-level urgency. Her voice carried through the diminishing opening of the door swinging closed behind her.

Sneaky little thing, Constance thought. Abigail must have snuck around the shed and into the woods while she was daydreaming in the sun. Constance turned away from the trees as if she didn't notice the younger girl crouching just inside the tree line.

The back door opened with a bang as Abigail exploded from the house in a gaggle of awkward limbs and shrill cackles. Apparently, she'd gotten one over on Mom and slipped by her.

If she was in the house, who was ...? Constance spun around toward the trees. The trees stood alone, with no young company in their rank and file. *That can't be. Geez, am I that tired?*

Abigail crossed the yard in a flash, quick for such an underdeveloped twerp. She was nothing but skin and bones, but she looked just like their dad, with brilliant blue eyes and chestnut hair. However, despite the complete awkwardness that only preadolescent girls possess, Abigail was beautiful. She simply needed a few years for her body to catch up to her face.

Delilah stormed through the back door with frustration and humor wrestling for real estate on her face. Constance loved watching her squirm under the conflicting emotions the girls evoked. Keeping their mom on her toes brought a twisted joy to Constance and Abigail.

"Can we get this over with?" Constance asked. "I want a nap."

Delilah huffed, "You and me both, kid. But we have more important things to tend to before sunset, so I don't see that happening."

They entered the cemetery in silence. Constance followed a few yards behind Abigail, who sped up and slowed down along the path with maddening frequency. Constance saw the narrow path open to a circular clearing amongst the towering trees. A dozen tombstones organized in three neat rows greeted her. Most markers appeared different from the next, a clear indication of the passage of time between burials. In contrast, she noted two identical headstones closest to the path's opening. She read the names and acknowledged the plots of her aunt Lydia and cousin Adeline, who was only nine years old when she passed earlier that summer. Constance had refused to attend Adeline's service despite Delilah's insistence. She just couldn't stomach burying a child. Her hesitation built when Aunt Lydia died only two weeks later. It'd been all too much for Constance to handle and being here revived that feeling.

Strolling in the cool, damp air hovering over the graves of her dead relatives, Constance focused on being present and aware. Something felt odd about the place, and it had nothing to do with her feelings for her aunt and cousin, the burial sites, and moldering headstones. She couldn't explain it, but it felt like fate and circumstance and an unfinished story haunted this place.

"Mom, why did you bring us here?" Constance asked, breaking the extended silence. "I understand you miss your family and all, but this place gives me the creeps."

"No, it doesn't," Abigail said. "This place is cool! And we'll end up here one day, so show some respect."

"I'm sorry to interrupt your busy life, Constance," Delilah said. "But it's important that we come here and learn about our family's rich legacy. This place matters."

Constance rolled her eyes. "Don't get wound up, Mom. We don't have a 'rich legacy.' We have a family like everyone else. There's nothing special about us. If there was, Dad wouldn't have left us."

She regretted the words the moment they left her mouth. She watched her wounded mother's eyes drop to her shoes before she lifted her face to her inconsiderate daughter.

"That was uncalled for, Constance. And your father left because *he* wasn't special. He wasn't smart enough to know how good *he* had it with the three of us. *You* included."

Constance dropped her eyes. Anger and embarrassment burned hot in her throat. *Touché, Mom.*

"Daddy *is* special," Abigail added. "And so are you two. Stop arguing. We don't want to upset the residents."

Constance moved past the moment, though she still felt the embarrassment coursing through her.

"Thank you, Abi," Delilah said. "I appreciate your affection for your father, and I'm sorry I said that. Now, let's talk about why we're here. Ladies, allow me to introduce you to my dearest cousin, Lydia."

Constance watched Delilah's hand dance across the top of the cleanest tombstone in the lot. Her fingers lowered and traced the letters of Lydia's name as they passed across the face of the stone.

LYDIA JONES

BORN APRIL 3, 1928

DIED AUGUST 18, 1966

BELOVED WIFE AND MOTHER

Abigail shot Constance a funny look as if to say, *what is she doing?*

Delilah spoke again, "You girls know how close Lydia and I were growing up. We lost touch for a bit when your dad moved us away for a few years. But it didn't matter. Regardless of how much time passed between us, when we saw each other, we picked right back up like we'd been together the day before. She was ... special ..." Her words trailed off.

Constance respected her mother's wishes to be here, to reminisce about her closest family member. But she couldn't shake the uneasiness within.

Delilah picked back up. "I sat straight up from my sleep the night she died, heart pounding, knowing something was wrong. I just didn't know what. Later that morning, I got the call that Wade had found her."

Constance saw the stern look on her mother's face and knew that asking to leave wasn't an option.

"What about Adeline?" Abigail asked.

Delilah bowed her head and shook it. "Her death was an utter tragedy. None of us could have seen it coming. A healthy young girl like that, dying of a seizure after nine years without a single serious medical ailment. Well, we were all surprised. No one took it harder than Lydia. That woman loved that girl more than life itself."

Her mother placed her hand on Adeline's tombstone. Constance read the inscription on the stone face below her hand.

ADELINE JONES
BORN MAY 10, 1957
DIED AUGUST 8, 1966
OUR DAUGHTER, OUR ANGEL

Constance felt more anxious. A jittery energy sent slight tremors across her abdomen. She wasn't cold, but hearing about Adeline's death pushed a shiver through her.

"I moved us here because I want you both to have a safe, welcoming home. Your father left us with nothing. This house is a blessing, and we are damn lucky Wade offered it to us. I can't imagine what that man is going through. And I wouldn't wish his loss on my worst enemy. But now, we have an opportunity that's too good to be true. We have a home that's been in my family for generations and a mortgage that is criminally low by any stretch of the imagination. We need to take this opportunity to recognize the blessings around us."

Constance felt Delilah's eyes on her. She looked up and confirmed as much. Her mother was talking to both girls, but she was directing her message to Constance.

"This house is ours and one day, it will be yours. One day, I'll be gone, and you'll carry on the family's legacy here."

Constance felt a warmth rise from her chest and fill her neck and face. Staying here was the last thing she wanted. She had plans to build a life in a place with far more promise than any small-town home with its own cemetery could ever offer. What kind of legacy did her mother think she was building here? Living for the dead was no way to build a legacy. It was more akin to dying alongside the people you worshipped.

She wanted out. She wanted a career of her own. Constance wasn't even sure she'd ever have kids or a family. She was meant for more than that.

Constance looked past her mother to Abigail, who kneeled in the grass before Adeline's tombstone. The scene, although innocent, bothered Constance. One girl sat before the headstone of the other, six feet above her in the land of the living, the sun, and the wind. Constance felt a swell of anxiety as she watched Abigail's lips emit little whispers of an imagination running wild. Constance wasn't sure why she found this all so troubling, but she couldn't stay there any longer.

"I'm heading back to the house," Constance said to Delilah. "I'll see you there." Then she turned and hurried down the path to the house as the wind whipped the trees into a dance around her.

CHAPTER TWO

T he girls spent the rest of the afternoon and early evening in the throes of normalcy. Like every other weeknight, Constance set the dinner table while Delilah prepared the meal and Abigail pretended to complete her homework in her bedroom. Constance could hear Abigail giggling and singing in her room, evidence of the younger girl's lack of focus and productivity.

While Constance feigned dislike before setting the table, a small part of her reveled in the organization and accomplishment. Every plate, fork, knife, napkin, and drinking glass had its place. Each setting appeared identical to the next. From empty to set in minutes, completing another task felt like a minor achievement to put behind her before moving to the next.

This behavior ran counter to what Constance observed of Abigail. Upstairs, the girl hid away, avoiding any genuine achievement or accountability. Each night, she'd sit on her bed with her textbooks, pencils, and her notebook splayed before her. However, the pages of the notebook contained doodles and scribbles of imaginary scenes rather than cursive writing or expanding equations. Constance would never confuse herself with the class Valedictorian, but she always completed assignments, academic or otherwise. She focused, she progressed. Abigail chose distractions over requirements.

She was likely talking with some imaginary friend. That's what it sounded like to Constance, the muffled discourse of a one-sided conversation between Abigail and whoever she invented in the moment.

"Connie, would you call your sister down for dinner?" Delilah asked, stirring the pot of macaroni and cheese.

Constance *hated* that nickname. "Got it." She dropped the last cloth napkin on the table and walked briskly to the stairs. "Abigail! Dinner!"

Behind her bedroom door at the top of the stairs, Constance heard Abigail engaged in an animated exchange.

Constance rolled her eyes, pitying her simple sister. She couldn't figure out how a twelve-year-old could still have such an active imagination.

Delilah yelled from the kitchen, "Abigail! Let's go!"

"I heard you! I'm coming!" Abigail replied, irritated.

Constance burned inside. She hated when her mother jumped into her tasks. Why ask her to do something if she was just going to do it herself, anyway? Delilah didn't even give her a chance to finish the job.

"I've got this, Mom!" Constance said. "I can handle getting her to come down. Give me a chance. Jeez."

Delilah shot her a stern look over her shoulder, hands busy over-mixing the macaroni and cheese. "Excuse me, ma'am. Want to watch your tone with me?"

Constance raised her hands to signal her confusion. "Well, I'm not incapable. I'm eighteen. How would you feel if you had another adult up your butt every time they asked you to do something?"

"Another adult? I'm still your mother, kid. And I am most definitely *not* up your butt."

A moment of silence while they stared at each other. Delilah stuck her tongue out at Constance. They both laughed, letting the tension out of the room.

Abigail's door flew open. She came bounding down the stairs, her footfalls unreasonably heavy for such a scrawny girl. She sounded like an elephant running down the stairs with bass drums strapped to its feet.

Constance asked her, "Who the heck are you talking to up there? Aren't you a little old for imaginary friends?"

"Wouldn't you like to know?"

"Um, yeah. That's kind of the point of asking questions, dufus," Constance said.

Delilah chimed in as she walked to the table, a steaming plate of food in her hands. "Grab your plates, girls. We can talk about these wild mysteries while we eat."

After dinner, Constance washed dishes while Abigail cleared the table. As she worked, Constance ran through the list of tasks remaining for the night. She and her mother planned to unpack boxes from their move. They were down to a few stacks of boxes in the sitting room containing knickknacks, small decorations, and books for their makeshift library. They could finish the task tonight if she could keep her mom from telling a story about every item they unpacked. While Constance admired her mother's affection for the past, she couldn't stand hearing another pointless story about a family member she'd most likely never met.

Constance glanced up to see her mom sitting at the kitchen table, sipping hot Irish Breakfast and Bengal Spice tea from an old ceramic mug she'd dragged from kitchen to kitchen for the past twenty years. Across the ten feet between them, Constance noticed the last tendrils of soothing spice and leaf waft from the dark brew in a wave of misty comfort. She ached inside for a tea of her own but drinking caffeine at night never ended well for her.

"I'm down to the last few dishes, Mama. You should get a head start on the boxes in the sitting room. I'll be there in a few minutes."

Constance saw Delilah nod her head in agreement. She downed the last of her tea and handed the mug to Abigail before slowly rising from her chair. Constance noticed her mother's age check her speed more and more these days.

"Abigail, wash up and get ready for bed when you're done clearing the table. Your sister and I will come up in a little while."

Abigail responded in a sweet tone, "Okay, Mama."

Constance rinsed the last plate, then pulled the stopper from the sink. The tepid mixture of soapy water and dinner particles wound its way down the drain in a murky spiral.

She tossed a drying towel to Abigail and the two worked together to dry and place the washed dishes, glasses, and silverware in the cabinet above the counter.

Abigail spoke up, "So, you think you'll get through a complete box without hearing a tale of mischief and mayhem from the past?"

Constance smirked. "I'm determined to distract her with one item while I unpack the rest. That's my strategy. Hopefully, we don't run across anything of Aunt Lydia's. She got pretty upset last time that happened."

"I can understand that." Abigail reached up and placed a cup in the cabinet.

Without a word, Abigail spun around, tossed her hand towel over Constance's shoulder, and scurried to the stairs, giggling. Constance sighed. "You rotten kid! Get up there before I snatch you up!"

Abigail disappeared up the stairs in a flash. Then, the sound of the bathroom door opening in the upstairs hall followed by the splash of water running into the tub. The door shut, choking the sound of the water. Constance heard Abigail singing the theme song to *The Monkees* television show. The show was new to television that September and Abigail couldn't get enough of it.

Constance ran the dishtowels into the holders fastened to the cabinet face below the sink. She fanned them out, exposing as much of the cloth as possible to speed their drying. She turned to exit the kitchen when something caught her attention in the sink window.

Someone was walking across the backyard.

Constance froze for a second, then centered herself in front of the window. She looked left to right but saw no one.

That's so strange. I know I saw someone.

She walked across the kitchen to the back door. Again, she panned left to right but saw no one. She opened the door and walked onto the porch. The screens wrapping the rectangular porch obscured the view in the twilight.

"Hello?" Her voice went out, but no answer came back.

"I'm right here."

Constance spun around, her heart jumping into her throat. Delilah stood in the back door's opening, a curious look on her face.

"Jesus, Mom!"

Delilah replied with genuine dismay, "What? Who else did you expect to see?"

Constance let out a tight breath, allowing her entire body to relax. "I thought I saw someone out here. I didn't think it was you. You scared me."

"Well, who is it?" Delilah asked, looking beyond Constance to the yard.

"No one," Constance replied. "Let's tackle the boxes."

Constance entered the sitting room first, pulling the top box from the stack beside the fireplace.

She kneeled on the floor, the box set before her. As she worked the top open, she saw Delilah reach between two short stacks on the opposite side of the mantle. She drew out a single, shallow rectangular box. Propping it on top of the stack, Delilah opened one tucked cardboard end and tipped the container upside down, allowing gravity to pull a framed photo from within.

Constance stopped working for a moment and looked up.

Delilah stood eye-to-eye with a striking portrait of Lydia and Adeline. In the portrait, Lydia's skin looked as flawless and delicate as porcelain, her eyes a brilliant blue. She wore her hair down, chocolate curls spilling over the shoulders of her sleeveless wool dress. Seated beside Lydia, hands folded in her lap, was Adeline. Like her mother, she possessed the same striking beauty, a youthful charm that had yet to fully blossom.

Constance felt everything slow as her vision narrowed. The downstairs became silent. She could no longer hear the constant tick-tock of the fireplace mantle clock or Abigail singing in the upstairs bathroom. She closed her eyes to steady herself.

What's happening?

Delilah's voice broke the silence. "Hello, Cousin Lydia. Hello, sweet Adeline." Her voice cracked, filled with emotion.

The mantle clock's mechanical rhythm thrummed in Constance's ear, and Abigail's muffled rendition rang through the house once again. Constance eased her eyes open to the room.

Delilah flashed a proud smile tugging at the corners of her mouth at the sight of the portrait. "Lydia and Adeline stood for everything beautiful in this life. Eternal love and enduring loyalty were their greatest gift. Lydia left this world willingly and tragically, for the indomitable love between a mother and her child."

Delilah lifted the portrait with reverence and placed it at the center of the mantle. She took a few steps back to get a better view.

Warmth drained from Constance's limbs. It felt like someone had pulled a plug from her body and drained the blood from her. She looked up at the portrait on the mantle. Lydia and Adeline stared back at her, their eyes vibrant behind the layer of thin glass protecting the photo from the elements.

Constance pulled herself together and stood up, leaving the box at her feet. "I don't know, Mom. Are you sure this is the right place for it? It's kinda weird having a portrait of my dead aunt and cousin on the fireplace mantle."

Regretting her words, she scrambled to rectify the situation before her mother became incensed. "What I mean is, maybe it would be better to put their portrait somewhere more private. Maybe your room. Maybe it would be better to store it, so it doesn't get damaged. I just don't know how to feel about it."

"Well, it means a lot to me to see them. We'll leave it here on the mantle for now. I'm sure you won't even notice it in a few days." A note of sarcasm sounded in Delilah's voice.

"Whatever you want, Mom." Constance leaned down, picked up the box at her feet, and turned. "I'm bringing this box upstairs. It's just a bunch of my loose things, anyway."

She rushed out of the room, turned the corner, and met the base of the stairs. She pivoted on one foot, lifting the other to the first step. As she did, her back foot broke loose from the floor as if skating across a sheet of ice. She crashed to the hardwood floor, her head smacking the planks. Her vision burst into starlight; her arms went slack. The box in her hands slammed to the floor beside her. The top ruptured and its contents scattered across the floor.

"Constance!" Delilah yelled from the sitting room.

Constance felt her at her side in what felt like a split second.

"What happened? How did you fall?"

Constance lay still, going through a checklist in her head.

Breathing. Check.

Seeing. Check.

Legs move. Check.

Squinting in pain, she sat up, bringing her left hand to the back of her head to check for blood. She looked at her hand—no blood.

Damn, that was a hell of a fall.

She propped her arm behind her like a kickstand and scanned the scene for the culprit. She had stepped on something slick. But, what?

Beside her on the floor was a single wet footprint. Her eyes were wide in disbelief. Her foot hadn't been wet, and Abigail was still in the tub upstairs. None of this made sense.

She saw another print. And another. A trail of wet footprints led from the stair landing, through the kitchenette, to the back door.

CHAPTER THREE

Constance stood before the mirror in the steamy bathroom, one hand parting her hair, the other cautiously probing the bump on the back of her head. She'd finished her bath and stopped to check her injury one last time before going to bed. It was unbelievable to her how hard she had fallen. Constance inspected her probing fingers for blood, but they were clean. She fumed inside about the entire ordeal.

After her fall, she'd stormed upstairs to the bathroom to confront Abigail. The girl must have come downstairs unnoticed, soaking wet from her bath. Why? Constance didn't know, but there was no other logical explanation for the wet footprints on the floor and stairs. The evidence was damning. The prints started at the bathroom door and were the size of Abigail's feet. As she'd expected, Abigail had denied everything.

However, one fact puzzled Constance. The prints only went one way, from the bathroom, down the stairs, and to the back door. They never tracked back to the bathroom.

"Whatever. I just need to get some sleep," she muttered to herself as she flipped the bathroom light off and exited.

As she left the bathroom, she entered the small landing at the top of the stairs. Abigail's closed bedroom door stood across from her. The hall was dark but the light escaping from under and around the doorjamb implied that Abigail was still awake. Constance gave a half-hearted knock as she opened the door and began talking.

"Hey, I'm going to bed. Mama is already in her room for …"

Constance went silent as she witnessed Abigail lying in bed, eyes closed, a copy of *A Wrinkle in Time* gripped in one curled hand. Her mouth hung agape, her chest rising and falling with each shallow breath. Constance exhaled, a little jealous that her sister was already asleep. Smiling, she removed the book from her sister's hand and placed it on the nightstand.

She looked around the small, organized room, admiring the progress Abigail had made over the past few weeks. She'd wasted no time unpacking and placing her things once they'd arrived. In the far corner sat the old oak dresser Constance had handed down to Abigail, its top adorned with small ceramic figurines of angels, a jewelry box, and a meager collection of paperback books. The jewelry box's lid stood open, a ballerina posed, waiting for the next cycle of the lid to dance. Next to the dresser sat a white wicker basket overflowing with stuffed animals stacked one upon the other.

As Constance reached with her left hand to close Abigail's closet door, she noticed several dresses, shirts, and light jackets hanging from metal wire hangers. The small clothes reminded her of Abigail's youth. Constance's heart warmed and her mood toward her sister calmed. She was stern and abrasive when she had confronted her about the footprints. Now, seeing the articles of youth around her and Abigail's sweet, resting face, she felt guilty for being so reactive.

Constance closed the closet door, walked to the night-stand, and turned out the lamp, casting the pink room into total darkness.

Lying in her own bed, Constance couldn't get comfortable. Normally, she slept on her back but that wasn't happening tonight thanks to the painful bump on the back of her head. She rolled onto her left side, huffed in frustration, and tried to still her thoughts.

Her mind bounced from the weird conversation with her mom in the sitting room to the argument with Abigail over the wet footprints.

She suddenly remembered seeing someone in the backyard as she'd finished the dishes.

No one was there. You looked, remember? Your mom didn't see anyone either. You're upset about your fall. Stop the madness or you'll never get to sleep.

Constance felt the weight of the day in every joint and muscle. Her tired body pulled her mind under, silencing the rambling queries fighting for her attention. Her breathing deepened and slowed, the darkness of her room lost its edges, and she drifted into a shallow sleep.

Constance walked across the backyard. The dew coating the grass dampened her cold feet. Crisp fall air seeped through her nightgown, kissing her skin. She looked up to the clear night sky and stared in wonder at the largest, most brilliant moon she'd ever seen. It filled the entire sky between the treetops and made everything feel miniscule, especially Constance.

As she dropped her eyes, she realized she'd traversed the entire yard and most of the narrow path between her home and the family cemetery. She shouldn't have traveled so far in such little time. How had she covered so much ground so quickly?

The path before Constance opened to the cemetery. Head-stones of her deceased relatives glowed like dim bulbs under the bright moon. The place felt surreal, the trees swaying in rhythm to a song she couldn't hear. She realized she was standing still, feet sinking into recently dug soil.

Constance panicked as she looked down, realizing that the sodden Virginia clay of a newly buried plot embedded her feet up to the ankles. She looked for a headstone but found nothing but grass between this plot and the next row of tombstones.

She tried to free her feet from the soil and her vision left her. Memories from the day flooded her mind. Constance saw her mother in the sitting room, staring with pride at the portrait of Aunt Lydia and her cousin, Adeline. She felt the fall, the crash of her head on the floor, and the impact of the box rupturing on the floor beside her. She stood in the bathroom mirror, mouth hanging open, hands covered in blood. Then she wandered into Abigail's room, ripping clothes from the hangers and dashing precious figurines against plaster walls while Abigail slept undisturbed.

She grabbed her head with both hands. Panicked breathing flooded her head with oxygenated blood and drove tiny needles into her lips, fingers, and feet.

Wake up, WAKE UP!

She opened her eyes to the clay. She crouched over the plot, hands pulling the earth away beneath her. Constance dug with purpose. She had to get to her. She had to save her.

Save who? Who is buried here?

Constance blinked and the steep walls of the grave surrounded her. How long had she been digging? Mud coated her arms and legs. Her hands cycled through the soil. She noticed another set of hands between hers. Then another. She looked around and saw no one.

She felt her fingernails breaking free from their beds, tossed aside with fists full of soil. The hands, both hers and those of her invisible helpers, crashed into the lid of a casket, flinging the remaining layer of dirt and rock from the surface. A dingy silver panel emerged—no doubt the upper half of an adult casket.

Constance stopped digging and sat back on her heels. She panted for air and looked up, the grave's opening hardly visible above her. She was deep in the earth, far deeper than any conventional grave. The moon sat between the high walls above her, casting all its light down in a single beam.

She looked at the casket lid beneath her and knew what to do. She fumbled around the left edge of the lid, found ample purchase to lift, and did so.

The lid crept open, hinges resisting as dirt ground into their surfaces. She pushed harder, twisting her body to prop the lid open. She paused, afraid to discover whose eternal slumber she'd disturbed.

Constance drew a deep breath, released it through a chattering jaw, and looked her mother in the face.

CHAPTER FOUR

C onstance sat on the edge of her bed, holding her head in both hands. Eyes down, she watched the early morning sun's rays illuminate the bedding crumpled around her.

That was the worst night of sleep I've ever had.

She suspected her head injury was the prime culprit with the odd events of the day as a supporting cast. Images from her dream spun in the soup of her morning thoughts.

That dream was vivid and disturbing.

Constance ran through the dream in her head. The walk to the cemetery, the moon dominating the sky, the mud and grime—finding her mother in the casket. She felt her stomach roll as bile pressed upward from her gut.

Shaking the disturbing image from her mind, Constance rose to her feet and stretched, pressing her hands toward the ceiling. The bump on her head throbbed with her heartbeat. She dropped her arms and went to her closet. She chose a pair of bell-bottom pants and a chiffon blouse and changed her clothes in silence at the foot of her bed.

Constance suspected the day ahead would be another rough one. Not only did she feel like a hammered nail, but she also dreaded school. She considered most of the students and teachers useless. Graduation couldn't come soon enough. The next seven months were bound to kill her.

She missed the life she'd built in her previous school at the other end of the county. She'd spent her whole life in that school system and although she never fit in with the popular kids, she'd established a few friendships and tolerated most of her teachers. Now, each day was fraught with ignorant kids who'd grown up together in incestuous cliques. In her mind, they considered her an unwelcome outsider. She accepted the label with pride. She planned to leave their ignorant little world the moment she could.

Constance tossed her bedclothes in the hamper in the corner of her room and headed downstairs.

As she entered the kitchen, Constance saw her mother standing at the counter pouring a bowl of cereal. She looked like Constance felt—unrested.

"Good morning," Abigail said from the kitchen table.

Constance shot her a blank look and refrained from responding. She went to the refrigerator and grabbed the orange juice from the top shelf. The cold bottle chilled her hand. Constance then retrieved the box of cereal from the counter next to her mother and ambled to the kitchen table where a bowl, glass, and spoon awaited. She plopped into her chair, poured her orange juice into the short glass, and realized she'd forgotten to grab the milk for her cereal.

"Can you bring the milk with you?" Constance asked her mother.

Delilah didn't respond. Constance looked across the kitchen. Her mother stood at the counter, eyes focused on the bowl of dry cereal sitting on the counter.

"Mom. Earth to Mom."

"What?" her mother said, a sharp edge in her voice.

"Can you bring the milk to the table with you?"

"Sure." Delilah yawned.

Constance watched her shuffle to the table, pull up her chair, and set her bowl on the table. As she took her seat, Constance noticed she hadn't brought the milk.

"Mom, you forgot the milk." Constance huffed and pushed her chair away from the table. She stood and crossed the kitchen, the bottle of orange juice in hand. She opened the fridge and exchanged the orange juice for an open carton of milk. Constance walked back to her seat and set the milk on the table in front of her mother. Her head pounded like a drum.

"Thanks," Delilah said as she picked up the milk and soaked her cereal.

"Leave some for me," Constance said.

"I'm not taking all the milk, Constance. Sounds like you didn't sleep well either."

Constance scoffed. "You could say that. I couldn't fall asleep and once I did, I had a crazy dream."

Abigail scooped a spoonful of multi-colored cereal from her bowl. "Tempers, ladies."

Constance sent a clear warning with her eyes. *Today is not the day to play peacekeeper, kid.*

Her head throbbed as her blood pressure climbed. She poured cereal into her bowl, then emptied the milk into the mix. Her frustration stoked as she looked for any sign of the milk level through her cereal.

She slammed the empty carton down in frustration. Out of the corner of her eye, she saw her mother look up with disapproval. Constance just wanted to eat and move on with her inevitably terrible day.

They ate without speaking. The sounds of mouths crunching cereal and sipping glasses between bites filled the quiet room.

Constance finished her cereal first and crossed the kitchen to wash her bowl and drinking glass.

"You girls don't miss the bus," Delilah said. "I can't drive you to school today. I have an appointment in town this morning."

"Why would I miss the bus?" Constance looked at her mother, who turned in her chair to face her.

"I don't know, Connie. I'm just saying I can't help you today."

"Well, it's a good thing I don't need your help. I'm a big girl. I can take care of myself." Constance felt the sting of her mother's glare. "You know, I only have seven months left of this routine before I graduate. Are you going to follow me to New York and make sure I get to work each morning?"

Delilah narrowed her eyes. "New York? You aren't going anywhere in seven months, especially New York. You couldn't afford to *breathe* in that city, let alone *live* there." She crossed her arms. "You have a lot to learn about life, Connie. If you think you have it tough here, just wait until you're paying your own bills and working sixty-hour weeks."

Constance tightened her hands into a fist. "I hate it when you call me that! My name is Constance. Connie makes me sound like a middle-aged housewife. And I *will* move to New York. It's where the entire publishing industry is. If you want to make it as a writer, editor, or publishing executive, your best shot is living in New York."

Abigail attempted to end the strife and lighten the mood. "Can you two wait until the afternoon to fight? I'd like to start my day on a more positive note."

"You stay out of this." Constance bristled as a smile spread across her mother's face. Delilah's eyes said it all—she didn't believe Constance could make it as a writer or editor. Outside of journalism, she didn't consider writing a real job. To her, Constance's dreams were nothing but fairy tales, misunderstandings about reality.

"We'll see about that, honey," Delilah said. "You don't even work here in little ol' James City County, Virginia. You think you'll just walk into a high-paying job and a sweet apartment overlooking Central Park?" Delilah shook her head. "That's not how reality works. You'll be broke and living in poverty in the projects. And you'll be alone, with no one to lean on when times are tough."

Constance rolled her eyes. "Breaking news, Mom; I won't waste my precious life working at the Pottery or playing make believe in Colonial Williamsburg. I'm leaving because I can't make it as a writer here. This place is a dead-end road for me."

"You know nothing about real life, young lady. Life is hard. You'd be lucky to have any of those jobs. The life you are running from would be a blessing for you. What do you know? You're eighteen years old and you don't even have a job yet."

Constance had heard enough.

"I don't want to be *you*. I don't want to rely on a man, spit out two kids, and wait for someone to die for me to move up in life."

Her mother erupted from her chair in a flash of anger. The chair tipped backward, crashing to the kitchen floor in a loud clap.

"Enough, Constance! That is enough. How could you say that to me after all that we've been through together? I can't stand to look at you right now. Go!"

"Gladly!" Constance spat back as she stormed out of the kitchen under the crushing weight of her mother's disappointment.

CHAPTER FIVE

Constance slipped through the door to Mr. Buchanan's English class as bells rang throughout the halls of Toano High School. She crossed the room and took her seat along the row of desks beside the windows. She dropped her backpack on the floor beside her desk and fished her textbook, notebook, and pencil from it as Mr. Buchanan stood to start his lecture.

"Good morning, everyone. Did we have a good weekend?" Mr. Buchanan asked. A few students responded with low grunts and angsty teen noises. Constance watched him loosen his necktie with one hand while adjusting his glasses with the other. Greasy fingerprints and specs of dust covered his lenses.

I don't know how he sees through those things, she thought.

He was nice to her, but Constance couldn't stand within three feet of him without reflecting on his lack of personal hygiene. Whenever she needed his help, she would wait until he sat at his desk so she could use the large wooden structure to maintain a healthy proximity. Half the time, she didn't trust the answers he gave her because of his persistent lack of confidence.

"Well, let's get this party started, shall we? Open your textbooks to page 136."

Constance flipped the pages of her textbook and placed her notebook on the right side of her small desktop. She felt a light tap on her left shoulder.

She rotated in her chair a few degrees to acknowledge Sandra Henderson without alerting Mr. Buchanan. Constance looked down and saw Sandra's extended hand holding a small, folded rectangle of looseleaf paper. Sandra passed her the note, rolled her eyes enough to make a point, and returned to her textbook without a whispered word. Her actions said, *Here's your stupid note, nerd. I don't have time for these interruptions.*

Constance faced forward in her chair, careful to keep the note under her desk where Mr. Buchanan couldn't see it. She would feel mortified if he stopped class and demanded she hand it to him. Especially since she was ninety-nine percent sure the letter came from Eli, the only friend she'd made since changing schools. The rumors about them being a couple had already made rounds, although they were simply two outcasts stumbling awkwardly through a new friendship. What if Mr. Buchanan read the letter aloud to the class? And what if Eli wrote something crazy in the note? She'd be more angry than embarrassed if that happened.

Constance considered whether to read the note and risk the exposure or hold the note for after class. She chose to live dangerously and unfolded the note in her lap, careful to avoid making any noise.

> *Looking a little tired loser. You need to catch*
> *me up at lunch. Also what are you doing this*
> *weekend? Wanna catch a movie?*
> *Eli*

She shot a squinty glance over her right shoulder at Eli seated two rows over and a few seats back. She registered his satisfaction with her response. He stuck his tongue out in a quick gesture, reinforcing the harassment.

"Is there something you two would like to share with the class?" asked Mr. Buchanan.

Constance whipped her head around as her pencil rolled off her desk to the floor. She reflexively reached for it, caught the edge of her textbook, and accidentally flipped it off the desk in a dramatic flurry of uncoordinated movement.

Laughter broke out all around her to exclamations of "smooth move" and "get a grip" from her classmates, led by Betty Chandler and her little circle of friends seated on the front row. Betty never missed an opportunity to belittle others.

Constance leveled her eyes at Betty. "Why don't you shut up, Betty?"

"Why don't you make me, loser?" Betty replied with a slight snarl.

"Mellow out, ladies," Mr. Buchanan said. "May I please continue with the lesson? Is that okay with you?"

Constance picked up her book and pencil, reorganized her desktop and tried her best to hide her flushing face. She stole one last glance at Eli before investing in Mr. Buchanan's riveting lecture.

It only took twenty minutes of Mr. Buchanan's monotonous droning to put Constance in a trance. She stared out the window to her left, consumed with thoughts of escaping this stupid school and the idiot spawn within it. Outside, autumn leaves cascaded from substantial maple trees dotting the field between the school and the running track. Their slow, drifting descent calmed her. The longer she watched them, the further away from the class her mind wandered.

Constance noticed a slight movement beneath one tree—something wrapped around the trunk. She looked more intently, seeking detail through the flimsy metal screen on the window's exterior.

Movement again.

Constance focused harder. She couldn't quite place what she saw—was it a hand?

As the hand moved across the trunk, a forearm emerged draped in a loose black sleeve. A woman slowly transpired from behind the tree.

Constance stopped breathing. Aunt Lydia stood in a shower of orange and brown leaves. She locked eyes with Constance.

Another hand on the tree trunk, this time coiling in the opposite direction. Again, an arm clothed in loose black emerged as the hand extended further.

Her pulse pressed into her throat, beating the breath from her airway.

Lydia turned her head toward the tree, took the creeping hand in hers, and coaxed the new woman forward. Constance sat up at her desk, her eyes growing wide.

Delilah, donning an identical burial gown, stepped forward and joined Lydia. The women looked lovingly into each other's faces before turning their heads in unison to meet Constance's unbelieving eyes.

This is not happening, repeated in her mind like a skipping record.

Her mother mouthed the words *I love you, baby*. Beside her, Lydia smiled at the proclamation. She dropped Delilah's hand, turned, and walked away. In moments, she disappeared behind the trunk of an adjacent tree.

Constance, now in a panic, looked back toward her mother. "How are you—"

Delilah raised her hand to her heart, fell backward, and burst into a blizzard of swirling leaves.

Constance stood abruptly, interrupting Mr. Buchanan mid-sentence.

"Can I help you, Miss Constance?" he asked, unhappy about another outburst.

She dashed past him, hiding her tears from the class behind one hand. She burst into the empty hall and picked up speed. Constance was running by the time she reached the exit doors to the parking lot beside the school.

Entering the harsh sunlight and cool autumn air, she drew a deep restorative breath and slowed to a rapid walk as she banked left toward the back field.

Constance stumbled to the field's edge. Her eyes shot back and forth among the maples, looking for any sign of her mother or Aunt Lydia. A light breeze stirred the leaves under the trees.

She stood alone under the rolling clouds and brilliant sun, a thick blanket of fresh fallen leaves before her. As she caught her breath and steadied her nerves, Constance considered whether she needed to see a doctor. Something was terribly wrong. First, the nightmare, now this. She felt helpless and somehow more alone than ever before.

She turned and faced the school. Amused faces stared at her through the windows of her classroom. Flush with emotion, she walked back to the school, the muffled sound of the hall bells screaming on the other side of the thick double doors.

CHAPTER SIX

Constance waited for her guidance counselor, Mr. Holcomb, to open his office door. She was there against her will, summoned after her disruption of Mr. Buchanan's class. She never cared for guidance counselors. They were all the same in her eyes, motivated to feed kids with money into expensive colleges and the rest of the student body into local service industries. She didn't fit their mold, and she felt they had nothing to offer her. When times were rough, she kept to herself; she didn't need a stranger to lean on.

The office door opened, expiring the conversation between Mr. Holcomb and a severely undersized freshman boy. The kid clung to a small stack of textbooks with both arms, his eyes and surrounding skin appeared red from tears. Constance assumed the young academic had experienced a tough time acclimating to the cruel environment of his new school and needed to vent. Her heart sank for him.

Mr. Holcomb towered in the doorway as the diminutive boy strode through the main office waiting area to the hall door. The kid struggled to pull the heavy door open with one hand while clutching his books to his chest with the other. The cacophony of teens moving between classes in the hall filled the quiet office with wild sounds. Then, the door shut as the poor freshman disappeared into the jungle that was the hallway. *He was never seen again*, she thought, and smiled.

"Come on in, Constance." Mr. Holcomb turned and took his seat behind his desk, leaving the door open for her.

She walked into the unremarkable office and took a seat in the chair across from him. The beige-painted cinder block walls and dingy false ceiling clashed with the new carpet and modern desk. A triangular wooden nameplate, a single notepad, and a small globe stood alone on the desk.

Mr. Holcomb was a large, kind man. He was also the first Black man she'd seen in a position of authority since moving to the more rural side of the county, where this was a rare sight. She liked him, she just didn't appreciate these circumstances.

He furrowed his brow. "You don't want to shut the door?"

"I don't have much to say, and I don't plan to be here long," she said.

"Very well." He leaned back in his chair and laced his fingers behind his head with a warm smile. "Want to talk about what happened in Mr. Buchanan's class? It's not every day that a student jumps up in the middle of a lecture and runs out of the school, although I suppose most would love to." His smile stayed put, his eyes alight with curiosity.

Constance stared at her hands and considered her response. Sure, she had to keep the vision of her mother and Aunt Lydia to herself. They'd lock her up in Eastern State if she spilled those beans. However, she hadn't felt the guilt of withholding the truth until now.

"I felt sick and didn't feel like puking all over the floor. That would have been a real interruption, wouldn't you say?" She made eye contact to reinforce her words.

His smile remained in place. "Well, sick students normally go to the nurse's office or the bathroom. Running to the field behind the school seems like an odd choice. Wouldn't you agree?"

"Not today, I wouldn't." She returned his smile.

A small laugh escaped him as he repositioned himself in his chair and crossed his forearms on his desk. "Okay, I get it. You don't want to talk about it. That's fair. How old are you, eighteen? There's not much I can do to persuade you to confide in me. However, I want you to know that you *can*." This time, his smile projected comfort and trust.

"Thank you, sir. I appreciate that. I promise there's nothing to worry about. I feel better now."

"I'm sure you do."

Silence stretched between them for what felt like an eternity to Constance before Mr. Holcomb took things to the next level.

"How are things at home? Getting along with your parents?"

"You mean *parent*," she quickly responded without thinking. Constance abandoned her smile, exposing herself without realizing it.

"Ah, that's right. It's just you, your sister, and mother. My apologies."

The silence stung this time. Constance regretted exposing her emotions with such a quick and uncalculated response.

"We're fine. And I'll be done with school in a few months, anyway."

Mr. Holcomb picked up a pencil and turned it in his fingers. He looked at her with prying eyes. "Then what? Do you plan on staying around here?"

Constance scoffed at his question. "Not a chance. I'm heading straight to New York and getting a job in publishing. I don't care if I work temp jobs and live in a slum. I'm getting the hell out of here."

Mr. Holcomb nodded his head and pursed his lips, contemplating his next words. She wouldn't give him much more time to dig for clues, and she suspected he knew it.

"I know that feeling. I felt the same way when I was your age. I had plans to haul ass and get into acting. New York was on my radar, too."

She couldn't believe her ears. She hadn't pinned Mr. Holcomb as the artistic type. Her unbelieving eyes and relaxed facial expression must have tipped him off.

"I don't look or sound the part, but it's true. I was on my way anywhere else."

Constance continued the conversation. "What happened?"

"*Life* happened. My wife and I married a bit earlier than anyone planned. We had our first son six months later." He smiled at her, allowing her to do the math with no further explanation. "I got a job with the county, then became a teacher, and eventually decided that helping students as a counselor was where I needed to be. And here we are." He opened his arms wide, beholding the kingdom of his office.

Constance nodded her head and slowly clapped for him. "Well done, sir. Well, I assure you I will not meet the same fate. I have no intentions of staying here, regardless of what happens before graduation. The longer I'm here, the more convinced I am of leaving."

Mr. Holcomb dropped his arms to his sides and made one last attempt to penetrate her defense. "Well, don't tempt fate. Sometimes life has a funny way of changing our plans for us."

Constance straightened in her chair and drew the conversation to a close with her reply. "Thank you for your time, Mr. Holcomb. I should get back to class."

He dipped his head and stood. "My door is always open if you need to talk."

"Thank you."

She stood and walked out of his office with no intention of taking him up on his offer.

***

Constance took her seat near the front of the school bus without speaking to the other kids. She dropped her book-bag on the seat beside her, sending a clear message to the mongrels climbing about the cabin that she didn't intend to share her seat. She pulled a paperback copy of *The*

Catcher in the Rye from her bag and leaned against the thin glass window. Constance hoped the sight of her reading would prevent others from talking to her.

The bus smelled like stale vinyl and puberty. A handful of boisterous kids occupying the back seats harassed a few passive kids in the seats ahead of them. Mrs. Ellis, the bus driver, had her nose in a book of her own as the last few stragglers climbed the steps and walked down the aisle to their seats. When the last of the kids got on, she sighed, folded the upper corner of her page, then tossed the book in a cubby to her left. Constance cringed at the thought of desecrating a book by folding the pages.

Mrs. Ellis pulled the bus door lever. "Okay, take your seats back there! We're rolling!" Her head spun about as she checked her mirrors for errant walkers. A few seconds later, the rolling began.

The chain of yellow school buses departed the school's loading zone, winding their way onto Route 60 like a herd of lumbering elephants. As they traveled, the occasional bus peeled out of line to barrel down a crossroad.

Constance neglected her book, choosing instead to watch the fall foliage whip by to the soundtrack of the bus's obnoxious engine and bellowing kids. She loved this time of year. The changing seasons filled her with a sense of peace and anticipation. Change was good, something she desired so much. For a few minutes, Constance forgot about the day's oddities. She let her mind drift with the kaleidoscope of foliage passing by. Blazing orange leaves mingled with brown and yellow castaways dotting the lawns and roads. The partially stripped canopies muted the afternoon sun, flashing her eyes as the bus rolled beneath the branches.

Mrs. Ellis piped up as the bus rounded a wide bend in the road. "What the heck is this? Oh, man, that doesn't look good."

Constance looked over the forest green seat back in front of her. Through the windshield, she saw a solid column of smoke rising from the median as cars stacked in the lane ahead of them. Dissipating smoke hung in the air between the trees. Constance stood up, depressed the tabs on both sides of her window, and lowered the pane until it stopped. With the upper half of the window open, Constance noticed the sharp, offensive smell of burned rubber and hot metal in the air.

Mrs. Ellis and the kids craned their necks in a futile attempt to see the accident ahead. Constance couldn't see around two hulking fire trucks blocking the road. She noted a police officer standing in the road behind the closest fire engine, directing cars onto the narrow shoulder of the right lane.

The bus driver glanced at her wristwatch and shook her head. "Everybody hang tight. There's no way for me to turn around. Please refrain from looking out of the windows as we pass the accident just in case it's bad. Okay?"

Constance recoiled as the kids in the back rows burst into exaggerated laughter at Mrs. Ellis's request. They were rude, simple little monsters. She wondered why people felt so compelled to live vicariously through the tragedy and suffering of others. The thought of enjoying someone's horrific car accident turned her stomach inside out.

An expanding nervousness crept into Constance's core as the bus crawled toward the scene. The flimsy walls constraining her thoughts collapsed as her hyperactive imagination jogged through progressively disturbing scenarios.

What if the drivers were young parents picking up their kids from school?

What if they were an older couple enjoying a leisurely cruise in the fall weather when a drunk driver plowed through the median and obliterated decades of love and dedicated partnership?

They were closing in on the scene. As they crept nearer, Constance saw the look of controlled concern on the face of the police officer directing traffic. The anxious sensation in her chest grew as a somber silence blanketed the bus. The backseat kids who clamored for thrills just moments before stood quiet as the gravity of the situation set in. There was no turning back. They were passing the scene of something bad, and Constance suspected they all knew it.

The bus hugged the shoulder, its right tires exploring the grass beyond the paved surface. The nose of the bus passed over a mess of firefighting water, stray automobile parts, and charred blackness. Constance held her breath and turned her head away just as the bus cleared the firetrucks and drove parallel to the scene. She didn't want to see whatever carnage lay there, smoldering and ruined in the road.

A boyish voice from the back broke the silence, "Whoa! Look at that fire!"

Constance whipped her head around, abandoning her inhibitions in a single jagged inhale. Through the adjacent windows, she saw her mother's windowless, smoking car.

"No ..." The word fell from her in a pained groan.

"Oh God," Mrs. Ellis exclaimed in a restrained voice. She shot a panicked look over her right shoulder at Constance.

"Stop!" Constance screamed. She jumped up from her seat, grabbed the door lever with both hands and pulled with no regard for the bus's movement.

Mrs. Ellis stomped on the brake pedal, propelling Constance into the windshield. She reached out with one hand to grab the girl, but Constance rebounded immediately and evaded her reach as she ran down the steps to the grassy, soaked shoulder.

Moving from the protected interior of the bus to the smoky air felt like jumping into a pool of water. Constance ran as if in slow motion, her feet slogging through an atmosphere so viscous it crowded the air out of her lungs. She realized she was inhaling smoke, her feet soaked in a torrent of running water.

Mom. Mom. Mom. Mom.

Her mind raced, her eyes skipping wildly around the scene before her. Smoke and steam poured from the car, obstructing the view of the cab. Firemen in firefighting ensembles worked hoses and dragged car parts from the scene.

She came to a sudden stop as a massive set of arms consumed her. "Stop, kid! You can't be here!" Constance halted inches from the soaked face of a fireman. He held her fast, immobilizing her. She thrashed, pressing her hips back and shoving as hard as she could with both arms. As she broke free from the fireman's wet grasp, an even larger police officer grabbed her from behind and spun her away from her mother's scorched vehicle.

Constance screamed until her lungs emptied. Full panic set in as she fought to free herself. Her ears rang with the booming voice of the officer restraining her from behind.

"Please, kid! Just relax so we can talk with you!"

Needles pressed into every inch of her exposed skin as her frantic breathing flooded her bloodstream with oxygen. Her screams flew out and away from her. Constance's vision narrowed to a point, then darkness collapsed on her.

Beneath her, the ground opened. She fell, uncontrolled, arms bound, into an endless sinkhole of smoke, cascading water, and loss.

CHAPTER SEVEN

Constance fought to move her arms. They pressed into her sides as if bound by tight cables. Her body jostled left to right under the influence of an invisible current. A stabbing pain radiated upward from her left arm, then lingered.

Hands grabbed her limbs.

Incomprehensible voices panned from ear to ear.

Constance tried to cry out but failed. She had no control over her voice, unable to utter a coherent sentence to the darkness.

She found her eyes with her mind. *Open. Now.*

Forcing her eyes open, Constance focused as blurs of color and light battered her vision.

Where am I?

"She's waking up, Dan," a female voice said.

A man responded, "Constance, can you hear me? You're in an ambulance on your way to Williamsburg Regional Hospital. We'll be there in a few minutes. Take your time waking up, okay?"

Constance found slurred words. "Hospital? Why?"

The memories hammered home in a blast. She was riding home on the bus when they came across the car accident. Her mother's car ...

"Where is my mom?"

Constance balled her fists and pulled her arms upward with all her might. Bands of pressure anchored her wrists and elbows. She lifted her head to identify the interference and saw they'd restrained her to a wheeled stretcher. She let her head fall to the thin pad beneath her.

Rocking her head from side to side, Constance dumped tears out of each eye socket in rivulets. The pain in her arm became more apparent as she grew more aware. She'd sustained an injury at some point. Or maybe she hadn't. She couldn't be sure. Constance didn't know what was going on.

"Where is my mom?" she pleaded with the paramedics.

"She's at the hospital, sweetie," the paramedic said. "We'll get you to her as soon as we can. Just rest."

Constance glanced at Dan, the male paramedic. He looked at his partner with a cautionary stare. Constance thought he was warning her not to say too much or over-promise. She looked back at the woman.

"She's dead, isn't she?" Constance asked.

The two paramedics exchanged another tense stare, then they turned back to Constance. Dan spoke up this time.

"She was still alive last we heard, okay? But she was very, very hurt. Please, just relax. We'll reach the hospital in a minute."

With no way to hide her face, Constance rolled her head to one side and cried until the ambulance came to an abrupt stop outside the emergency room.

Constance flirted with consciousness, a dance of dark and light. One moment she plunged into the dark, surrounded by flames and the sounds of her voice cracking as it broke into screams of disbelief at the sight of her mother's burning car. The next, she burst to the surface, exposed to glaring lights and bustling hospital staff. Back under she went.

Eventually, she emerged in a quiet, dim room. Her thoughts lagged as she pieced together fragmented memories of the previous hours.

School interrupted by Lydia and Delilah.

Bus ride interrupted by a horrific accident.

"Mom."

Constance pulled her thoughts together, weaving them into a cohesive tapestry in her mind.

"She's awake," an eager voice carried from beyond a drawn curtain surrounding her bed. A probing hand explored the fabric, seeking an opening through which to cross over. Then, as if by magic alone, Abigail appeared at the foot of the bed. Constance saw trails of tears tracing unruly paths down her sister's cheeks.

Abigail moved like a flash and threw herself onto Constance, desperately embracing her. Constance tried to wrap her arms around her little sister but failed when thick, buckled restraints arrested her movement. Realization crept in again. They'd restrained her in the ambulance. But why? Was she hurt?

The car. The fire. The smoke choking out the world.

Constance pleaded in her haze, "Mom. Where is she? Abigail, tell me."

Just then, Aunt Jenny and a young nurse breached the curtain. Aunt Jenny, her mother's older sister, looked both troubled and relieved. The nurse was all business under a thin layer of empathy, clothed in a tight-fitting white uniform. She pulled the curtain open, exposing the foot of the bed to a small recovery room. Aunt Jenny approached Abigail from behind and coaxed her off Constance with soft words and a gentle tug of the shoulders. Abigail obliged, freeing Constance to breathe more freely.

"I need to check her out before we do anything else, okay ladies?" The nurse approached the left side of the bed, a slight smile on her face. Constance read the smile as an honest attempt to ease her concern about the current and future state of things. Her heavy eyes told Constance that she understood the stress of being restrained and confused about her mother's health.

Aunt Jenny took Abigail by the shoulders and guided her to a chair opposite the bed.

"Let the nurse take care of your sister. We can talk with her in a few minutes, okay?"

The nurse drew the curtain closed before Constance could see Abigail respond.

"I need to see my mother. Where is she?"

"We'll get you to her soon, Constance. I need you to spend a few minutes with me beforehand. Is that okay?"

Constance scoffed. "What choice do I have?"

"Fair enough," the young nurse replied. Constance saw a name tag pinned to her pressed uniform identifying her as Nancy. "Let's start with the most obvious discomfort. The paramedics restrained you when you became combative at the scene. We kept you restrained because we were concerned that you'd hurt yourself or someone else by accident as you came in and out of consciousness. It's not personal. I'm sure you understand."

Constance nodded her head in confirmation. "I promise I'm good," she said, making eye contact with Nurse Nancy to show her honesty.

"I know you are. Now let's get those off."

Nancy removed the wrist cuffs first. Constance felt tremendous relief, but observed a burning sensation along the back of her left arm. She rotated her arm to inspect the painful area while Nancy removed the cuffs from her ankles. Bandages blanketed the stretch of upper arm between her elbow and shoulder.

"What happened to my arm?" Constance furrowed her brow, trying hard to recall how she had injured herself.

"You took a pretty hard spill when the police and firefighters tried to restrain you. You have a gnarly case of road rash under those bandages. You're lucky you didn't break your arm the way you fell. How does your head feel?"

Confused by the question, Constance raised her left hand to her head and found a pronounced bump just above her ear. Angry pain bloomed under her fingers, scattering like fleeing spiders across her scalp. She winced and drew a sharp inhale through clenched teeth.

"You hit your head pretty hard when you fell, kid," Nurse Nancy said, walking to the head of the bed. "Let me look at that." Nancy carefully parted Constance's hair to inspect the damage. "Yeah, you lucked out. Didn't lose much hair or skin, just a nasty hit. I'll give you something for the headache."

"I don't have a headache."

"That's because we gave you meds through your IV. When that wears off, you'll wish you had that needle back in your arm."

Constance looked down and saw the needle and tubing affixed to the crook of her right elbow. How had she not noticed it until now?

She turned back toward Nancy. Their eyes locked, arresting Constance's attention. The nurse appeared tough, yet compassionate. Crow's feet stamped the skin at the corner of both eyes. Constance supposed she'd seen some things in her profession, the least concerning being a teen who mixed it up with the asphalt.

Outside the curtain, she heard Aunt Jenny shuffle Abigail out of the room. The door to the hall closed with a soft thud.

"Are you clear-headed enough to talk about your mom, Constance?"

The question stole the breath from Constance's lungs. She felt unprepared for this conversation despite begging for it since she'd witnessed the burning car.

"Yes, ma'am." Her eyes dropped to her hands. She felt tiny, like a little girl. Tears encroached on her eyes despite her best effort to suppress her emotions.

"You saw the accident, so you know she was involved in a very bad collision. Her car was engulfed in flames when the firetrucks arrived. They got her out of the car, but she was badly injured."

"She's alive though, right?" Constance asked.

Nancy drew a breath. "Yes, she's alive. But we're not sure she can survive her injuries. The doctors will give you the official prognosis before you leave today but ..." Nancy looked to the door beyond the curtain for a moment. "They'll talk with your aunt because she's the uninjured adult in this situation. But she asked me to talk with you as soon as you were ready."

Her eyes told Constance volumes. Aunt Jenny couldn't break the news to Constance. She didn't have the stomach for matters such as these. Constance assumed that Aunt Jenny knew she'd rather get the news now from a female nurse than wait several hours to hear it from some buttoned-up doctor.

Nurse Nancy dropped her head forward, maintaining strong eye contact. "Do you have any questions?"

Constance replied without hesitation. "Is my mom going to die?"

Nurse Nancy nodded her head without saying a word aloud.

CHAPTER EIGHT

Constance, Abigail, and Aunt Jenny sat in the waiting room outside the Intensive Care Unit. Constance looked up at the clock hanging above a corner table littered with well-worn magazines. An artistic rendering of Senator Robert Kennedy graced the cover of the September 16, 1966 issue of *Time Magazine* sitting atop the pile. A frail janitor floated like a ghost through the room, emptying the ashtrays beside the seats bordering the only window in the space. He left without saying a word or making eye contact. It was nine thirty in the evening, but it may as well have been three o'clock in the morning. Constance felt exhausted despite her nap earlier that afternoon.

She shifted in her chair and every nerve in her body protested. The skin on the back of her arm felt tight and sensitive to the slightest contact with her bandages. The bump on the side of her head felt like a time bomb ready to explode the moment she doubted its existence.

Her wrists and ankles throbbed from her persistent fighting while restrained. Although she couldn't deny her injuries, they didn't matter at the moment. She was too worried about her mother to worry about herself.

One of the substantial double doors to the ICU ward unlatched and Nurse Nancy leaned through the doorway. "Ladies, I can bring you back."

They rose from their seats, Constance considerably slower than Aunt Jenny and Abigail. They each lent her an arm to steady herself, which she gratefully accepted as they walked toward the door.

Entering the ICU demanded silence and solemn reflection. Constance felt the weight of the place the moment the door shut behind them. Here, doctors and nurses cared for the worst ailments, the direst medical cases. The atmosphere bore the sterile silence of sensitive events and heavy discussions.

As they walked to the nurse's station at the front of the long, rectangular room, Constance heard quiet beeps and low voices escape from the series of curtained bed stations spanning the unit. Nurse Nancy collected a file and clipboard from the desk, exchanged a few words about their intentions with a nurse seated behind the desk, then asked the girls to follow her. As she passed the desk, Constance caught a look of pity on the seated nurse's face. *They all know it's bad, but they aren't saying it*, she thought. The nurse returned to the papers on her desk, turning away from them as they entered the belly of the unit.

They walked between the rows of patient beds, Nancy leading the way followed by Aunt Jenny, Abigail, and Constance. The nurse glanced back at her to make sure she approved of the pace. Constance showed her satisfaction by maintaining her pace despite her discomfort.

Abigail turned to see each patient's bed as they passed. Constance couldn't fault the girl's curiosity. Each bed and its unfortunate inhabitant lived behind a curtain. Despite this attempt at privacy, the curtains did little to hide the occasional moaning and troubled cries escaping the more aware patients.

They passed several beds occupied by older patients fighting for the little time that remained of their expiring lives. In one bed, Constance saw a middle-aged man who, based on the large stitches holding his chest closed, must have had a serious heart condition. In another bed, she saw a woman around the same age as her mother. The woman's bald head, sunken eyes, and gray skin implied that a terminal illness was taking its sweet time draining her of life.

The woman stared at the ceiling, mind somewhere else and most likely somewhere better. As Constance passed her, the woman looked in her direction and muttered unintelligibly before mustering a grim smile. Constance smiled back, unaware if the woman recognized her presence.

The smile dropped from the woman's face as their eyes locked. Constance slowed her pace, stopping just before passing the edge of the curtain bordering the woman's bed. The sick woman's lips moved without sound, sending a message that Constance would never hear.

At a loss for words, Constance stood frozen in place, focused on the woman's face. Although she couldn't hear the woman's voice, she tried to read her lips. The repetitive phrase became hypnotic. Constance heard herself whispering the words as she found them.

"They ..."

"They all ..."

What is that last word?

"They all burn."

As the words left her mouth, the overhead lights went dark. All sounds stopped. Suddenly, the woman burst into blinding flames. She sat upright, her neck stretched to its limit, and her face turned up to the ceiling.

Constance watched with wide, unbelieving eyes as the fire flew upward, curled off the ceiling and spread into the surrounding curtains. Flames consumed every surface within sight.

The radiant heat stung her face and pulled the moisture from her eyes, nose, and mouth. The smell of burning hair and cloth rushed into her throat. Deep in the base of her lungs, Constance felt the sharp pangs of combusted gas snuffing out.

Fully engulfed in hungry fire, the woman leveled her head and locked eyes with Constance again.

Recognition blew through her mind like a bullet fired at point blank range.

It was her.

Speaking over the roaring flames and raining embers, Lydia held Constance hostage with every word.

"They all burn."

"Constance. Hey. You can't be here."

Constance jumped as she turned to face Nurse Nancy. Another nurse rushed to the ill woman. Constance couldn't believe her eyes. The sickly woman appeared drugged, leaning perilously over the side of her bed. The attending nurse lifted the poor woman back onto her pillow and used her foot to lower her bed while she wiped drool from the ill woman's chin. Nancy pulled the privacy curtain around.

"I ... I'm sorry," Constance said, searching for words. "I thought she was in trouble and didn't know what to do." A lie, but anything to get her out of this awkward situation.

"I appreciate that. She'll be fine." Nurse Nancy guided Constance back down the corridor toward her mother's bed.

Constance felt numb from head to toe. The experience at the ill woman's bed left her feeling foreign to the harsh reality of the hospital. A surge of emotion rose in her as she grappled with the horror of what she'd just experienced coupled with the difficulty of her mother's situation.

Exhaustion set in *hard* as her adrenaline crashed. Gravity pressed every square inch of her body toward the ground she crossed. Each step took tremendous effort under the weight of the day's events. As she looked forward, she wiped tears of fatigue and frustration from her eyes before any member of their death caravan could see.

Nurse Nancy stopped at a drawn curtain surrounding the last bed on the unit. She turned to address them before moving forward.

"I want you to understand the extent of her injuries before we go in there. Delilah suffered significant burns to over eighty percent of her body after the collision. We believe she was unconscious from the point of contact with the other vehicle, and she's remained unresponsive since. We assume she can hear us, but we can't confirm that until she's responsive. The doctors will tell you whether they think that's possible. You know my thoughts on that."

Looking away, Constance allowed the tears to come this time. She reached deep to find strength. She needed to be strong for Abigail. Up to this point, she hadn't considered how her sister would handle all of this. Now, she wasn't sure Abigail could.

Constance stepped forward. "Thank you for the care you've shown us today, Nurse Nancy. I'd like to see her first if that's okay with everyone."

Aunt Jenny's hand landed on Constance's shoulder. Their eyes met and she saw the pain and fear in the older woman's expression. Her breathing sounded labored between bouts of subtle groans. The woman leaned on her, the eighteen-year-old, for strength.

"It's okay, Aunt Jenny. You don't have to see her if you don't want to."

She turned her attention to Abigail, placing her hand on the girl's shoulder. "That goes for you, too. Don't feel pressured to see her if you aren't comfortable."

"No," Abigail said through her own tears. "I want to *see* her. I need to."

Nurse Nancy turned and held the corner of the curtain open with one hand. They entered one by one, Constance leading the way with Abigail at her heels and Aunt Jenny close behind.

There, completely still in the bed, lay Delilah. The volume of bandages and wraps protecting her mother's body astounded Constance. She couldn't see a bare inch of flesh among the white and brown cloth wraps. Tubes ran into her mouth and nose. IV tubing ran into the wraps on each arm. Nurse Nancy must have realized Constance's surprise.

"Infection is the greatest threat to a severe burn victim. We spent the entire day cleaning and treating her burns while fighting to control her vitals. She lost a tremendous amount of blood. We don't know how she'll respond to the treatment she's received so far. Dr. Davies will explain your options when he arrives in a few minutes."

Constance couldn't peel her eyes from the wrapped mound of her mother. Her only visible skin lay behind the unwrapped area over her eyes. Her chest heaved with every mechanical breath provided by the ventilator. *She can't breathe on her own*, she thought. *She can't talk, can't see us, this is terrible.*

"We're here, Mama," Abigail said. She placed her hand on the edge of the bed. "I'm sorry this happened to you. We'll be here when you wake up. We love you."

Constance wrapped her good arm around her sister and pulled her close. At the foot of the bed, Aunt Jenny sniffled as she watched the girls with their mother.

Behind her, the curtain parted as a short, round man entered.

"Good evening, ladies."

Nurse Nancy replied, "Good evening, Dr. Davies."

He smiled and nodded his head in acknowledgement. He pushed his oversized glasses up the bridge of his nose with his free hand while holding a chart at a safe reading distance with the other. A soft pack of cigarettes crinkled in his breast pocket as he adjusted the height of the chart in his hand.

"You must be Jenny. And you must be Constance and Abigail. Very good. Well, as you can see, we have a tough situation on our hands. Mom is tough; most people don't survive accidents of this magnitude. Despite her strength, burns this advanced are very difficult to treat and, frankly, it's anyone's guess how she'll respond. There's a significant risk of infection with burns this extensive. As soon as she's stable enough for a transfer, I'd like to send her to the burn ward at VCU in Richmond. Yes, I believe that will be best."

Constance stared at Dr. Davies, her blood pressure rising. How dare he give them a false sense of hope? Beside him, Aunt Jenny nodded her head, buying the pitch wholesale.

Abigail looked at Constance, confusion set behind her eyes. Constance looked past her and engaged Dr. Davies.

"We appreciate you talking with us about our mother's condition, especially since we've been here for nearly five hours without a single visit by a doctor."

Constance watched Aunt Jenny's hands lower to her sides, a look of disbelief emerging on her face. Her mouth hung open, her eyes clearing by the second. Nurse Nancy went to the ventilator, pretending to tend to her mother's equipment.

She'd caught Dr. Davies flatfooted. A smile hung on his face, but his eyes reflected his confusion.

"I-I apologize about that. We've been extremely busy and short-staffed tonight. That's not an excuse. I am sincerely sorry."

He looked from Constance to Aunt Jenny, who feigned concern for the staffing issues by narrowing her brow and nodding her head.

"Why don't the three of us convene outside and give the girls some time alone with Mom?" Nurse Nancy suggested.

Constance stood with Abigail as Nurse Nancy corralled Aunt Jenny and Dr. Davies out through the narrow opening in the curtain.

Abigail smiled. "I like her."

Constance smiled and brushed the hair out of the girl's face with her right hand. She exhaled a big, shaky breath and lowered her guard a little. She turned her attention back to her mother.

Seeing her mother like this made Constance think about how unpredictable life could be. Their day had started like any other, but now their mother fought for her life in the hospital.

Constance tried to remember the last time she'd seen her mother before the accident and realized with dread that their last conversation had been the argument at breakfast.

Her heart broke, all the frustration, fear, and anger spilling forth. As the fresh tears came, Abigail moved to console her sister.

Constance tried to ease Abigail's concern. "I'm okay. I just thought about our argument this morning. That was the last time we spoke." She then turned to Delilah. "I'm so sorry, Mama. If you can hear me, know that I'm sorry. I am so incredibly sorry." She wiped her face and swallowed hard. "I wasn't trying to push you away. I don't want to leave you; I just want to start my life and do my best to make you proud. I didn't mean to insult you. I'm a terrible daughter." She put her face in her hands and sobbed.

Abigail leaned into her and gripped her right arm for support. Constance drew a deep breath, cleared her eyes, and continued with conviction.

"Don't worry about us. I promise to take care of Abigail while you get better. If you can fight, fight. Stay with us if you can. But if you must go, go without regret or concern. We'll be okay. I'll watch after Abigail. I promise."

Constance looked for any response from the damaged woman before them. "Come on, Mom. *Please.*"

Delilah's chest rose and fell under the power of the ventilator. Otherwise, she remained somewhere else. Somewhere alien to Constance. Wherever she was, her daughter prayed she heard her promise and forgave her for her indiscretions.

The curtain opened and Aunt Jenny and Nurse Nancy entered.

"Let's get you girls home," Aunt Jenny said. "You need a good night's sleep."

Constance and Abigail conceded without protest. They placed their hands on the wrapped body of their mother and wished her a good night.

Before Constance passed through the curtain, she turned to look at her mother, the woman who birthed and raised her. She needed her now more than ever.

Unfortunately, she feared she was on her own.

CHAPTER NINE

Constance, Abigail, and Aunt Jenny trudged through the front door of the house just after 11 p.m. The sound of their shoes striking the foyer's hardwood floors woke Uncle Hank from his nap on the sitting room couch. He sat up, dropped his feet to the rug, and pressed sleep from his mind as the girls kicked their shoes off near the front door.

He rattled off a series of questions as if he'd been awake when they entered. "Hey, do you need me to get anything out of the car? Constance, do you need help with anything? When did you last eat?"

Aunt Jenny raised an open hand to halt his flow of queries. "We're fine. Thanks."

Constance noticed a shade of guilt in his eyes. While they'd endured the hospital and the trauma of the day, he'd napped in the silence of the sitting room. Her bitterness fell apart as her eyes found the portrait of Aunt Lydia and Adeline watching her from the fireplace mantle. Lydia's eyes burrowed to her core. Constance closed her eyes to halt the effect. Lydia's voice penetrated the dark behind her lids.

They all burn.

"Constance? You okay?"

She opened her eyes to see Uncle Hank's concerned face. The large man stood before her, his hand steadying her right shoulder, his broad shoulders and chest obstructing her view of the sitting room behind him.

How long have I been standing here with my eyes closed?

Constance turned her head to see Aunt Jenny and Abigail walking past the stairway and into the kitchen. She glanced back to Uncle Hank, assuring him with her eyes.

"Yeah, I'm okay. It's just been a very long day. I could sleep standing up."

Uncle Hank smiled and lowered his hand from her shoulder. She felt sorry for him. She knew he wanted to help but couldn't. And she didn't have the words to ease his concern.

"There's some food in the kitchen if you're hungry," he said. "I understand if you'd rather go straight to bed." He paused, eyes downcast. "I'm sorry about what happened today. I'm here if you want to talk about it."

"Thank you, but I'm going straight to bed. I want to wake up early enough to head back to the hospital when visiting hours start."

Uncle Hank nodded in understanding and accompanied Constance to the foot of the stairs. She paused there, one foot on the first step, listening to the mild bustle of Abigail and Aunt Jenny in the kitchen. Uncle Hank continued on to join them.

She felt a level of physical exhaustion she'd never experienced before. Every muscle in her body ached, and the road rash on the back of her left arm felt tighter and more sensitive than it had all day. The welt on her head spoke up to remind her of its presence. The stairs before her looked endless and overwhelming as they disappeared into the dark upper level of the home. She lowered her head and took them one at a time.

Constance struggled to keep her eyes open as she entered her bedroom half an hour later. Bathing and dressing had required more effort and time than she'd expected. She'd dressed and carefully wrapped new bandages to protect her wounds, then made her way down the dark hall to her unlit room, head aching in protest at the movement and lack of sleep.

She walked by memory through the dark room to her bed and climbed beneath the cool linen sheets. Exhaling, she relaxed her weary head to her pillow, staring up at the ceiling in the complete darkness. Constance sank further into the mattress under the weight of the day's memories. Despite her exhaustion, she couldn't stop the movie from rolling in her head. Soundless memories played out in a series of broken scenes.

The argument at breakfast.

The vision of Lydia and Delilah in the field behind the school.

Black, acrid smoke pouring from the burning car.

The shell of her mother lying behind a curtain at the hospital, every inch of her broken body hidden under seeping bandages.

Lydia in the hospital bed, engulfed in flames, eyes locked with hers, mouth moving rhythmically.

They all burn.

Constance opened her eyes to the dashboard of her mother's 1962 Chevy Impala. She struggled to control her blurred vision. A red vinyl dash pad came into focus between her hands. Her arms stretched out before her, elbows locked. She'd been bracing for an impact she couldn't recall. Had she been in an accident?

The accident.

Panic awoke within Constance. She was in the car moments after her mother's accident.

She whipped her head to the left, hands still anchored to the dash. Her mother sat erect and alert in the driver's seat, hands firm on the steering wheel, eyes fixed on the windshield before her. Constance tried to speak, but her mouth refused to move. Instead, a pathetic whimper found its end in her throat.

Her mother sat catatonic, suspended in time—until she wasn't.

Delilah's jaw slowly lowered, parting her lips in a silent "OOOOO." A deep, unfamiliar voice grew in her chest and poured from her open mouth, sending Constance into hyperventilated breathing. Wild terror overtook her.

She couldn't pull her eyes from her mother's face. In her peripheral vision, the windows filled with billowing black smoke. An offensive mixture of burning caustic materials flooded her nostrils, stinging her eyes, and attacking her throat with a thousand penetrating needles. The interior of the cab dimmed as the smoke beyond the vehicle obscured the outside world.

Constance coughed uncontrollably, head locked in her mother's direction. She ripped her right hand from the dashboard and grabbed frantically at the door handle. Her fingers found the handle, but the smooth metal lever failed to budge.

Heat kissed her feet where the firewall met the floorboard. The temperature in the cab climbed fast.

My God, we're going to burn, she thought. *We need to get out.*

What felt like two invisible hands slid up each side of her face and came to rest at her temples. The sluggish hands turned her head away from her mother and toward the passenger window. She tried to fight their grip and was rewarded with crushing pressure in opposition. The force pulled her forehead to the passenger window.

She tried to close her eyes and pull back from the glass, but she'd lost all control of her mechanics. She'd become a puppet manipulated by some invisible force.

Blinding pain exploded in her head as her mother's groan morphed into a booming command.

"Loooook!"

Two fiery eyes opened a fraction of an inch from her face on the opposite side of the window, separated only by the thin layer of glass between them.

Constance's bladder let go. Warmth spread in her lap, the sharp smell of urine mixing with the cab's toxic atmosphere.

Hungry flames danced in the brilliant, glowing eyes. They held Constance captive as they moved away from the glass into the smoke.

She recognized Lydia. Her heart pounded in her chest, threatening to rupture the arteries feeding blood to her extremities.

Her aunt stood proudly in her black burial gown, rich chocolate curls spilling over her shoulders. Constance recognized the undeniable pain in Lydia's face. Yes, her eyes burned bright, but her face was slack and depressed. Constance thought it was the saddest face she'd ever seen. Lydia embodied loss and longing.

"Without my daughter, they all burn." Tears poured down Lydia's face as the words left her.

Constance matched Lydia's tears with her own. Her heart burst with a ruinous froth of misery, grief, and fear. Her face remained pressed to the window. In the driver's seat beside her, out of view, another guttural proclamation escaped her mother's throat.

"Loooook!"

A figure stepped forward from the smoke surrounding Lydia. A girl.

Constance's cousin, Adeline, took station beside Lydia. The nine-year-old took her mother's hand and turned her face up to her in adoration.

Another figure appeared from behind Lydia—Abigail.

Behind Constance, a piercing scream erupted from Delilah.

Held firm to the window, Constance fell apart, her screams blending with her mother's as flames crept into her legs from the car's combusting interior surfaces.

On the other side of the impenetrable glass, Lydia huddled the younger girls to her bosom and burst into blinding flames.

As promised, they all burned.

Constance woke to sunlight piercing the sheer curtains of her bedroom window. Wet nightclothes clung to her overheating body. She'd sweat through her clothes and sheets. She sat up and pulled her sheets back in a panic.

"What the ...?"

Constance stared at her lap in disbelief. She'd wet herself in her sleep.

Images from her dream surfaced in her mind. In the dream, she'd been so terrified that she'd lost control of her bladder. Frustration surged in her as tears appeared at the corners of her eyes. She wiped them from her cheeks and looked to the window, mustering her strength in the growing dawn light.

She was losing control of everything. Her mind had played tricks on her at school, her mother had been in a life-threatening accident, and she was losing control of her body.

Determined and ashamed, she climbed out of bed, stripped her soiled bedding, and deposited the evidence in her hamper. Then she cleaned up in the hall bath, changed into fresh clothes, and headed for the kitchen. She planned to eat a quick breakfast before going to the hospital with Aunt Jenny.

She entered the kitchen as Aunt Jenny and Uncle Hank were coming into the house from the back porch. Constance slowed her stride as she saw the dour look on Aunt Jenny's face.

Uncle Hank spoke first. "Constance ..."

Aunt Jenny broke into tears and leaned on the back of a kitchen chair for support.

"... the hospital called. Your mom passed this morning."

The world fell silent. Constance saw Uncle Hank's lips move but heard nothing. All feelings left her.

Numb and deaf, she walked past Aunt Jenny and Uncle Hank, through the back door to the porch, and out into the backyard.

Constance stood strong in the center of the yard, facing the trees and the morning sun.

She closed her eyes, inviting memories of her mother to pour over and around her. She felt her mother's embrace as she reached up to her after falling as a child. Her mother's warm, soft skin comforting her as they cuddled together in front of their new RCA color television, her little sister crawling on the floor. She watched her face light up as they entered their new house in the summer. Constance recalled her mother's words on that day in the cemetery.

We have a family; we have strength.

Warm sunlight settled onto Constance's face to the sound of leaves falling under the influence of the autumn breeze.

More of Delilah's words from that day in the cemetery reached her again.

This house is ours, and one day, it will be yours. One day, I'll be gone, and you will carry on the family's legacy here.

CHAPTER TEN

Still stunned by the news of her mother's passing, Constance entered the house through the back door to find Aunt Jenny and Uncle Hank seated at the kitchen table. Without a word, she closed the door behind her and took a seat.

"Are you okay, honey?" Aunt Jenny asked.

Constance ignored the question, wiped tears from her cheeks, and responded with a question of her own. "When should we tell Abigail?"

Uncle Hank replied, "We figured it would be best to let her sleep and talk to her after you'd had some time to think."

"I appreciate that." Constance glanced toward the stairs and thought of her poor little sister sleeping in complete ignorance of their mother's passing. Her heart ached. *This'll devastate her*, she thought. They'd faced significant adversity over the past year, starting with their parents' divorce, moving houses, and starting new schools. Now this.

"When you're ready, we have some things we need to discuss with you," Uncle Hank said.

Aunt Jenny shot him a disapproving look. He shrank under the pressure of her stare. Uncle Hank put his hands up.

"I'm getting ahead of myself. That can wait a few days. For now, you and your sister need time to process this."

Aunt Jenny continued her silent assault on him with her narrowed eyes.

"Thank you, but I'd rather not wait for the inevitable. Are you talking about funeral arrangements?"

Uncle Hank frowned. "Well, I was talking about you and your sister."

Aunt Jenny interjected. "We'd like for you girls to come stay with us for a few weeks until we figure out what to do next."

Constance drew her brow in curiosity. "How long have you been thinking about this? Wait. When exactly did you get the call from the hospital?"

Aunt Jenny dropped her eyes to her fidgeting hands and pursed her lips, trapping any potential reply.

Constance pressed Uncle Hank for a response with her eyes.

"We got the call last night."

Constance contained her expanding anger. *You knew last night?*

"*When* last night?"

He lowered his head, avoiding Constance's gaze. "Just past midnight."

Constance closed her eyes as anger spread through her like a virus infecting her thoughts, composure, and emotions.

Aunt Jenny cleared her throat. "You needed your rest. You had an especially brutal day and—"

Constance cut her aunt's words. "I can't believe you didn't wake me." She spat the words through clenched teeth. "I understand not telling Abigail. She's just a kid. But you should have told me right away."

"*You* are just a kid," Aunt Jenny replied.

"I am *not* a kid. I'm eighteen years old. I can handle this." Tears threatened again, but she choked them back.

Uncle Hank placed one palm down in the center of the table to lower the tension in the room. "Let's not do this. You have a right to be upset with us, Constance. I'm sorry I didn't wake you last night." He leaned forward. "You and your sister have a lot going on. We just want to help. We're not trying to rip you out of your house while all of this is going on."

Constance crossed her arms. "How does this work? You stay here with us for a few weeks, *then* rip us out of our house? Or you move in here with us for good?" When Hank didn't respond, she continued. "We're not moving. And no one is moving in with us either. Abigail and I will be fine on our own."

Aunt Jenny laughed. "That's not happening."

Constance turned her attention to Aunt Jenny. "I can assure you it is." She placed both hands on the table and stood. "I appreciate your concern, but we'll be fine after the funeral on our own. If we need help, I'll ask for it."

"What about your dad?" Uncle Hank asked.

The question set Constance on her heels. "What about him?"

"What about him staying with you girls?"

Aunt Jenny exhaled in displeasure at the proposal. Constance sensed the misalignment between them.

"No, thank you. And I'm comfortable telling him that if necessary." Constance responded as respectfully as she could.

Hank replied, "Well, you'll have your opportunity to do just that when he arrives this afternoon."

The news rocked Constance and left her speechless. She hadn't seen her dad in months. Ice crept into her veins.

Aunt Jenny jumped in. "Geez, Hank! What are you doing?"

"I'm treating her like an adult." Then he stood and exited through the back door. Constance realized that she'd hurt him by being so resistant to their help.

She turned, walked up the stairs to her room, and left Aunt Jenny sitting alone at the kitchen table with her head in her hands.

Constance spent the next two hours in her bedroom with the door shut. She bounced between bouts of crying, frustration, anger, and resolution. Each cycle brought new issues to the surface, stomped them to muddy pulps, then pressed them back into the murky waters of her emotions to search for the next target.

In her grief, she cried for her mother. Then she cried for Abigail. Eventually, she cried for herself.

Her room was suitably dark for the task, and the silence of the home provided the sonic reprieve she needed to think. She contemplated what life would be like for her and her sister. Where would she get a car? How long before she would need a job to support them? No wonder Aunt Jenny and Uncle Hank doubted her ability to carry this burden. Constance was ill-prepared for independence, less being a guardian to her little sister.

She needed guidance and support. Why did she reject those willing to provide it?

Because you see it as a sign of weakness. And you are unwilling to admit that you're wrong, which is also a sign of weakness. You are weak despite your strength.

She pressed her palms to her temples in frustration. A bolt of searing pain shot across the left side of her head. In her self-loathing, she'd forgotten her very real head injury.

Constance rolled onto her right side, removing the pressure from her throbbing head. She felt dejected and alone in a way she'd never experienced before. She had no parents, no one to be proud or confident in her, no one to protect her from herself.

A gentle knock at the door interrupted her self-destruction.

"Constance? Can I come in?" Abigail asked through the door.

Constance sat straight up in the bed, her breath caught in her throat. Her pulse climbed in anxious anticipation of the conversation ahead. She felt terrible for not going to Abigail sooner, for not checking on her. What if she'd heard them talking and had to process the news alone in her room, with no support?

She lost her stomach for the mission. Her mouth betrayed her. "Yes. Come in."

Abigail opened the door, careful not to disturb the silence. She closed the door behind her and walked to the bed, climbing in and laying her head in her older sister's lap. It was her way of giving and receiving comfort without saying a word. Constance, still sitting up, looked to the ceiling for strength. She checked her nerves and swallowed hard. Lowering her head, she brushed her sister's hair from her upturned cheek. The time had arrived.

"Abi, we need to talk. There's something you need to know."

Without hesitation, Abigail admitted, "I already know about Mama."

Constance sat rigid and unmoving. *What?*

"Oh, Abi, I'm so sorry. Did you hear us talking downstairs?"

"No," the girl said flatly. "Mama told me last night. Aunt Lydia brought me to her in my dream."

Constance lost her nerve and slid her legs out from under Abigail, who shot up in response. Now sitting face-to-face, Constance noticed her red, swollen eyes for the first time since she'd entered the room. Abigail must have been crying all morning.

"But, how? What are you saying, Abi?"

Abigail's face twisted into a silent cry as she leaned her face into Constance's shirt. Constance did nothing in her shock.

The girl spoke in muffled sobs. "It was so real. I saw the accident. You were there, trapped in the car with Mama. Then Aunt Lydia and Adeline brought me to her in the hospital. She was healthy, Constance. She looked perfectly fine. She was waiting for me. She told me she was gone and this morning when I woke up, I just knew it was true. I just knew it."

Constance overcame her surprise and wrapped her good arm around her sister. She pressed her head into Abigail's hair and managed her own silent tears as her heart broke with her sister's.

"Promise not to tell anyone about my dream," Abigail pleaded. "Promise me."

"I promise," Constance whispered. "Don't worry about that. It's just you and me now. We'll be fine."

Abigail sniffed hard. Constance wiped tears from her sister's face with her shirtsleeve and looked into her bloodshot eyes. Before she could further console her, Abigail spoke.

"You don't understand. This is as real as you and me. Adeline wouldn't lie to me. Mama will visit us soon, but only if we keep this secret."

Abigail exhaled. Constance took her sister's clammy hands in hers and reiterated her vow.

"I promise."

Despite her comforting affirmation, Constance worried about how Abigail had been so convinced by a dream. *And why is she talking about Adeline like the girl is here with us?* At the moment, the experience seemed like a natural progression in the strange world of the past twenty-four hours. But deep down, a jagged kernel of fear nestled into Constance's gut.

The girls walked downstairs together after their conversation in the bedroom. They held hands, Constance comforting Abigail, who insisted on her big sister's protection as she faced her aunt and uncle. As they reached the bottom step, Abigail shot her a glance that said, *Remember our promise.*

Constance registered her aunt and uncle's awareness the moment they saw Abigail–they knew she knew.

"Come here, baby. I'm so sorry." Aunt Jenny opened her arms to Abigail.

Constance released her sister's hand but stayed close for comfort. She turned to Uncle Hank, who looked hesitant to engage her. Maybe she'd been a bit too hard on him earlier.

"There's some coffee on if you want some," Uncle Hank said. "Want me to make you breakfast?"

Constance smiled, appreciating his offer, and shook her head. "I'll pass on breakfast, thank you." She intended to partake in the coffee, though.

Aunt Jenny turned to Abigail. "I'm sure Constance told you that your dad is coming to see you today. He is driving into town from D.C. Can you be good for me when he gets here?"

Abigail nodded her head in agreement, gave Aunt Jenny one more big hug, then went to Uncle Hank for a hug. Constance watched all of this from the kitchen counter, where she mixed her coffee.

An hour later, Constance heard Roy's Cadillac rumble into the gravel driveway beside the house. The car was a rolling status symbol with its big fins and gaudy chrome covering everything. It was the perfect image for a man who left his family behind for a life of gambling and de-bauchery with questionable women. Constance tensed up when she heard his footsteps climbing the wood stairs to the front porch.

Roy walked through the front door like he lived there. He didn't knock or call out to them, he simply strolled in. *Who does he think he is?* Constance grew more anxious at the sound of him in her home. This was not his place. His presence here, on this day, turned Constance sour.

Hank stood and walked out of sight to greet Roy in the foyer. She heard the low mumble of their voices just out of earshot as she made herself busy in the kitchen, suddenly very concerned with the excessive quantity of dishes in the sink and the crumbs littering the counter.

Over her shoulder, Constance heard Aunt Jenny stand to welcome the men into the kitchenette, the legs of her wooden chair groaning across the dry floorboards.

"Hey, kid," Roy said, presumably to Abigail. Constance heard her younger sister mutter a low reply as she stood to greet her father. Constance ran the water in the sink, placing another barrier between her and the imminent conversation with Roy.

"Hi, Connie."

She bristled at the sound of his voice. She hated that nickname and hated him more for giving it to her.

"Hey," she replied, keeping her attention on the faux chores at hand.

Aunt Jenny led the way. "Why don't we catch up a bit in the sitting room? The girls can join us when they are ready. Want a cup of coffee?"

He smiled. "Sure, that sounds great."

Constance kept her hands and eyes in the sink, scrubbing dishes under scalding hot water. The more she scrubbed, the more agitated she became. She couldn't fathom what he thought he could accomplish by being here. He'd left them. Why couldn't he stay gone? Did he think he could swoop in and save them? How did he expect them to respond to him being here?

I've lost the only adult that I respected. We're on our own.

Aunt Jenny emerged beside her, grabbing a washed coffee mug and a small spoon from the drying towel beside the sink. She leaned close.

"He looks just as small and worthless as the last time I saw him."

Finally, something to smile about.

Constance walked into the sitting room, Abigail trailing one step behind her. They sat beside Aunt Jenny on the couch while Roy and Hank filled chairs flanking the fireplace. The normally stuffy room felt especially stale and flat, in contrast to the tension and angst in the air.

Now forced to sit in the same room as her father, she could no longer avoid seeing him. He somehow appeared sleazier than the last time she'd seen him. He wore new bell-bottom jeans, an obnoxious floral-patterned button-up shirt (open at the neck to show a gold chain, of course), and brown Chelsea boots. Constance fought the urge to scream, seeing him dressed like a twenty-year-old hippie with money.

Needing a break from the view, Constance looked at Abigail, who stared at her father with a mixed look of longing and disapproval. Despite Constance's well-known opinions about her father's behavior, she realized that she'd heard little from Abigail about him since he'd left them. She supposed her younger sister lacked the hormones and experience to develop a true distaste for the man he'd become. Constance thought Abigail stood too close to her youth to fully tarnish the image she held of her father. Constance held faith that these conditions wouldn't prevent the inevitable from happening. One day, Abigail would detest Roy as much as she did.

"So, how are you girls doing?"

Constance lifted her eyes to Roy, her face slack and unimpressed. "How do you think we're doing? We're devastated. Our mother is gone." She maintained steady eye contact with Roy.

"You know what I mean, Connie. I'm just as upset as you are. I love your mother, you know."

This time, Abigail spoke up. "No, you don't. You don't have to lie to us. You left us too, remember?"

Constance held her response, satisfied with her sister's reply. She watched Roy struggle to reset the conversation. He shifted in his chair, assumed a less casual stance by uncrossing his legs, and leaned forward, lacing his hands.

"I'm sorry. I deserve that. Can we start over?"

"I suppose." Abigail glanced at Constance with a look that implied she'd set things right for the moment.

Roy continued, "I know I made a huge mistake and I'm punished for it every day. Your mother and I shared a love for you that can never be undone, no matter what happened between us. If you'll have me, I'm here for you. I'll do whatever it takes to pick up the pieces and move forward."

Silence played the room for a minute. Constance couldn't take much more of this. She spoke up.

"So, what, Roy? You want to move in? Make us pancakes every morning? Leave the girlfriends and gambling behind for a life of domestic bliss?"

"If you'll have me. You may not believe me, but I've changed. I would give everything to be back with you girls. I stopped drinking, gambling–all of it."

Her heart hurt hearing him plead his case. Maybe he'd changed. Maybe he'd realized how much he'd messed things up. Only he knew. Perhaps having a father around would benefit Abigail more than a naïve sister figuring things out on the fly.

A small hand rested on her leg. She looked up and found Abigail consoling her with her eyes, as if she'd heard every thought running through her big sister's mind.

"It's okay." Abigail said with a small, comforting smile. "Go on."

Constance gathered a deep breath and continued. "If that's true–I'm proud of you. But we prefer to do this on our terms, just me and Abigail. If we need help, we'll ask for it sooner rather than later. I promise."

Roy looked up and opened his mouth to reply but hesitated. Instead, he smiled and looked for answers in his nervous, fidgeting hands. *He's embarrassed*, she thought.

He spoke, "I understand. I suppose talking you into moving in with me–in our old place–is out of the question?"

Constance stalled. She hadn't expected him to drop this bait in the water. *You know how much we miss living there,* she thought. *You know we miss our friends and our school. You're playing dirty pool.*

Again, Abigail placed a hand on Constance's leg, showing her silent support for the decision to stay, to press on as discussed. Words flooded Constance's mind, obstructing her thinking and crowding out any acceptance of his offer. She felt like someone had entered her mind and flipped a switch, jamming the signals with static. Clarity emerged, like a telegram broadcast in her mind on a dominant frequency.

"Mama loved it here. She wanted nothing more than to carry on a legacy in this house–to build a new life on familiar ground. As much as we appreciate everyone trying to help, we must honor her desire for that life." She looked at Abigail, who beamed with approval. "Maybe one day in the future, we'll be open to having you with us, Roy. But we have a lot of trust to rebuild before that's possible. We want to be here. We want to do this." Confidence and pride radiated from Constance in streams of warm energy. Saying the words out loud, committing to this path, lifted her diminished spirits.

She looked past the men sitting in their chairs and at the portrait of Lydia and her cousin positioned over the mantle. She felt alive, empowered by the momentary claim of independence. Under her feet, the floors hummed with an energy she'd never felt before.

CHAPTER ELEVEN

Constance and Abigail spent the rest of the afternoon in the privacy of their bedrooms. Aunt Jenny and Uncle Hank entertained Roy for another hour before he left in his Cadillac. *He's on his way back to our old place, our old life*, Constance thought.

She lay on her bed, wrapped in blankets, heartache, and a new sense of independence. In her confidence, she also found conflict. She'd pushed all her chips into the center of the table, gambled big on their future, and won the hand. Now what? She had a week to figure out the basics before her aunt and uncle returned to their house twenty minutes away at the other end of the county and left the girls to their own devices. Uncle Hank interrupted her stacking questions by hollering up the stairs.

"Supper is ready, girls!"

"Coming!" Constance replied, projecting her voice toward her closed bedroom door.

Constance kicked her blankets off and departed her room. She started for the stairs, but then realized something.

Why didn't Abigail respond?

She suspected her sister had fallen asleep on her bed in the afternoon's silence.

Constance walked down the dim hall and arrived at Abigail's bedroom door. She knocked and listened for a response. After a moment of silence, she opened the door.

The room stood empty. Warm sunlight streamed through the window, reflecting pinks, greens, and blues from the bed's comforter onto the walls. Abigail's bed looked undisturbed. Constance glanced into the open closet door to her left and found it void of life. Abigail must have left her room without Constance hearing her from down the hall.

She turned and headed downstairs. As she entered the kitchenette, Uncle Hank asked, "Did you see your sister on your way down?"

"She's not in her room." Constance furrowed her brow. "You haven't seen her down here?"

She could tell by the confused look on her uncle's face he hadn't seen Abigail. He shook his head, setting a stack of clean plates on the table.

"I'll find her. She's around here somewhere." Constance turned toward the front of the house to begin her investigation.

She walked past the stairs and peered into the family room to the right of the front door. No Abigail. She turned and investigated the adjacent sitting room to the left. Again, Abigail was nowhere to be seen.

Constance stood in the sitting room entrance for a moment, contemplating where her sister may be. Quiet, still, dusty–the room held no energy, yet it felt strangely enticing. She stepped into the room and approached the portrait on the mantle. The cool floorboards expanding from the stone mantle cooled her socked feet.

"Hello, ladies."

Lydia and Adeline responded with silent stares from the portrait.

"Have you seen my sister? I figured she may visit you here, but apparently not." Constance smirked, spun on her heels, and set out to expand her search when her vision left her in a blinding flash. She stopped mid-step, stumbled, and caught herself on the arm of the couch. Frigid fingers pried her brain open. A sudden rush of images flooded her mind as she cowered against the couch, too terrified to draw a proper breath.

Blinding sunlight.

The backyard.

The path to the cemetery.

Abigail standing over an open, freshly dug grave.

Abigail pitching forward in a freefall into the gaping hole in the earth.

A casket slamming shut, the sound of the lid crashing down.

Constance tried to call out but fell to her knees, mouth wide in a silent scream. Her hand shot up to the angry wound on the left side of her head. She thought of it as an open portal through which flowed an onslaught of torment.

This is crippling. It'll kill me.

Constance moved into the vision. She stood where the path met the cemetery. Frozen in place, she stared ahead at the grave imprisoning her little sister. She tried to lift her arms, take a step–to do *anything*–but failed to budge. Her breathing escalated as she watched the crown of a head slowly emerge from the mouth of the grave. Floating upward, Lydia emerged, her hair matted with wet soil. She looked like a puppet lifted by its strings, arms hanging at her sides, toes pointing downward. Constance read the anguish in Lydia's eyes.

She opened her mouth to scream, but her voice had abandoned her. Mouth agape, exhaling every bit of breath in silent terror, she lost any sense of being in the sitting room. She was there, in the cemetery, her dead aunt suspended in mid-air before her.

Lydia's eyes found her, and the look of anguish turned to unmistakable adoration. Constance felt completely exposed. She couldn't fight or revert to flight.

"She's with me, Constance. I'll care for her. You wouldn't know where to start. You've never been a mother. You've never truly loved. True love is deeper than any grave."

Lydia's words landed like stone slabs in Constance's heart. They challenged her decision to care for Abigail, to love her like a mother loves a child. They challenged her readiness, her discipline, her ability to sacrifice for someone else.

Desperation bloomed in her gut.

She closed her eyes as her voice emerged from her throat with an anguished groan.

Constance opened her eyes to the waning light of the backyard. Abigail sat in the grass at her feet, her face shadowed with concern.

"Stop! You're scaring me!" Abigail pleaded with her.

Constance stood rigid, eyes locked on her sister, groaning in despair. Abigail sat cross-legged with a pile of harvested fall leaves in her lap. She shielded her eyes from the setting sun with one hand while the other tugged at Constance's pant leg.

How in the world did I end up out here?

Constance struggled to clear the confusion in her mind. Overwhelmed and suddenly aware, she stopped groaning, took a step back from her sister, and brought her hands to her head. The pain in her head had abandoned its post.

Aunt Jenny's voice, heavy with concern, carried from the back porch. "Constance, are you okay?"

"Yeah, I'm fine!" Constance looked around the yard, getting her bearings. She pulled the cool, clean fall air into her lungs and exhaled a shaky breath.

Aunt Jenny challenged her. "Are you sure? You just walked through the kitchen, slack-faced like a zombie. I spoke to you, but you just walked right by me. You girls come in and get washed up for supper." She disappeared into the house to attend to the kitchen.

Abigail narrowed her eyes. "What was that? You were groaning." She stood up from her spot in the grass, then bent to gather the leaves she'd collected.

"I said I'm fine," Constance replied. "What were you doing out here, anyway? I never heard you leave your room. I couldn't find you."

Abigail looked at her like she'd lost her mind. "Am I not allowed to come outside without permission?"

Constance heard subtle rebellion in Abigail's question, and she didn't care for it. "No, but no one knew where you were. I was looking all over for you. You should tell people when you leave the house. Aunt Jenny and Uncle Hank also didn't know where you were."

Abigail let out a stunted laugh. "What are you talking about? I told Aunt Jenny I was coming out here."

Constance stood speechless. *What the hell is going on?*

"You're the one who zombie-walked out of the house without telling her where you were going."

Abigail turned, arms extended straight in front of her like a zombie and walked with exaggerated straight legs across the yard. She stopped at the foot of the steps to the back porch and turned to Constance.

"Come on. You probably just need a good night's sleep after the day we've had. Let's go, weirdo."

"I'll be along in a minute," Constance replied, flashing a fake smile. Abigail shrugged and crossed the porch to the house.

As soon as the door shut, she turned toward the cemetery, tempted to walk down the path to prove that she'd only experienced a terrifying daydream. Her guts bubbled at the thought of being proven wrong. She recalled the sound of that casket slamming shut and the image of Lydia suspended above the open grave.

Had she dreamed the whole thing? Had she not spoken with Uncle Hank? Was the entire trip between her bedroom and the backyard just one big hallucination?

Supper unfolded in uneventful bliss. The girls ate their meals with little conversation. Afterward, they helped Aunt Jenny clear the table and clean the dishes. Uncle Hank sat at the kitchen table with his reading glasses perilously perched on his broad nose. He filled a notepad with a list of obligations for the coming week. As Constance finished drying the last dish, Abigail drained the sink and rinsed the turbid water down the drain.

Aunt Jenny pulled three coffee mugs from the cabinet. She turned to Constance and asked, "Are you comfortable discussing the next few days with us?"

Constance lowered her eyes, her heart sinking in her chest. It was time to discuss funeral arrangements and family schedules.

"Yes, ma'am. I suppose we must."

Aunt Jenny nodded and handed Constance a mug. "Here, pour a cup for you and Uncle Hank. He takes his black."

Aunt Jenny turned and leaned into Abigail's bony little shoulder. "You head upstairs and wash up for the night. You don't want to listen to this boring adult stuff."

In that moment, Constance appreciated Aunt Jenny's calm temperament. The woman may have lacked fire and motivation, but she was always level and sensitive and that worked for the role she'd carved in their lives.

"That works for me," Abigail said with a relieved look.

Constance poured the coffees, hers with cream, and took her seat at the table. Uncle Hank took a sip with a nod and a smile.

"That is a fantastic cup of coffee. Thank you, ladies," he said, placing the mug next to his lined notepad.

Constance read his scribble from her upside-down perspective.

One heading titled FUNERAL HOME stood out at the top of the page. Beneath the morbid heading, a short list of items to discuss with the staff at Gracey Funeral Home descended. The next heading read FAMILY COMING INTO TOWN. Constance knew most of the names, but a few unknowns piqued her curiosity. Aunt Jenny must have read her face.

"Your mom knew lots of people, many you never met. She was quite popular in her youth." A warm smile crossed her face, lifting her cheeks and drawing wrinkles at the corners of her eyes.

"I can't wait to meet them and hear their stories," Constance said.

Uncle Hank pointed his pen at an indistinguishable list on his pad and asked her, "So, just confirming, you and Abigail are *not* attending school this week, correct?"

"Correct," she replied, Aunt Jenny nodding in agreement.

"Okay. We just need to talk to your school, let them know what's going on, and get a list of any assignments that you may need to complete from home while—"

"They'll be fine without keeping up with their studies this week," Aunt Jenny interrupted. "The schools know what's going on."

Uncle Hank looked over his reading glasses at Constance. "Okay, sounds good. Let us know if that changes. We can drive you up there if you need us to. That brings me to my next item: I want to lend a car. It's no Ferrari, but it'll get you girls safely from point A to point B and it's free."

Constance smiled. "I appreciate that. I'm not picky. I'm grateful for whatever I can get. Honestly, I hadn't thought much about any of this, so ... yeah, thank you." Her mind spun, considering the list of responsibilities a car introduced. She'd have to get car insurance, take care of maintenance, and keep the gas tank full. She anxiously bit her lip. *What else have I not thought about?*

Uncle Hank answered her question without her saying a word aloud. "We'll take you grocery shopping every Sunday afternoon starting this weekend. Unfortunately, you are about to find out how expensive and not fun grocery shopping can be."

Aunt Jenny said, "We don't need to go over all these things. This poor girl has enough on her mind today. Let's discuss what we're doing tomorrow."

"Right," Uncle Hank said, shifting gears. "Tomorrow, we meet with the funeral home director at nine sharp. Constance, you and your sister don't have to go. Aunt Jenny and I will talk with them about ... well, about a casket and the burial. We'll host the viewing, funeral, and wake here. They'll get your mom ready there and transport her here the morning of the funeral."

His words hung in the air, impressing their significance on Constance. She hadn't considered having her dead mother in the house. This news robbed the warmth from her body. She felt conflicted. On one hand, she couldn't wait to have her mother back where she belonged. The thought of her being in a refrigerator in the morgue didn't sit well with her. On the other hand, having her dead mother in the house took the wind from her lungs.

"Where will they put her?" Constance asked.

"We thought the sitting room would be a fitting place for the viewing. She loved that room." He looked to Aunt Jenny for support.

She nodded. "As long as that's okay with you, of course."

They turned to Constance for her approval.

Mustering her courage, she said, "Yes, of course."

She looked down the hall to her right, toward the sitting room beyond the staircase. A single lamp in the room cast light and shadows into the adjacent foyer. She imagined her mother there, lying in her casket, waiting for her girls to spend time alone with her.

Come sit. Mama missed you.

Her supper rolled over in her stomach.

"It'll be nice to have her back home."

CHAPTER TWELVE

Constance excused herself from the table, her head spinning with details of the coming week. The conversation with Uncle Hank and Aunt Jenny had left her feeling overwhelmed and queasy. She needed a relaxing bath and a good night of sleep, but she had a few things to take care of beforehand. Uncle Hank remained at the table, continuing his work on the list while Aunt Jenny cleaned the counter around the coffee pot.

"I'm going upstairs for the rest of the evening. Thanks for all you are doing to help us." Constance walked to the kitchen sink, washed her coffee mug, then gave Aunt Jenny an honest, sustained hug. Holding Aunt Jenny, Constance realized that she'd hugged her mother for the last time. This realization twisted like a rusty knife in her stomach and drained the little remaining energy she'd held. She laid her head on Aunt Jenny's shoulder, hugged her a little tighter, and fought back tears. She acknowledged her days ahead involved deep grief over her mother's death. Time seemed unbelievably cruel.

Loosening her grip on Aunt Jenny, Constance stepped back, bringing her hands up to wipe the emotions from her face. Aunt Jenny turned to the counter. She suspected Aunt Jenny needed to distract herself to keep her own emotions under control.

Constance turned and left the kitchen without another word. She headed up the stairs, contemplating whether she should join Uncle Hank on his trip to the funeral home the following morning. As she reached the landing at the top of the stairs, she saw Abigail's partially open bedroom door to her right. The light creeping out of Abigail's room amplified the darkness of the hall. She heard her sister's low voice somewhere in the room. Constance stopped and opened the door. She took one tentative step into the room, looking around for her sister.

The girl was nowhere to be seen.

Constance listened as she looked toward the closed closet door. Abigail's muted voice escaped through the door, revealing her location. Constance stepped toward the door and considered opening it as fast as she could to scare her sister, but she resisted her natural urge to torment her. Such fun didn't fit the day's dour mood.

Instead, Constance placed her hand on the closet's doorknob and opened it. An expanding arc of light crept into the darkness of the small closet as the door opened wider. Sitting in the middle of the closet floor, Abigail seemed oblivious to her sister standing in the doorway. Constance readied her words and immediately stopped when she saw the stack of items before Abigail.

Abigail sat, eyes closed, muttering to a stack of shoe-boxes. Sitting atop the stack was the portrait of Lydia and Adeline.

Constance stood dumbfounded, her mind skipping like a record. She couldn't rationalize what she was seeing.

"What are you doing?"

Her voice interrupted Abigail's muttering. She opened her eyes and looked at Constance with a dreamy stare.

"Hey, what's going on? And why did you take that portrait from the sitting room?"

Constance watched the clouds clear from her sister's eyes. Awareness dawned on Abigail's face, her forehead drawing tight as she looked around the small closet for clues to her predicament.

My God, is she really unaware of what's going on?

She started to kneel when Abigail stood. Constance shuffled back to give her sister enough room to step out of the closet. Abigail bent and lifted the portrait from the makeshift shoebox altar.

"I was just playing around. I honestly don't know why you're freaking out."

Constance didn't know how to respond. *This is so odd.*

Without another word, Abigail exited the closet with the portrait in hand and disappeared into the hallway. Then she galloped down the stairs and walked to the sitting room, most likely to restore the portrait to its home on the mantle.

She must be embarrassed that I found her playing make believe in the closet, Constance thought as she left the room to avoid adding insult to injury when Abigail returned.

As she walked down the hall to her room, her mind fought to balance the stressful week ahead with Abigail's odd, immature behavior. Frankly, she needed to keep her head in the game and didn't have time to worry about Abigail playing worship leader to the shoebox altar in her closet. Constance tried to put the odd experience behind her and spent the rest of her evening preparing for the next day and reading in bed.

She caught herself nodding off within minutes of opening her book. Giving in without a fight, she placed the book on her nightstand and turned out the light. Sleep pulled her into the mattress like an anchor.

As she drifted into sleep, the last thing she thought of was Abigail's closed eyes and soundlessly moving lips as she kneeled in the closet before the portrait of her dead relatives.

When she woke the next morning, Constance felt physically refreshed but mentally drained. Although she couldn't recall her dreams, her mind had been hyperactive throughout the night. She gathered her thoughts as she sat on the edge of her bed. She suspected an emotionally demanding day awaited her on the other side of her morning routine.

After dressing and brushing her teeth, she met with Abigail, Aunt Jenny, and Uncle Hank for breakfast in the kitchenette. They ate an uneventful breakfast before piling into Uncle Hank's four-door Bel Air. Constance and Abigail sat on the expansive bench seat with enough space between them for another person. Constance normally enjoyed the car's cushy baby-blue-and-white vinyl interior, but it felt at extreme odds with her drastically deconstructed reality. The bright, plush surfaces exuded upbeat comfort while her world felt shadowed and uncomfortable.

Ten minutes later, Uncle Hank steered the Bel Air into the small parking lot behind Gracey's Funeral Home, parking one space over from the only other car in the lot. Constance suspected the stretched black Lincoln belonged to the funeral home director, Norman Daniels.

Uncle Hank turned in his seat to look at Constance and Abigail. "You girls okay?"

Constance shared a look with her sister before nodding to acknowledge her uncle. Then they opened their respective doors and exited the vehicle.

They crossed the small lot to the patron entrance at the back of the building. An ornate wooden door and wrought iron sconces stood out against the surrounding flat brick wall. A hunter green awning with *Gracey's* scrolled in sweeping cursive letters protected the entrance. Uncle Hank held the door open as Aunt Jenny and the girls stepped into the carpeted foyer.

As the door closed behind them, Constance heard a chiming deep in the building. She suspected a bell had notified Norman of their arrival. Moments later, footsteps crossed the wooden floorboards behind one of several doors in the long, wide hall before them. Norman emerged from a set of doors on the left side of the hall.

Constance thought he must be at least eighty years old the way he moved. His small, wet eyes and prominent ears reinforced her assumptions as he approached them. He moved well for a man his age and carried himself with pride. Mr. Daniels extended his right hand to Uncle Hank and kept his left hand tucked in a small pocket of his gray vest. He wore matching gray slacks and a buttoned white collared shirt with the sleeves rolled up his forearms.

"Good morning, Hank."

"Good morning, Mr. Daniels." Hank carefully gripped the older man's hand. By the slight wince on his face, Constance thought Uncle Hank had underestimated his elder's strength.

"And you must be Jenny, Constance, and Abigail."

They responded, one after the other, as he offered each a more subtle handshake than he'd lent Uncle Hank.

"I'm sorry for your loss. Delilah was such a lovely lady. Always so nice to me, especially during everything with young Adeline and, well of course, also Mrs. Lydia." His eyes drifted in thought to the wall over Abigail's shoulder for a moment before he found focus with them again. "Well then, shall we? Right this way."

Mr. Daniels turned on his heels with exceptional grace and stepped toward a set of double doors at the end of the hall. They followed, the sound of their shoes quieted by the substantial carpet pile beneath them.

Abigail whispered behind her, "This is the nicest carpet I've ever walked on. Feels like a dream."

Constance half-smiled over her shoulder. She turned her head back just as they rounded through the double doors and into a comfortable room containing a couch, a large coffee table, and several chairs. A few narrow tables bordered the room, each containing picture frames and photo books. It dawned on Constance that this room contained the discussions, details, and decisions that filled the adjacent rooms with events. She drew a shaky breath in anticipation.

Mr. Daniels took a seat in a chair as Uncle Hank and Aunt Jenny sat on the couch across the table. Constance and Abigail sat in chairs at the ends of the coffee table, completing the square. Constance saw several large picture books on the table and resisted the urge to pick one up.

"Thank you for meeting me first thing in the morning. We have a lot to discuss but I believe this conversation won't take more than the allotted time. I assume you've considered burial options but knowing your family's history, I also assume Delilah's resting place will be the family cemetery. Is that correct?"

"Yes, that's correct," Aunt Jenny replied.

"Very well. And you prefer a traditional casket burial, correct?"

"Yes, please," Constance replied before Aunt Jenny or Uncle Hank.

Mr. Daniels gave Hank and Jenny an inquisitive look, as if confused about who held the decision-making authority for the family.

Uncle Hank spoke to allay the older man's concern. "Yes, sir." He gave Constance an apologetic smile and a nod to apologize for the uncomfortable situation.

Stewing in the ageism's aftermath, she sat on the front edge of her chair, resting her elbows on her knees and lacing her hands. She didn't intend to give in to the unspoken norms at play.

Mr. Daniels resumed, "I propose we schedule the viewing, burial, and wake for this upcoming Saturday morning, if that works for you. Is 10 a.m. reasonable?"

This time, Uncle Hank, Aunt Jenny, and Constance all agreed in unison. Abigail smiled at the chorus, saying nothing but sending support to Constance with her bright, adoring eyes. Constance wondered if Abigail understood the meeting's significance. She appeared unphased by the gravity of the situation.

Mr. Daniels nodded at each of the respondents, jotted some notes on a small green notebook, and pressed on.

"Very well. Sandy, my assistant, will put together the invitations. I'll need some information for the obituary and a picture of Delilah by tomorrow afternoon, please."

Mr. Daniels reviewed a few notes, then he closed his notebook and turned his attention to Abigail.

"Sweetheart, would you be comfortable here by yourself if I took your aunt, uncle, and sister to the room next door for a few minutes?"

Abigail smiled. "That's fine, sir. Thank you."

"Great. Would you three please join me in the next room?" Mr. Daniels gracefully stood, respecting his old bones.

Constance, Uncle Hank, and Aunt Jenny rose from their seats and followed Mr. Daniels into the hall and through another set of wooden double doors. They entered a room of similar size to the last but void of furniture. Caskets of various finishes and colors bordered the room. Constance had predicted this moment, yet she felt uncomfortable and unprepared.

Needing a minute alone to gather her thoughts, she crossed the room to a beautiful, dark wood casket. Mr. Daniels had Uncle Hank and Aunt Jenny's undivided attention at a silver metal model on the opposite side of the room. They spoke with hushed voices as if to avoid disturbing someone at rest in one of the room's many closed coffins.

Constance tentatively placed her hands on the smooth lid of the casket before her. The coolness of the glasslike surface pulled the warmth from her exposed palms. She closed her eyes as her imagination set its hooks in her. She thought of the burial to come, the people all dressed in black, the coffin descending into the grave, the family's cemetery welcoming another cadaver to its cohort.

The coffin grew colder beneath her hands. Constance tried to lift them but something firm, something *foreign*, rooted them in place. She opened her eyes, panic swelling in her chest. She watched her hands submerge into the coffin's mirror-like surface, which solidified, trapping her up to the wrists. Through the lid, she felt fingers interlock with hers.

Constance looked over her shoulder in a panic. The trio of older adults remained engaged in low conversation, oblivious to her predicament.

From the corner of her vision, the upper half of her coffin's split lid crept open. Her head snapped forward against her will. She tried to clamp her eyes shut but lacked any control of her body.

As the lid raised, she saw them—Lydia and Adeline, lying on their sides, face-to-face, mother cuddling child.

Lydia opened her eyes and turned her face toward Constance.

"This is love. *You* will burn for it. The girl will be mine."

She watched as Adeline became Abigail. Her sister lay in Lydia's embrace, dead and graying.

Constance's head swam as oxygenated blood flooded her body, her chest heaving in hyperventilation. She felt her knees weaken. She feared blacking out and being suspended by the wrists from the coffin.

A voice from behind. "Constance?"

The coffin lid slammed shut, blowing her hair back as her hands emerged.

She spun around and faced Aunt Jenny.

"Hey ... you don't look too hot, kid. Hank, I'm going to take her to the other room."

Constance broke down and sobbed as Aunt Jenny ushered her out of the showroom.

CHAPTER THIRTEEN

No one spoke on the car ride home. Constance watched the trees and scenery whip by through the window as she fought to regain her mental footing after the experience in the casket showroom. Since her mother's accident, overwhelming visions and surreal experiences had haunted her. At first, she'd contributed these experiences to the shock of her mother's accident. Now, she feared something more significant, more troubling.

She feared she was losing her mind.

As Constance's heart sank, she felt Abigail's hand on her right leg. She turned from the window and toward her little sister.

"We'll be okay. Things will calm down once it's just us," Abigail said in a low voice. Her eyes left Constance to make sure Aunt Jenny and Uncle Hank hadn't heard her. She turned back to Constance and mouthed the words *I love you*.

Constance feigned a smile, placed her hand on Abigail's, and said, "I love you too."

Her sister's maturity took Constance back. *She sounds so ... grown.*

As Uncle Hank eased the car into the gravel driveway, Aunt Jenny announced, "Looks like we have a visitor."

Constance looked ahead to see Mr. Holcomb, her school's guidance counselor, standing on the front porch.

The car rolled to a stop and Constance exited the car before Uncle Hank secured the engine. She wanted to greet Mr. Holcomb before Aunt Jenny or Uncle Hank delayed their conversation with small talk. As she rounded the back of the vehicle, Mr. Holcomb descended the front porch steps to meet her.

"Hello, Constance."

"Hello, Mr. Holcomb."

It was surreal talking with him here, at the house, and not in that godforsaken school. He seemed taller, more present here than at any time in the school.

"I wanted to stop by and check on you. I don't know what to say, Constance. I'm so sorry about what's happened."

"Thank you, sir. I'm surprised they let you out during school hours," she said, making a small joke to lighten the mood.

Behind her, car doors opened and closed, and feet crossed gravel to where Constance stood near the convergence of the drive and the front walkway. Constance looked over her left shoulder and saw Uncle Hank, Aunt Jenny, and Abigail approaching. A curious smile decorated Abigail's face. Aunt Jenny and Uncle Hank appeared less happy with their visitor.

Mr. Holcomb turned his attention to the arriving party. He extended his right hand to Uncle Hank.

"Good day; you must be Uncle Hank and Aunt Jenny. My name is Calvin Holcomb. I'm the guidance counselor at Toano High School. My condolences for your loss."

Uncle Hank nodded and shook Mr. Holcomb's hand. "It's nice to meet you, Calvin."

Aunt Jenny asked, "Would you like to come in, sir? Can I interest you in something to drink?"

"That sounds nice. But only for a few minutes. I'm playing hooky and need to return to the school before anyone knows I'm gone." He smiled at Constance, adding the punchline to her joke.

Abigail stepped to Mr. Holcomb and presented her hand before he could turn to follow Uncle Hank and Aunt Jenny.

"Hello, sir. My name is Abigail. I'm the better of the two sisters, just in case you were wondering."

Mr. Holcomb's smile spread wide and bright on his dark face. He took her small hand in his and shook it with vigor, as if she were a similarly sized man rather than a twelve-year-old girl. "Well, it's a pleasure to meet you, Abigail. It's not every day that I get to meet someone better than Constance. This makes my day."

Abigail laughed as Constance interjected. "This way, Mr. Holcomb. You'll have to excuse my sister. She has a strange sense of humor."

Mr. Holcomb pointed his right arm toward the front door. "After you, ladies."

They ascended the front steps and entered the cool shadows of the silent home. Constance drew a heavy breath as the door closed behind them. She hoped nothing odd would happen with Mr. Holcomb in the house. Having a new soul in the home brought a sense of unexplainable risk that she couldn't quite identify.

They stepped beyond the foyer and past the entrance to the sitting room on their right. Constance glanced over her shoulder, watching Mr. Holcomb as he explored the sitting room with his eyes from the safety of the hall. She noticed a look of discomfort stretch across his features, his eyes tightening. She wondered if he was uncomfortable being in their home because of what he'd heard about their family in the past year.

They arrived in the kitchenette after Uncle Hank and Aunt Jenny. Aunt Jenny pulled a glass pitcher of iced tea from the refrigerator and Uncle Hank brought several drinking glasses to the table.

"Please, take a seat," he said as he set the glasses down and pulled out a chair.

"I'm going to my room, if that's okay," Abigail said.

"That's fine, dear." Aunt Jenny filled four glasses and set one aside.

"I appreciate the hospitality." Mr. Holcomb settled his large frame into a chair and admired a tall glass of iced tea. "I've taken care of Constance's absence from school this week. There's no need to send a note or visit the office to explain."

Uncle Hank nodded. "We appreciate that. It's been a tough few days."

Mr. Holcomb spoke to Constance. "Is it premature for me to ask whether you'll stay with us at Toano?"

"Against my better judgment, yes, I'm staying in Toano."

"That's good. Are you moving in with your family?" He gestured to Aunt Jenny and Uncle Hank.

"Abigail and I will stay here. Just the two of us."

He raised his eyebrows in apparent surprise. "Okay. Well, that'll be quite the adjustment for you."

"We'll be fine. Abigail is housebroken, I know how to cook popcorn, and the house is paid off. What could go wrong?"

He smiled wryly and sipped his tea. He sought agreement from Aunt Jenny and Uncle Hank in a glance and got it.

"Well, I'm here for you if you need any support. I spoke with your teachers, and they will do whatever it takes to get you back on track when the time comes to return."

"I'm coming back next week," she replied.

Aunt Jenny opened her mouth to speak, but Uncle Hank beat her to it.

"We'll play it by ear. We scheduled the funeral for Saturday morning here at the house. We'll see how the girls feel afterwards."

Constance leaned forward and placed a hand on Mr. Holcomb's left forearm. "I'll be there Wednesday. Thank you."

He looked down at her hand, apparently surprised by the contact. He smiled and lifted his eyes.

"Great. I look forward to seeing you on Wednesday."

Constance saw genuine concern in his eyes. *I believe he truly cares. He's a good man, one of the few people I trust outside of this house*, she thought. She drew her hand back and lifted her tea for a sip.

A knock at the door interrupted their conversation. Aunt Jenny stood. "I'll get that."

Uncle Hank watched her walk to the front door. Constance thought he looked guilty. She craned her head to look down the hall toward the front door.

Roy crossed the threshold in a wall of daylight.

"Great," Constance said, cutting her eyes at Uncle Hank. He looked deflated and flushed. "You knew he was coming over and didn't tell me?"

"He wanted to come to the funeral home, but I didn't think it was a good idea, so I told him to come over this afternoon instead. I meant to tell you, but surprisingly, he's early for the first time in his life."

Mr. Holcomb looked unsettled. "I should get going. I'm available if you need to talk. Just call the front office and they'll put you through to me."

"I will. Thanks."

They stood in unison, pushing their chairs away from the table as Roy and Aunt Jenny entered the kitchenette.

Constance hated the petty look on her father's face as he sized up Mr. Holcomb.

She *knew* what he was thinking. Among his shortfalls of gambling and cheating, he also harbored ill feelings toward the county's Black residents. Delilah never held the same feelings. She raised her girls to show respect to everyone in their small community, regardless of race or income. However, Roy often verbalized his discontent for the county's Black folk during the girls' upbringing. He'd thrown a small fit two years earlier when "that useless slug" President Johnson had signed the Civil Rights Act into law and ended legal segregation. She never understood why he felt the way he did. Why hate someone you don't even know?

Constance held her breath as Mr. Holcomb extended his hand to her much smaller father. "Hi, I'm Calvin Holcomb, Constance's guidance counselor at the high school. It's nice to meet you."

Roy looked frail compared to the much larger man before him. He took Mr. Holcomb's hand without making direct eye contact.

"Likewise, Calvin. I'm Roy, Constance's father." He released Mr. Holcomb's hand with awkward quickness, rubbing them together as if trying to wipe away his discomfort.

"I'll show you out, sir," Constance said.

She walked Mr. Holcomb to the front door, thanked him for the visit, and watched him climb into his car from the front porch.

———

Back in the kitchenette, Uncle Hank gave Roy the details of the morning's visit to the funeral home. Constance caught only the tail end of the conversation as she returned from sending off Mr. Holcomb.

"He seems like a very nice man," said Aunt Jenny.

"He is." Constance registered a disbelieving look on Roy's face before he realized she was looking in his direction. *Busted*, she thought. *You can't hide your ugliness from me.*

Roy adjusted in his seat. "Can we talk about this week's plans for folks coming into town? I have plenty of room at my place if anyone needs somewhere to stay."

"We appreciate that, Roy. I believe most people are staying at the Parkway Inn, but I'll let them know in case they want to save a couple of bucks." Uncle Hank nodded.

Roy exhaled and slumped in his chair with relief. "Sure thing. The offer stands if anyone is interested."

Of course you're relieved, Constance thought, taking her seat at the table. *You don't really want people staying at your place, you just feel obligated to offer so we won't think less of you.*

"When will the fellas from town start their work out back?" Aunt Jenny asked, skirting the ugly details.

Uncle Hank looked from her to Constance, then answered. "They'll bring their equipment and prep the site Thursday afternoon, but they won't dig until Friday."

Silence ruled the room for what seemed to Constance like an eternity before Aunt Jenny spoke up again. "I may take the girls into town to pick up the flowers Friday morning so we're not in the way."

She's trying so hard to protect us from the ugliness of it all. Constance considered pushing back against the obvious sheltering but decided against it. Aunt Jenny was probably right. It was best to avoid exposing Abigail to the grave digging. That may be a bit much for a twelve-year-old preparing to bury her mother.

Roy stepped in. "I'll be here to help the guys. I'll bring lunch on Friday, so you don't have to stop what you're doing to feed everybody."

"That would be great," Aunt Jenny replied.

"Are you coming to Mama's service?"

Constance's question to Roy stole the oxygen from the room. She could tell by the dumb look on his face that she'd surprised him. He reeled in the spotlight suddenly shone on him.

"Well, yeah ... yes, of course I'm coming. Is that something we need to discuss?" He looked at her in frustrated disbelief.

"Yes, it is," she replied with confidence, maintaining uninterrupted eye contact with her father. "I want your word that you're coming before I get Abigail's hopes up that you'll be there."

He looked shocked by her stern shift. Constance refused to take her eyes off him, taking full control of the situation. *You've got this. Stay strong. He's let you down too many times before. Don't let him hurt you again and especially don't let him hurt Abigail.*

Roy cleared his throat, his face filling with color as his embarrassment escalated. "I'll be there. That is, if I'm welcome."

Constance felt pride and exhilaration surge in her. She was holding him accountable for his commitments, something her mother tried to do for half her adult life. Now she had to protect them from his lies and failures, and she felt jaded and bitter from past mistreatment.

"I would like that very much, but I need you to promise me you'll be here on time. And you'll be sober and alone."

Roy's hands shook with anger as he processed her demands. Her *justified* demands. He pressed his lips together, restraining himself while he mustered a calculated response. Finally, he gained his composure and made eye contact again.

"I promise I'll be on time, sober, and alone."

Unexpected tears threatened as the week's emotions roiled in her. Normally, confrontation with him wouldn't upset her this much but she'd been dealing with so much—it was all so much. And damn him for putting her in his position. He was supposed to be the more responsible party here.

"Okay. Thank you." She stood, smoothed her clothes with both hands, and left the room before she lost the upper hand.

CHAPTER FOURTEEN

With the funeral approaching, the next two days passed in a rotation of consoling visitors and preparation of the home for Delilah's return. Constance felt like an ephemeral ghost in the home, floating amongst the madness, quiet and unusually introverted.

She awoke on Thursday, two days before her mother's funeral, under the same melancholic blanket of mourning and silence as the days prior. She hadn't suffered from nightmares or traumatic visions since the experience at the funeral home. The recent ceasefire convinced her that those terrifying events were likely caused by the stress of her mother's passing. Now, time was at work, probing her heart and suppressing her spirit under the forceful hand of grief.

Constance went about the morning with studious focus. First, she joined Aunt Jenny to rearrange the sitting room to accommodate her mother's body and casket, which was scheduled to arrive in the early afternoon. They spent the rest of the morning dusting, sweeping, and organizing the main floor of the home. According to Uncle Hank's most recent estimate, they expected close to a hundred family, friends, and acquaintances to attend the services. The rotating body of visitors would start Friday morning as they opened the house to close family who wished to pay their final respects with a brief, private visitation before half the town showed up for the funeral.

After her lunch, Constance retreated to the screened back porch to breathe some fresh fall air. She needed a moment to think. She felt unsure about the emotional prospects of the next two days. The funeral home would deliver Delilah within the hour and her mother would lie in wait in the sitting room until her burial on Saturday morning. The casket would remain closed because of her extensive burns, but how would Constance and Abigail feel about their mother's dead body sitting there in the home? This was strange territory for the girls.

What about the visions, daydreams, and nightmares? Will you avoid those little gifts while your mother spends her last hours above the dirt with you? What if they start again?

Constance dashed the concern from her mind before she considered an answer to the question. She wouldn't allow the machinery of her anxiety to start.

The sound of a car pulling into the driveway interrupted her thoughts. Uncle Hank appeared in the side yard as a stretched black hearse pulled forward to position its rear door closest to the front walkway. Chrome bumpers, light bezels, and ornamental accents adorned the front of the car, lending elegance to the hearse's ominous posture.

Constance squinted as sunlight reflected from the polished surfaces. She shielded her eyes against the sharp light with one hand as the front doors opened and Mr. Daniels and a younger gentleman exited the vehicle. They closed their doors and met Uncle Hank at the rear of the car. Constance heard their voices but couldn't decipher their words. The back door to the house opened and Aunt Jenny appeared.

"Hey, Mr. Daniels is a bit earlier than expected. Would you like to join me in the sitting room, or do you prefer to wait?"

"I see that. I'll come with you." Constance stood and crossed the porch for the home's stuffy interior. Once inside, she pressed the door shut and followed Aunt Jenny through the kitchenette, short hall, and foyer. The front door opened behind them as they entered the sitting room on the left. Constance looked back as Uncle Hank graced the foyer, speaking in an elevated voice.

"We'll be in here to the right, Mr. Daniels. Oh, sorry for the intrusion, ladies."

"It's no bother," Aunt Jenny said. "We're here to welcome our lady home." She huddled close to Constance, shuffling toward the far end of the couch. They stood across from the space they'd cleared for Delilah to the right of the fireplace hearth and under the windows looking onto the front porch.

"Did you tell Abigail?" Constance asked in a low voice.

Aunt Jenny replied without looking away from the foyer, "She's napping in her room."

Uncle Hank held the front door open as Mr. Daniels and his young helper navigated the front steps out of view. Soon, they passed through the door, light pouring in around the two men and the narrow, blonde wood casket spanning between them.

Constance held her breath as the men wheeled her mother's closed casket into the room. *She's finally home.* Uncle Hank maneuvered past the men to close the door behind them as Mr. Daniels backed into the room. He guided their payload as his twenty-something helper gently pushed, navigating the clear path from the sitting room entrance to the place before the windows. Once there, they locked the cart's wheels to keep it from rolling off station. Mr. Daniels pulled a handkerchief from his back pocket and dabbed his forehead. His lips moved in short, jittery fits as he caught his breath and muttered to himself. He turned and addressed Aunt Jenny and Constance.

"A blessed afternoon, ladies. Thank you for your patience. We got here as early as we could."

"You arrived at the perfect time, sir. We appreciate you accommodating our request for a home viewing," Aunt Jenny replied.

"It's no trouble at all, dear," he said. "Have you met my grandson, Kenneth? Kenneth, this is Mrs. Jenny and her niece, Constance."

The boy bowed his head. "It's a pleasure to meet you, ladies. My condolences for your loss."

"It's very nice to meet you, Kenneth," Aunt Jenny answered.

Constance glanced in his direction, nodding and smiling before returning her attention to her mother's closed casket.

"Well, we'll be on our way. I'll be in touch tomorrow morning, Hank. Excuse us, ladies." Mr. Daniels shuffled his grandson out of the room toward the front door. A minute later, the hearse roared to life and backed out of the driveway.

Aunt Jenny and Constance stood before Delilah's concealed body. The afternoon sun shone through the front windows, accentuating the swirling patterns of the casket's wood grain.

"It's smaller than I thought it would be. Is she ... wrapped up in there? Like she was in the hospital?"

Aunt Jenny sighed. "No, dear. They removed her dressings at the hospital before Mr. Daniels picked her up. I brought him one of her best dresses on Tuesday."

Constance nodded in understanding. She heard footsteps in Abigail's bedroom overhead, followed by footsteps descending the stairs. Constance walked out of the room to meet her little sister. She arrived just as Abigail came into view on the lower half of the stairs.

"Hey kiddo," she said.

"Hi. Is someone here? I heard a car engine in the driveway and woke up."

"Mr. Daniels just left."

Understanding settled into Abigail's sleepy eyes as she reached the main floor. She looked past Constance to the sitting room entrance.

"So, she's home?"

Constance exhaled a heavy breath. "Yes, she's home."

Abigail looked back to Constance, her eyes alight, a broad smile stretching across her youthful face. "Mama's home."

Constance spent the rest of the afternoon cleaning the downstairs with Abigail and Aunt Jenny. They had an early dinner of meatloaf and mashed potatoes with Uncle Hank in the kitchenette, then spent an hour in the sitting room, reminiscing about fond memories of Delilah. As the sun set behind the house, Aunt Jenny convinced the girls to turn in early, knowing that the next day would be tough on everyone. Constance expected Abigail to object, assuming her earlier nap had rejuvenated her, but the young girl willingly complied.

Constance took a hot bath, slipped on a soft cotton nightgown, and slid into bed. She lay still in the silence, moonlight painting a rectangular path across the room. The day had been surreal. They'd walked around the house, completing menial tasks and having normal conversations while her mother's dead body lay in a wooden box.

She's down there right now, resting in the lightless sitting room.

Quieting her mind, she refused to allow her imagination passage into dark territories. She fell asleep to the persistent ticking sound of her bedside clock's second hand.

Constance awoke in the middle of the night to the sound of voices downstairs. She strained her hearing to overcome the pounding of her elevating heartbeat in her ears. Soon she heard the voices again.

Yes, that is definitely Abigail. Who is she talking to? Holy ... is that ... Mom?

Constance got out of her bed and on her feet in a flash. She seemed to fly rather than walk, her feet never touching the cool hardwood floor in the hallway. Light from the hall bath near the top of the stairs illuminated her path. As she approached the end of the narrow hallway, she saw lights burning in Abigail's bedroom.

The voices sounded much louder from the top of the stairs. She peered into Abigail's room and saw the bedsheets tossed back as if her sister had exited her bed in haste.

Constance slowly descended the stairs. Her heart pounded away, filling her ears with rhythmic panic. What would she find down there?

She reached the landing at the bottom of the stairs, drew a shaky breath, and turned left. Light poured into the hall from the entrance to the sitting room. Abigail's voice carried once again.

"We missed you so much. Constance will come around soon. She just needs to see you the way I do."

What the ...?

"I know, dear. I know," Delilah responded.

Constance broke into a sprint as she rounded the corner to the sitting room entrance, breaching the harsh barrier between light and dark.

She shot up in her bed, gasping for air in the band of moonlight cascading through her bedroom window. Her heart raced in her chest. Constance was safe in bed, not downstairs in the sitting room.

It was just a dream, she thought, flopping back onto her pillow. Relief settled on her as she stared up at the ceiling, slowing her breathing. *Abigail's strange behavior must be influencing my dreams. She's been odd but "talking with our dead mother" odd? Maybe I'm the odd one.*

Returning to sleep seemed like an impossibility, so Constance sat up and swung her legs out of bed. She sat there for a moment, straining her ears to the silence of the sleeping home. No voices, no ghosts, nothing out of the ordinary.

I need you.

Her mother's voice cut through the silence like a radio transmission. Constance froze on the edge of the bed. Had she heard her mother's voice with her ears or her mind?

Constance didn't budge. She did her best to remain calm, but her senses ran wild. Her fingers and toes tingled, and her gut rolled as adrenaline flooded her bloodstream.

Fascinated and perplexed by the dream, she stood and crossed her room. She opened the door and peered into the pitch-black hallway beyond. No light poured forth from Abigail's room or the hall bath. All was dark.

Dream zero, reality one, she thought, keeping a meaningless score in her head.

Constance walked down the hall, leveraging soft footsteps to keep her late-night transit a mystery to the sleeping souls of the home. She didn't want to explain her actions should she wake Uncle Hank or Aunt Jenny, who slept in her mother's former bedroom. Constance reached the top of the stairs without incident. She stood there, listening for several intense seconds as she contemplated her next move.

Should I go down there, into the dark, where my mother's dead body awaits?

Her adrenaline cranked, scrambling her thoughts. She raised one foot and extended it out over the stairs–then paused.

She looked back over her shoulder at Abigail's closed bedroom door. The faint glow of a night light illuminated the space under the door.

She's in there sleeping like a baby.

Constance committed and allowed her foot to drop to the first step. She descended the stairs, doing her best to limit the groans and barks of the old wooden planks underfoot. Reaching the main floor, Constance turned her head toward the sitting room. No lights, no sounds, no concerns so far.

She walked down the short hall and reached the sitting room entrance without incident. She stood at the opening, breathing in slow, shallow breaths to steady her nerves and lessen the sound in her ears. Cool moonlight bathed the shadow-laden sitting room. Her mother's casket sat undisturbed under the illuminated window.

"Hi, Mama," she whispered.

She crept into the room. Nearing the casket, Constance placed her right hand at the foot of the polished wood box. Her eyes crawled up the casket from where her fingertips rested on the cool wood, past the closed lid, to the fireplace mantle beyond. There, in the portrait, Aunt Lydia and

Adeline stood watch over her mother's body like soldiers guarding the body of an eminent citizen laying in honor.

"Hello, ladies. Thank you for keeping Mama company. Please watch over her."

She felt stupid talking to a portrait, especially when her mother's body lay mere inches away beneath the closed lid of the casket under her fingers. But she had faith that somewhere, her aunt and cousin heard her words and that somehow, those words mattered.

"I'm so sorry we didn't have more time together, Mama. Please give me the wisdom to care for Abigail. I promise you I'll show her all the love I can."

Her bottom lip quivered, and her throat tightened as tears threatened. She spread the fingers of both hands across the foot of the casket.

"Tomorrow, everyone will come to visit you. They'll cry, tell us stories, and then they'll leave. But we'll be here. We'll *always* be *here*. I won't leave you." The tears came, slow and steady. "We'll keep you where you belong, with us, with your family. Please, just be there when I need you. I've …"

She paused, embarrassed to continue. She lowered her voice more.

"I've been struggling with things I can't explain. I've had vivid and disturbing visions and dreams. They started around the time of the accident and I'm afraid that they'll get worse." Her hands shook in unison with her voice, tremors radiating throughout her body as she suppressed her emotions. "I know I'm not crazy, but I wouldn't be surprised if I'm still in some type of shock. Abigail is handling things much better than I am, although she's been acting super weird. Anyway, I need you to guide me. Be my guardian angel if that's an option."

She released a relieved breath, wiping the tears from her face with her nightgown sleeves. Her hands returned to the casket lid, this time feeling more comfortable with the arrangement. Her eyes returned to the portrait.

"I hope that you're with Aunt Lydia and Adeline in heaven. I hope that you're happy and warm and bathing in love–I hope it's real."

She hoped because the alternative seemed unbearable. She couldn't imagine her mother dying so brutally, only to be cast into eternal emptiness, a lightless abyss void of warmth, love, and familiar souls. That sounded like hell to her. And the thought of a hell existing without a heaven seemed unbearable. If nothing good existed beyond the inevitability of death, how could she view life as anything other than a gift leading to an inescapable punishment?

You'd better live it up while you can. Your reward for a life well-lived will be the same eternal emptiness that awaits those who waste their precious time. Your reward is the life you live, not what awaits you in death.

The thought pulled her into a pool of depression that threatened to swallow her whole should she not find hope in this new life to buoy her. She never considered living here on this property as the best use of her precious time on earth, but now she'd accepted that fate. Constance needed confirmation that she was making the right decision. She closed her eyes and drew a deep, therapeutic breath.

Calm down, you are overreacting. Take one thing at a time. Mama's gone. You're still here and no matter what awaits on the other side of death, you're alive now.

In response, a repulsive voice slipped into her ear.

"Well, you don't *have* to do anything. Death is *always* an option, whether or not you make the decisions."

Constance jerked her hands back from the casket. She frantically searched the room for the voice's owner and found no one. She was alone except for her mother's corpse and the residents of the portrait mounted upon the mantle.

Gathering her courage, Constance approached the portrait. She stared into Aunt Lydia's eyes. *Was that her voice I heard?*

She leaned closer, reaching beyond the portrait with her mind and heart, seeking Lydia. If she was there, Constance wanted to know now and not in a horrific vision later.

Come on ...

Nothing.

Constance stepped back and exhaled a held breath. She buried her suspicions and turned to leave the room. She ran her fingers along the length of Delilah's casket before exiting the sitting room. As Constance reached the stairs, she wondered if she'd find sleep before sunrise.

CHAPTER FIFTEEN

Constance woke early the next morning, unrested and sluggish from the previous night's exploits. She spent the first hour preparing her mind for the morning's scheduled viewing hours. She exchanged small talk with Abigail, Aunt Jenny, and Uncle Hank over breakfast before she returned to her room to change into a solid gray cable-knit pullover sweater and black slacks. After she dressed, she helped Abigail pick out a dark blue skirt and white blouse. Before leaving Abigail's room, the girls shared a moment of normalcy while Constance braided Abigail's hair.

Family and close friends rotated through the house like troubled spirits until noon. Constance knew most of their visitors, especially the local family and close friends. Those she hadn't met were distant relatives from across the state. She'd likely never see them again, so she didn't dedicate too much energy to memorizing their names or hometowns. Regardless, the conversations were similar.

"We're so sorry for your loss."

"This is such a tragedy. You poor girls must be going through so much."

"Is there anything we can do to help you? Please call if you need anything at all. We're not too far down the road."

Eli's visit was the highlight of her morning. She hadn't seen him since the day of the accident. She felt a tinge of guilt for not realizing this sooner, but she kept it to herself. They spoke on the front porch before he left.

"I don't even know where to begin. How are you?" he asked.

"I'm doing okay, I guess. I'm not sure when it'll all hit me, but I feel like it's coming after the funeral tomorrow."

He didn't reply, probably because he didn't know how to respond to such an ominous proclamation. She wasn't sure how to talk about these things without making it awkward for the other person.

"I'm planning to come back to school next Wednesday, but we'll see how the next few days go. I'm not convinced any amount of time away can prepare me for a return to that prison." She snickered and nudged him with her shoulder to loosen the mood. He smiled and relaxed his shoulders a little.

"Look, I want to be here for you–if you'd like, of course. Is it okay for me to call you or stop by before Wednesday, or should I just wait my turn like all the other prisoners?"

She smiled and pulled on his sleeve. "I hereby authorize you to call or visit at will. Just don't expect me to be normal."

He faked a surprised laugh. "You? Normal? That's the last thing I'd expect."

"Okay, that's enough out of you," she said. "You may want to get out of here before one of my relatives asks if we're dating."

He pulsed his eyebrows up and down to tease her.

She laughed and pushed his arm. "Get out of here, nerd. Will I see you tomorrow?"

He dropped the comedy act, averting her gaze. "I'm not sure I can handle an actual funeral. I've ... I've never been to one. But if you want some support, I'll be here for you."

Constance replied without pause. "That would be nice."

"In that case, I'll see you tomorrow. Now, if you'll excuse me, I need to rummage through my father's closet to find a suit."

"Isn't your dad like twice your height and weight?" she asked.

"Yes. Yes, he is."

They both laughed as he walked down the stairs in a defeated gallop, climbed into his parent's Ford Falcon, and backed out of their driveway as other cars pulled up.

At noon, Abigail helped them prepare a simple lunch of sandwiches, chips, and dill pickles. Constance had noticed her sister's silence over the past days mirrored her own. They'd passed each other throughout the days without saying much other than the occasional word of support during tasks. Now, they sat at the kitchenette table, chewing their food while their minds processed all that had happened and what would happen in the coming day.

As Constance ate, she caught movement at the periphery of her vision. She looked up and out the back door, through the screened back porch, and into the sunny backyard. Two men walked across the yard from the cemetery path, their hands gloved and carrying digging tools. Terracotta clay stained their pant legs and shirt sleeves.

Gravediggers.

They had been hard at work for two days, mostly out of sight. She'd heard their muffled voices as they'd hollered to each other over the mechanical noise of their production or when they had emerged from the trees to access supplies in their truck parked in the driveway.

Uncle Hank appeared from the doorway of the shed on the back left corner of the property, a baseball cap precariously tipped back on his head. He walked over and wiped his brow with an old rag while exchanging words and gestures with the two men. There were nods of agreement and pats of encouragement on the arms to go around as they parted. The diggers made their way to their truck and moments later, their engine roared to life and carried them away.

Constance pulled her attention back from the yard and realized Abigail had been watching her. Constance stopped chewing. Something was *off* about her sister's gaze.

She looked at Aunt Jenny who flipped through a *Better Homes & Gardens* magazine, oblivious to the two girls sitting with her at the table. She looked back to Abigail, swallowing her masticated sandwich.

Abigail slowly chewed as she stared at Constance–*beyond* her. Constance glanced over her shoulder, confirming the absence of anything troublesome or notable. She returned her attention to Abigail, locking eyes and attempting to break her apparent trance.

What's that ...?

Small flames burned deep in Abigail's eyes.

Constance's hands violently slammed to the table under the control of a foreign agent. Her heart fluttered as it kicked into gear. Her eyes remained locked with Abigail's. Abigail's pupils expanded to dominate her corneas. Constance tried to pull her eyes away—to speak; she accomplished neither.

Abigail had full control of her.

Pressure settled into Constance's chest as if someone stood on her, driving the air from her lungs with their full bodyweight.

Abigail's pupils spilled over her corneas' boundaries, emptiness and hungry flames consuming the entire surface of her eyes. Glossy black tears poured in steady streams down her supple cheeks. Her chewing grew more aggravated and animated.

Abigail spoke through a mouth of macerated food. "It's almost time to burn, Constance. Will it be you or me?"

Constance tried to cry out but whimpered pathetically instead. She sat rigid, unable to turn her head or lift her limbs. Her panicked breathing filled her ears. In her peripheral vision, Aunt Jenny read her magazine as if nothing out of the ordinary were happening.

Abigail leaned forward, food spilling from her mouth as she screamed through mad, shaking lips.

"You or me?" Her eyes got wide and she screamed, "You or me!"

<hr>

"Constance. Are you okay?"

Aunt Jenny's voice startled her. Constance sharply inhaled, choking on the food in her mouth.

"You're freaking me out, Constance." Abigail pushed her sister's tea closer, urging her to sip the drink and clear her throat.

Tears welled up in Constance's eyes as she cleared her airway with coughs, her hands planted on the table for support. She reached for her drink and almost tipped the glass over. Abigail countered the clumsy grasping and pressed the glass into Constance's hand.

She paused, drew a deep breath, then drank her tea. She used the exercise to buy her time while she thought about what had just happened.

This can't keep happening. It just can't.

Clearly, something was wrong with her. She'd developed a false sense of security over the four days since her last episode at the funeral home. Apparently, her crazy had gone dormant for a little while before showing up unannounced to crash lunch with the girls.

Constance lowered the glass to the table and placed her left hand on her chest. She flashed an artificial smile to set Aunt Jenny and Abigail at ease. On the outside, she appeared to have regained control. On the inside, despair, bewilderment, and fear wrestled for dominance. She closed her eyes and calmed her breathing. She opened them, calm and collected.

Aunt Jenny's face was a mixed mask of concern and confusion. Probing eyes sat beneath dropped brows, her head cocked to one side. She held a page of her magazine mid-turn between two fingers of her right hand, a quarter sandwich held in her left.

Beside her, Abigail looked calm and entertained. Her giggles subsided as she reached for another potato chip. Constance didn't quite understand what she saw in her sister's face. Abigail looked both concerned and wildly satisfied. The concern dominated the muscles and flesh of her face, but her eyes *glowed* with the satisfaction.

Constance grew cold. She had to regain control.

"I thought you were going to burn a hole in your sister with that stare. Either that or choke to death." Aunt Jenny shook her head and turned back to her magazine.

Constance and Abigail finished their food in silence. Constance's mind raced, pulling apart the details of the apparent daydream, looking for meaning in each obscure detail. She was no wiser by the time she'd finished her food. Aunt Jenny stood first.

"Well, that was enough fun for one meal. I'm going upstairs to clean the hall bathroom. What do you have planned?"

Constance spoke up before Abigail answered. "We're going to visit Uncle Hank in the yard before we straighten up our rooms."

"Okay. Bring him a sandwich while you're at it. That man will skip lunch, then badger me for an hour before supper." She shook her head while she carried her empty plate to the sink.

"Just leave it there on the counter. We'll clean up before we head out," Constance said, pushing her seat back and standing.

"That sounds good to me," Aunt Jenny said, turning to make a sandwich for Uncle Hank.

Five minutes later, Aunt Jenny went upstairs, and the girls left the house for the backyard with Uncle Hank's food wrapped in a paper towel.

Stepping into the afternoon sun invigorated Constance. The sun's warmth filled her with invisible energy as they walked across the yard to the oversized shed on the back of the lot. She couldn't remember the last time she'd felt the sunlight. She realized she hadn't left the house since the trip to the funeral home.

"It's so nice out," Abigail said.

"I agree. The sun feels amazing."

The girls reached the shed and found Uncle Hank singing poorly to himself. He shifted tunes to The Monkees' "Last Train to Clarksville" when he saw them darken the shed entrance.

Constance scrunched her face as if bracing for shock, sending Abigail into wild laughter.

"You know, that's my favorite song. Try not to kill it," Abigail said.

Uncle Hank made an exaggerated frown at the joke. "Fine. I'll stick to singing the blues. It's better music anyway," Uncle Hank said, tossing his hands in the air in fake frustration.

"We made you a sandwich. Aunt Jenny says no complaints until dinner," Constance said, passing the wrapped sandwich to Uncle Hank.

"Thank you, dear. What are you girls up to?"

"We are going for a quick walk to enjoy the sun for a few minutes before we head back in and finish cleaning up."

Abigail turned her head and cast a curious eye at Constance. She winked at Abigail, pausing her sister's curiosity. Distracted by his sandwich, Uncle Hank nodded and unwrapped the paper towel.

"You girls have fun and don't wander too far."

"We won't. We're just going to visit the graveyard and come back." Constance turned, hoping Uncle Hank wouldn't probe further.

Uncle Hank looked up from his exposed sandwich, opened his mouth to reply, then stopped. His facial expressions flashed from confused to understanding.

He nodded and turned back to the shed's interior without speaking another word. Constance prompted Abigail with a silent nod toward the walking path at the edge of the woods on the opposite side of the yard. They stepped across the damp, freshly cut lawn.

The girls walked in silence as they journeyed down the narrow path between the towering trees. The expansive canopy of the woods blocked much of the dominant sunlight they'd enjoyed in the backyard. Constance prepared her heart as she realized the risk she was taking by visiting the family cemetery. She felt vulnerable, her experience at the kitchen table that morning fresh and vivid in her memory.

Is this a terrible idea? Should I be in such a uniquely haunting and spiritually charged place so soon after that?

A new concern clambered to the forefront of her anxious mind—she would be alone with Abigail here. Normally, that wouldn't warrant concern, but Abigail had been so odd lately. Her response after this morning's vision had left Constance unsettled. It was almost as if Abigail had acknowledged something happening without saying it.

Don't forget all the other strange things she's been doing. Remember the altar in her closet? How about talking to herself in her room or how comfortable she'd been in the funeral home and how oddly she behaved on the ride home?

She wrestled her mind into submission. Constance was in the driver's seat, not her little sister or psychological damage from her mother's sudden, violent passing. She wasn't a helpless passenger in a car driven by a rotating cast of ill-conceived visions.

Constance glanced over her shoulder at her sister. Abigail smiled to assure her a tree-dweller hadn't snatched her from the path. Constance turned her eyes back to the freshly maintained trail. The gravediggers who visited that week had cleared the path of fallen limbs, stray tripping hazards, and an impressive dense blanket of leaves which had fallen over the past month.

The cemetery welcomed them in a column of sunlight breaching the opening in the canopy. To the right of the path, beside Aunt Lydia's unspoiled place of internment, their mother's freshly dug grave awaited them.

Constance swallowed a sharp lump in her throat, mustered her confidence, and approached the opening in the earth. Images from her recent nightmare threatened to surface, but she suppressed them. Still, she instinctively placed herself between the hole in the earth and her sister. She closed her eyes and summoned memories of her mother. *I'm in control.*

Delilah came to her in the darkness. Mother holding child, smiling with pride, loving with a heart only a mother can possess. Squeezing her eyes tight, fighting against the sunlight, Constance spurred more vivid memories. She longed to hear her mother's voice in her ear, to smell her hair as they cuddled in her youth.

Nothing more came. Only mottled colors imprinted through closed eyelids.

Small, cool fingers intertwined with hers. Abigail closed the distance between their bodies, sharing in Constance's moment of mourning.

She opened her eyes as Abigail laid her head on her shoulder. Before them, their mother's grave stretched out in anticipation. Tomorrow they would join their friends, family, and acquaintances to lay their mother to rest. For now, the empty grave was theirs alone.

"It's much deeper than I thought it would be," Abigail said.

"Yeah. It sucks," Constance replied as she stood in awe of the massive pile of soil resting a few yards beyond the grave. Seeing all that removed soil revealed with harsh clarity how much earth the men had moved over the past two days. That massive pile would soon separate them from their mother's buried body.

Constance turned to Abigail, taking her hands in hers. For the first time since their mother's death, the sisters stood face-to-face together with only the reality of their future between them. They spent a quiet few seconds looking at their interlocked hands, easing the other's emotions through touch and proximity. Constance spoke first.

"This week has been brutal. I've tried to give you some space to process everything that's going on. Are you okay to talk about what comes after tomorrow?"

Abigail lifted her tear-filled eyes. "Yeah, I guess so."

My God, she looks so young. She's just a kid, Constance thought. Her heart ached for her little sister. She couldn't imagine handling all of this at her age. She forgave Abigail's odd behavior and felt a tinge of guilt for being so hard on her.

"Look, I should have asked you if you were cool with being here alone with me before I stood my ground with Dad, Aunt Jenny, and Uncle Hank. I should have discussed it with you first. Are you sure you're still good with this?"

"Yes," Abigail replied confidently.

"Good." Constance drew a relieved breath and continued. "I'm planning to go back to school in a few days. I told Mr. Holcomb I'd return on Wednesday. That means you'd go back to school on Wednesday as well. Is that okay?"

This time, Abigail hesitated to respond.

"Be honest with me. I'll understand if you don't want to go back so soon. We can work it out with Aunt Jenny."

"No, that's fine," Abigail replied with hesitation.

"Abi, what is it?"

"Well, I just wish you'd talked with me before you decided what you were doing." Abigail released Constance's hands and dried one damp cheek with her shirtsleeve. "If I didn't go back this week, would you just leave me home alone all day?"

Constance wasn't sure how to respond. She hadn't considered how her decision to return so soon would impact her sister. The situation unearthed unasked questions. Regardless of the reason, was it okay to leave Abigail home alone? For how long? Their mom didn't have an issue leaving her alone in the house for quick runs to town, but a whole day alone? Was it even legal to leave her home alone all day?

"Look, I don't want to be a burden. We can both go back on Wednesday, and I'll go stay with Aunt Jenny during the day if I change my mind. I guess I'm just not sure how I'll feel after tomorrow. I'll be fine by Wednesday."

"Okay. I'm sorry about that. I promise to ask next time something big comes up. I'm still figuring out things myself."

They let silence have its moment between them before advancing the conversation. Constance led.

"I want you to know that I'll always put you first. I can never replace Mom, but I'll do my very best to give you everything you need."

"I know you will. I love you, too." Abigail paused. "You may not have thought about this yet, but what happens after you graduate in the spring?"

There it was. The big question. She'd caught Constance off guard, and her lack of an immediate response spoke volumes.

Abigail jumped in to save her. "We don't need to figure that out now. We have so much going on. Let's talk about it some other time."

"No. I'm staying with you." Just like that, Constance committed to Abigail.

"Con—"

"I'm staying. That's it. I'm not leaving you. New York can wait. Maybe I'll never go. Maybe I'll stay here for good." She took Abigail's hands a bit more firmly this time. "It's me and you from here on. That's the way I want it."

Abigail looked up into her face, the tears welling again. "I love you. Thank you." She pulled her hands from Constance and threw her arms around her. They embraced each other, their worlds inextricably reinforced, two girls on the precipice of a terrifying new life together while towering before the precipice of their mother's yearning grave.

They separated and looked in unison into the gaping pit. Simmering just beneath the surface of Constance's fragile reality, bitterness, anger, and fear swam in wild circles as she readied herself for the terrifying unknown ahead.

CHAPTER SIXTEEN

Constance woke the morning of the funeral with a stone heart. Every breath felt like a chore, each thought anchored by grief. The previous day's conversation with Abigail in the family cemetery rang in her thoughts.

She moved through her morning routine in silence, her head low, her mind occupied with an intentional reflection on their life with their mother. They'd reached a bleak milestone in life where death preceded burial and burial preceded a dispiriting period of acceptance. The funeral would force her to accept the permanent loss of her mother, a prolonged period of grief and coping. Now, she'd adopted the compounded challenge of leading herself and Abigail beyond this milestone.

Before their guests arrived, Constance floated down the stairs in a black silk dress. She'd pinned her hair up, ready to receive a pillbox hat. Abigail stood at the bottom of the stairs, wearing a matching dress. Constance embraced her as she reached the main floor.

"You look beautiful, kid. Did you get any sleep last night?"

Abigail replied, "Yeah, it took me a while to fall asleep, but I slept okay. How about you?"

"Not so good."

I definitely didn't *visit Mama in the sitting room last night*, she thought, diverting her eyes to the kitchen in search of Aunt Jenny and Uncle Hank.

"They're on the back porch having coffee," Abigail said.

"I could use a cup myself," Constance replied, taking Abigail's hand and guiding her to the kitchen. She continued to the counter where the partially drained coffee pot greeted her. Aunt Jenny had placed several rows of mugs on the counter to accommodate their guests. Constance picked one up, made sure it was clean, then filled it with coffee and creamer. Abigail sat at the kitchen table before a plate of half-eaten toast and a glass of orange juice.

Constance sipped her coffee as she assessed the weather through the kitchen sink window. The sky held a perfect balance of blue atmosphere and light gray clouds. The trees stood still, their branches clinging to the final vestiges of fall color. On the right side of the property, the path to the family cemetery separated the forest, ready to accept the caravan of mourners promised by the day's service. Constance turned from the window and made her way to the back porch where Aunt Jenny greeted her.

"You look beautiful, dear."

"Thank you." Constance forced a thin smile of gratitude for the compliment. "What can I do to help you before visitors arrive?"

"Oh, nothing at all, thank you. We're as ready as we can be. Father Pritchard should be here any minute. I don't want you or your sister doing anything today, you hear me?" Aunt Jenny tipped her head forward, pulling compliance from Constance with upcast eyes.

"Yes, ma'am," Constance said and drew a mouthful of coffee from her mug. She could already feel the caffeine sharpening her thoughts.

Abigail's face appeared over her right shoulder. She must have been standing on her tippy toes. Constance could feel her swaying against her back to get her chin high enough to clear her sister's shoulder.

"I think someone's here," she said.

"And so it begins," Uncle Hank exhaled, straightening his back as he stood. He wore his charcoal-gray suit and black tie over a starched white shirt. Aunt Jenny stood as well, adjusting her black macrame lace dress.

Abigail darted to the foyer. She opened the front door and the silhouette of Father Pritchard materialized in the doorway as the flow of mourners began.

An hour later, Constance stood in the backyard watching the driveway. To her left, the procession walked down the path to the cemetery in a single file. She wiped her sweaty palms across the back of her legs as her anxiety and frustration mounted.

There'd been no sign of Roy yet.

I knew I couldn't trust him. I just knew it.

Eli stood beside her, his father's suit draped over his bony frame. Constance appreciated him for showing up despite his initial hesitation. She needed some semblance of normalcy in her life, especially that day.

"I'm sure he'll show up," Eli said, trying his best to ease her escalating concern.

"And I'm sure he won't," she replied. She didn't fault him for his poorly informed hopefulness. He'd never lived with Roy's negligence, and he wanted to help her. She'd admired his steadfast optimism since the day they'd met.

It was one of his most endearing qualities. But today, that optimism had no chance of survival.

The back door opened, and Uncle Hank appeared on the uncovered section of the back porch. His pursed lips and furrowed brow showed his concern for her.

"It looks like we're heading to the cemetery in a minute." Constance turned her full attention to Eli. "Why don't you head down there ahead of us? I'll catch up with you afterwards."

"Of course," he replied, his intense eyes overrunning with empathy for her.

Uncle Hank walked down the wooden steps to the yard and closed the distance between them as Eli departed for the path. Constance returned her eyes to the driveway. Her neck and face felt flushed. There was no way to hide her anger and disappointment.

"I'm sorry," Uncle Hank said as he met her.

"You don't have to apologize. You didn't neglect to show up at your ex-wife's funeral to support your children."

"Jenny and your sister are on their way out. The service starts in a few minutes." He soothed her upper arm with his heavy hand.

At first, she felt the urge to pull away and keep her guard up, but she knew that wouldn't be fair to him. Also, she craved support, especially today. It was a shame she'd never receive it from the man who created her.

"I'm ready," she huffed, abandoning hope of Roy's arrival. She pushed the bitterness down into a pocket of her heart reserved for the disappointment of their relationship. Her anger gave way to sorrow. She realized that she'd allowed justified indignation to replace her grief in an ineffectual attempt to hide from the fear and pain waiting for her in the cemetery. She'd subconsciously chosen distraction over facing the inevitable.

I'll never forgive him for doing this to Abigail.

On cue, Aunt Jenny and Abigail appeared on the back porch and joined them in the yard. Aunt Jenny had been crying, her makeup marred by tears. She sniffled and smiled at Constance. Uncle Hank put his arm around her and hugged her before turning to the girls.

"Are you girls okay? No one will be upset if you decide not to attend."

The girls exchanged a quick look and nodded to affirm their readiness. Constance took Abigail's hand in hers and rubbed the back with her other hand. They walked to the path, leading Uncle Hank and Aunt Jenny.

One moment, the journey down the path felt dreamlike, but the next moment, it became brutally real. The trees swayed despite the absence of a noticeable breeze. The sun danced in and out of the clouds, casting mammoth shadows one moment, then disclosing every detail of the surrounding forest in brilliant light, the next.

Constance held up well until she noticed the throng of mourners at the head of the path. Suddenly, she felt exposed. The sun became a massive spotlight disclosing her location to the world. There was nowhere to hide, no way to shed the identity she now wore as the oldest surviving child of a deceased mother.

As they reached the cemetery, the crowd parted to allow their passage. People wept as they passed, huddling together for comfort. Constance felt pitied and awful. She loathed the attention but accepted the inevitable focus that came with being the immediate family of the deceased. As the mourners parted, Delilah's grave came into view in harsh detail. Her mother's coffin sat over the gaping earth like a snack dangling over a ravenous mouth. Constance heard a diminutive groan escape Abigail as they took their places alongside their mother. She pulled Abigail close and pressed her head to her shoulder. Abigail wrapped her arms around Constance's waist and squeezed for comfort.

Father Pritchard's words plowed through the autumn air, each word accentuated with intense reverence. "Dear friends and family, today we gather to commit our dear Delilah to the earth ..."

Those were the last words Constance heard. She stared at her mother's coffin, blocking out the people, the lamentations, everything but her mother and dear Abigail clinging to her arm. Silent sobs racked their bodies as misery devoured their hearts. Tears coursed down her cheeks, blurring her vision and burning her skin. Constance couldn't concentrate. All at once, her mind flooded with every memory she'd shared with Delilah over eighteen years of childhood.

Panic took root in her sour gut. This was it. This was the end. She opened her mouth to draw more breath as the casket swam in her vision. Every knot and wave in the wood grain carried her to another memory, another conversation, another sensation. The thoughts came faster, sweat dampening her dress against her young skin. Too young for death, too young to adopt a preteen girl, too young to lose her own youth.

Time turns now. *Time hammers you with brutality* right now. *What you knew is no longer, what you'll come to know will terrify you. You've just begun to mourn. You've just begun to burn.*

Constance tried to pull her eyes away from the casket but could only stand there in shock as Father Pritchard walked in a circle around Delilah's suspended casket.

Get a hold of yourself. You're missing the most important moment in your life.

The coffin jostled in the tight aperture of her vision and Constance felt her knees melt under her. Abigail caught Constance as Uncle Hank stepped in to brace her.

The lid jumped and Constance groaned.

Please ...

Darkness took her.

CHAPTER SEVENTEEN

Constance flitted in and out of consciousness like a powerless swimmer pulled out to sea in a rip current. One moment, the current pulled her under, enveloping her in an ocean of shadow, numb paralysis, and helplessness. The next, she surfaced, gasping for air, blitzed by sunlight as she bounced in Uncle Hank's arms. Then back under.

She surfaced again on the sitting room couch. Dr. Adams, the family's physician, squatted next to her and exchanged muffled words with Uncle Hank, who stood at her feet. The sitting room spun, urging her return to unconsciousness. She looked around for anything stable and found the portrait of Aunt Lydia and Adeline fixed above the mantle. Everything else pivoted and spun around the fulcrum point of the portrait. Her stomach turned as she returned to the dark.

She surfaced for the last time. The portrait of Aunt Lydia and Adeline greeted her again as she fought to understand how she'd arrived there from the cemetery. She tried to sit up, but Dr. Adams interceded.

"It's okay, Constance. It's me, Dr. Adams. You're in the house. You passed out, dear. Lie here and get your wits about you before you sit up, okay?"

"What happened?"

She remembered standing in the cemetery. She remembered feeling that daydream sensation again, then … Abigail's arms wrapped around her.

The coffin lid moved.

Her mind cleared. She struggled to repress a well of emotions boiling up inside her.

"I'm missing the burial. I need to see her. I need to be there for Abigail." She forced herself into a seated position.

Dr. Adams shot Uncle Hank a desperate look. Uncle Hank opened his mouth to speak, then stopped.

"Give me one moment, Doc." He walked down the hall toward the back of the house.

"Well, you look much better than you did a few minutes ago, kid." Dr. Adams stood and gave her some space. "I'm just glad your sister could hold you until your uncle got to you or you may have fallen and been injured."

Constance swung her feet off the couch and planted them on the floor. She pressed her hands to her eyes and blinked, clearing her vision and her thoughts. Uncle Hank's heavy footsteps echoed down the hall as he returned to them.

"It looks like the procession is on its way back. Abigail is fine. She's with Aunt Jenny. Rest, honey."

It's over. She's finally at rest, Constance thought as her welling emotions ran over. She stood, tears streaming down her face, and walked to her room as fast as she could. Constance laid on her bed for the rest of the night and wept until she'd run out of tears to cry.

Constance woke the next morning with fire in her veins, having reached a breaking point in the past twenty-four hours. She'd confronted the finality of her mother's burial, suffered Roy's predictable neglect at her most vulnerable moment, and experienced another disturbingly vivid vision. She was struggling to determine just how mentally damaged she'd become and refused to bring it to anyone's attention for fear of losing Abigail. She needed silence to think. Constance needed the healing hand of time.

She heard Roy's car grace the driveway from her bedroom. Apparently, Roy thought he could roll in at his convenience to drop empty apologies and promises at the feet of his wounded children.

Not now. Never again.

Constance stood and closed her eyes.

Okay, Mama. I'm cashing in on that motherly guidance and strength. Please guide me through this. Give me the words to get through this conversation. I'll try my best not to lose my temper.

She opened her eyes and left her room on a mission. She arrived downstairs just in time to see Uncle Hank pass through the back door and onto the porch. Constance assumed he wanted to intercept Roy before he tried to enter the house, trying his best to protect her from a contentious conflict and she loved him for it. However, Constance's desire to set Roy straight far surpassed her concern for herself. She reached the front door and stormed down the front porch steps to the walkway.

Constance reached the edge of the driveway before Roy had exited the Cadillac, locking eyes with Uncle Hank over the length of the massive car. He tried to intercept her.

"I've got this. Let's get you back insi—"

"Uncle Hank," she said, stopping him in his tracks. "I love you for all that you've done to care for and protect us, but *I've* got this. Please." She felt the heat in her face and the intensity in her eyes. Her thoughts raced and her heart pounded as her confidence soared. She was a huntress and the dishonest man exiting the car was her prey.

Roy turned in her direction and raised an open hand to Uncle Hank.

"It's okay, Hank." Roy closed the car door and briskly walked toward Constance.

"Don't take another step, Roy," Constance ordered.

Roy stopped, wincing at the sound of his daughter saying his name in such a condescending tone.

"You shouldn't have come here. You should have just stayed away for good. I can't believe you'd—"

"Let me speak," he demanded.

"Don't interrupt me! You have *no* right to speak."

"Watch it, Constance. You may be upset but I'm your father."

"Not anymore, you aren't. Me and Abigail—we don't have a father. You are *nothing* to us. In fact, I don't want to hear whatever lame excuse you have for not being here yesterday." Her body shook with anger. "We needed you yesterday more than ever and you could not care less. You never cared."

"That's not true. I love you girls more than life. I just couldn't bear to put your mother ..." He squeezed tears from his eyes.

"Because you're weak." Constance spat the words. "You left us to do the dirty work without you. Just like when you left us and we had to pick each other up without you. You never put us first because you're selfish."

"That's enough!" he snapped, taking a heavy step toward her. "How dare you speak to me like that?"

Constance matched his step with one of her own, closing the gap between them. The move surprised him. From the corner of her vision, Constance saw Uncle Hank move into position behind her father–just in case.

"What are you going to do, Roy? Nothing, that's what. You're going to run away from us just like you always have. You don't need to share a story on the way out; just go. This time stay gone. I *never* want to see you again."

She saw heartbreak and desperation in his eyes. A small piece of her buckled but she stood firm. This had to be done. "Look, I know you have problems, but we can't help you. Goodbye, Roy."

Constance turned and left him standing speechless in the driveway with Uncle Hank. She released the tears of frustration and relief that she'd been holding back. And through those tears, she wore the biggest smile she'd had in over a week.

She quickly climbed the front steps and entered the house, closing the door behind her. She stopped as she passed the opening to the sitting room. Abigail sat upright on the couch, her eyes searching Constance's tear-streaked face.

"I'm sorry, kiddo. Did you hear all that?" She sniffled and braced herself for her sister's response.

Abigail smiled. "Thank you. And good riddance, Roy."

And that was enough to throw both girls into a well-deserved fit of laughter and hugs.

Later that afternoon, after an uneventful supper, Aunt Jenny served leftover pound cake and coffee. Throughout the afternoon, Constance had noticed Uncle Hank staring at her when he thought she wasn't paying attention. However, he hadn't said a word to her about what had happened with Roy in the driveway. He broke his silence while they enjoyed the dessert.

"I know you probably don't want me to bring it up, but I've been dying to tell you something all day," he said as he lifted a sizable piece of cake with his fork. He smiled from across the table, encouraging her to consent to the discussion.

"Okay, let's hear it," she said, matching his fork load with hers.

"I'm proud of you," he said, opening his mouth wide to receive his fork's payload.

"Thanks. I appreciate you being there with me." She devoured her piece.

Aunt Jenny raised her eyebrows in surprise. "I may be prouder than both of you. I thought for sure one of you two would come back with his head, but you exercised admirable restraint."

Constance and Uncle Hank nodded at each other, earning a genuine giggle from Abigail. Constance felt a hundred pounds lighter than she had in weeks. Blowing off steam had been tremendously therapeutic.

Aunt Jenny turned to Uncle Hank. "Why don't you run to the house after we clean up from supper? We need to get the mail from the past few days, and you should check on the heat lamp in the well house. It's supposed to dip below freezing tonight and I can't remember the last time we checked that light."

He nodded in agreement while he chewed the massive bite of pound cake.

"Why don't you both go? You need a break from this place for a little while, don't you think?" Constance asked.

"You're not getting rid of us so soon," Aunt Jenny replied.

"You know what I mean. Enjoy a cruise across town. We'll be fine here by ourselves for a few hours. I promise. What's wrong? You don't want to be alone with your husband?" Constance smiled.

"I don't trust him as far as I can throw him. And he's even less trustworthy when we're alone." Aunt Jenny replied, nudging Uncle Hank. He shot her a scandalous look, lifting one eyebrow while tipping his head in her direction.

"Seriously, we'll be fine here," Constance insisted. "I have to go through some of Mama's things, anyway. We'll be fine."

Aunt Jenny and Uncle Hank looked at each other, then at Abigail. She confirmed Constance's claim.

"We'll be fine. You love birds go have fun. Just make sure you're home before your curfew."

Thirty minutes later, Constance and Abigail watched Uncle Hank and Aunt Jenny roll out of the driveway and onto Route 60 as the sun dipped behind the treetops across the street. Standing on the front porch in the cool air of the fall sunset, Constance breathed a sigh of relief.

The girls were alone in the house for the first time in weeks, and she welcomed the isolation.

"I'm going to go through some things in Mama's room. Do you want to take your bath while I'm up there?"

"That sounds good to me," Abigail replied, turning for the front door.

Once inside, the girls walked through the foyer to the stairs. Their footfalls on the wooden steps sounded amplified in the silence of the empty home. Abigail reached the upstairs landing first, diverting into the hall bath. Constance continued down the hall to their mother's room. She heard the water for Abigail's bath running into the tub from down the hall as she entered the primary bedroom.

She could hardly tell that Aunt Jenny and Uncle Hank had stayed in the room over the past few weeks. Everything was as Delilah had left it. Constance sat on the padded stool in front of her mother's vanity. She pressed the switch on the antique lamp resting on the left of the vanity's top, casting her reflection into the wood-framed mirror before her. Her mother's jewelry box stood on the right.

She inhaled as she opened the wide, center drawer. The familiar smell of the aged wood soothed her as she looked over her mother's cosmetics. She carefully sifted through the makeup tray, admiring the natural shades of the lipsticks, powders, and eye shadows. She wasn't looking for a particular item, but she needed to make a mental inventory of her mother's possessions. Starting with her makeup and keepsakes sounded like a good starting point.

Constance removed several white letter envelopes from the right side of the drawer. The first envelope contained several folded letters from a much younger Abigail to her mother. The first was a Valentine's Day letter decorated in vivid crayon and shedding glitter. Constance's heart warmed as she read her sister's creative spelling.

I love you Momma. I'love you for ever evin if you make me eat greens. Just no pigs feat.
- Love, Abigail -

Constance snorted as she folded the letter and returned it to its envelope. She took the next envelope from the drawer and turned it over to open it. She could tell this letter was from an adult by the neat cursive handwriting bleeding through the paper. Constance unfolded the letter and looked through the pages for clues to the author's identity. Wade's signature graced the bottom of the last page. She assumed he'd left this letter for Delilah when he sold her the home.

Dear Delilah,

I hope this letter finds you healthy and happy in your new home. I am thrilled that you and the girls will continue the family's legacy there. Lydia loved reading in the sitting room, long summer afternoons in the back-yard, and walks to the family cemetery. Perhaps you will find the same joys during your time in the home.

I only wish our last days in the home were differ-ent. Our world collapsed the day we lost Adeline. I lost everything that day, my daughter, my wife, the home, everything. I feel like a chain reaction started and there was nothing we could do to stop it.

I want to share some things with you I've never shared with anyone else. No one truly understands our final days together after Adeline's funeral. Lydia was a mess. But something changed the last day or so before she passed. We were mourning Adeline's death so I didn't think much of her mood swings but Lydia started sleep-ing in Adeline's room, walking the house at night, and spending time staring at the backyard. I guess by the time I realized what was going on, it was too late.

On her last night alive, I found Lydia in the hall bath in complete darkness, drowning in the tub where we'd lost Adeline the week before. I couldn't understand how it was physically possible for her to drown herself. I saved her before she succeeded but something crazy hap-

pened when I ran to our bedroom to call an ambulance. I couldn't get the phone to work and somehow, the bedroom door was locked from the inside and I couldn't get the lock to move. I tried opening a window to call out for help but the windows wouldn't budge. It was like the house had come alive to trap me in the room and allow Lydia to finish the job she'd started in the tub.

I begged her to help me through the door and she told me that she'd seen and heard Adeline in the house. Then she told me she loved me and she left. Minutes later, I saw her walk across the yard to the cemetery in the moonlight. I screamed for her until I lost my voice. I tried breaking the window but couldn't. I tried breaking the door down but couldn't. I was helpless. It was the worst feeling in the world. I couldn't save them. Do you know what that's like for a husband and father? It's the worst feeling in the world.

The house freed me just after sunrise. I was lying on the floor crying and bleeding when the door unlatched and opened on its own. I couldn't believe what I was seeing. I ran as fast as I could through the house to the cemetery. The rest, you know. We buried Lydia beside Adeline a little over a week later. You were there, you could probably tell that I was completely in shock. I didn't know how to process or talk about what I'd experienced.

The police asked me to keep the details of Lydia's last night to myself as they carried out their investigation. At that point, they weren't fully buying my story but I had nothing else to tell them. You are the only other person I've shared this with.

I'm telling you this because I want you to know what you're getting yourself into. This house is more than a house. It's alive somehow. Lydia is still here. She comes to me every night and I just can't keep going like this. I pray you have peace here. You know where to find me if you want to talk about anything from this letter.

Wade

Constance sat stunned, the letter shaking in her hands as her mind raced and her heart pounded in her chest. She looked up from the letter, craning her neck to see down the hall past the open bedroom door. Abigail had closed the bathroom door and turned off the water. Constance listened to the house.

She looked at the bedroom door and thought about Wade trapped all night, unable to pry the door open to save his wife. She stood, almost knocking the stool over, and rushed to the window looking out on the backyard.

This was his view as he watched Lydia walk across the yard to her death. He stood right here.

Her heart pounded away in her chest as her breathing grew labored. She almost closed her eyes to calm herself but stopped, suddenly afraid that if she closed her eyes, she'd be unable to reopen them.

She looked at the door again, this time with great distrust. If the door shut and locked itself, she would be separated from Abigail while the girl bathed alone–in the same tub that took Adeline and almost took Lydia.

Go now.

Constance moved as fast as she could across the room. The door seemed to respond by slowly closing. She made herself skinny and darted through the dwindling opening, afraid to touch the door in her escape. As she entered the hall, the door closed behind her, blocking the light from the hall.

Panic bloomed in her chest as she hurried down the hallway toward the bathroom. A few feet ahead of her, she saw Abigail's door standing open, a soft light illuminating several wet footprints between the bedroom and hall bath.

I never heard Abigail leave the bathroom. She should ...

Constance heard thrashing water in the bathroom.

No!

One, two, three rapid steps and she burst into the bathroom.

Abigail lay naked in the tub, eyes closed, her arms extended with her palms up. Her eyes shot open as Constance burst into the room. She sat up, covering herself in surprise.

"Constance! What are you doing? I'm trying to take a bath!" Abigail reached for a towel hanging on the rack beside the tub.

Constance stuttered, embarrassed and confused.

"I'm ... I'm so sorry." She fled the room, slamming the door shut behind her.

Back in the dark hall, she gasped for breath and fought to regain control of her emotions. Reading the letter had done something to her. She leaned forward with her hands on her knees, breathing deep, calming breaths.

I know I heard her thrashing in the water. I know that bedroom door shut itself. I know I saw footprints ...

The wet footprints remained in the hall. But they also tracked to the stairs. She walked slowly to the top step to confirm her suspicion–the footprints trailed down the stairs to the bottom floor.

Constance squeezed her eyes shut tight, then reopened them. The footprints remained. She crept down the steps, careful to avoid fouling the wet prints as she went. When she reached the bottom level, she turned with the footprints and crossed the house to the back door. She reached for the doorknob, then stopped.

Do you really want to open that door? Do you really want to know where these prints go?

She shoved her fear aside and opened the door to the back porch. The footprints continued across the deck and down to the grass. Constance stood on the porch in disbelief. She knew Abigail hadn't left the bathroom to come out here. She scanned the yard for signs of life and found none. The trees at the edge of the yard swayed in the brisk fall breeze.

Constance turned her head upward to the primary bedroom window above her. The lamp on the vanity filled the room with warm light. As the breeze picked up and the trees danced, the light dimmed, then went dark.

CHAPTER EIGHTEEN

Constance slept in fits and spurts, bouncing in and out of dreams inspired by Uncle Wade's letter. In one dream, she stood behind him as he pleaded with his broken wife, unable to help him or prevent her from meeting her fate in the cemetery. Pain radiated through her hands, wrists, and arms every time he struck the door, wailing and begging Lydia for help. His voice thundered in Constance's ears as he screamed at the window, cursing Lydia as she walked to her death beneath the moon. Constance's heart died along with his as he lay on the floor afterward, blithering and soaked by tears and spittle. They broke together.

In another episode, she stood in the dark upstairs hall, gritting her teeth at the sound of someone–Abigail? Adeline? Lydia?–drowning in the tub on the other side of the bathroom door. In this dream, she screamed through clenched teeth, eyes pinched shut, hands pressed to her ears. None of it worked. She heard every sound the tub emitted as it took its inhabitant under.

She also dreamed of sitting in a semicircle with Aunt Lydia, Adeline, Mama, and Abigail on the tall grass of the backyard. They shared tales of how the house spoke to them–*through* them–to each other. The property, the home, all of it, connected them. It *whispered* to them. It was their communicator, their network spanning time and planes of existence, limitless and powerful.

They were the girls of the Whispering House.

As she woke the next morning, their hushed voices clung to her ears. They fell off, one at a time, as she blinked against the harsh sun streaming through her bedroom window. Aunt Lydia's was the last voice to visit her.

"We're the girls of the Whispering House."

Constance rolled onto her back and released an exhausted, frustrated sigh. None of this could be happening. Uncle Wade's story couldn't be real. Her dreams weren't real, they were just dreams.

Yet, she believed.

Uncle Wade wasn't right. Losing his daughter and wife damaged him. Can't you see that? There's no way this house is haunted. You're damaged by grief, too. Your visions, dreams, and assumptions are products of your damage. None of it is real. How can you trust what you see or think with a damaged mind?

She heard Abigail in the hall outside her closed door. She had to talk with her sister. She had to find out if Abigail was experiencing visions or dreams. Constance had to separate the truth from the damage.

She got up and readied for the day. It was Monday, two days before her planned return to school. Constance had to figure out if she and Abigail were fit to return as planned on Wednesday. She also had to figure out if they should be alone in the house. She'd asked Aunt Jenny and Uncle Hank to stay with them until Wednesday. Now, she doubted whether she could watch over her sister and the house without them. Maybe they were right. Maybe she needed more time.

She hurried through the upstairs. Abigail must have already gone to the kitchen, as she wasn't in her room or the hall bath. Down the stairs, she went.

She found Abigail preparing a bowl of oatmeal in the kitchen. She saw Aunt Jenny and Uncle Hank enjoying their morning coffee on the screened porch.

"Good morning," Abigail said, yawning.

"Mornin'. You sleep okay?"

"Not really. I had crazy dreams all night," Abigail said.

Constance considered her next question.

"What kinds of dreams? Boys chasing you again?"

Abigail giggled half-heartedly and flashed a mischievous grin. "No. I dreamed of us. We were with Aunt Lydia, Mama, and Adeline in the backyard. We sat out there all-night telling stories."

Constance felt her body temperature plummet as goosebumps spread across her arms and legs. *Holy smokes. Don't tell her you had the same dream. Play it cool.*

"Interesting. What kinds of stories?"

"I can't really remember. I guess they weren't stories. It was more like they were trying to teach us, but nothing they said made much sense to me. Something about communicating through the house." Abigail shook her head.

Constance's arms went limp at her sides. She couldn't believe what she was hearing. She'd reached a point of realization and vulnerability with her sister. Telling Abigail that she'd had the same dream would require admitting that all these strange happenings were real. If she kept it to herself, the questions and denial would continue. That felt like torture to Constance.

"I had the same dream," Constance blurted.

They locked eyes and a million words passed between them in a brief but impactful moment of silence. Potential points of understanding flashed through Constance's mind in a stream of consciousness.

I know.

I've seen things, too.

They aren't just dreams.

The voices are real.

This place is different.

Something powerful is happening here.

I'm scared.

The back door opened and Aunt Jenny leaned through the gap.

"Good morning, ladies. You two must have been exhausted last night. By the time we got back, you were passed out."

"Yes," the girls replied in perfect stereo.

The girls wolfed down their breakfast and retreated to Abigail's room to talk. They sat cross-legged on the floor at the foot of Abigail's bed. Constance felt relieved to discuss things with Abigail, but she also felt apprehensive. She couldn't share too much. She had to protect Abigail from her more alarming experiences, and she didn't want Abigail to question her mental state. Abigail had to trust her or she'd never consent to Aunt Jenny and Uncle Hank leaving them.

"So, tell me what's been different for you since Mama's accident," Constance said.

Abigail stared down at her hand as she twisted the long pile of the avocado-colored shag throw rug in her fingers. Constance fought the urge to speak again.

Patience, she thought. *Maintain control by taking what she gives. Don't force this.*

Her patience paid off.

"I guess it's mostly been dreams and feelings," Abigail admitted.

Well, what the heck do you call that chanting in the closet last week? Or how you floated in the tub last night like a rigid board after I heard you thrashing in there?

"Me too," Constance confided.

"Really? Because I thought maybe you were experiencing a bit more than that." Abigail shot her a condemning look with her dark, round eyes.

Is she testing me to see if it's safe for her to admit to more?

Constance held her position. "I've had a few daydreams, if that's what you mean."

"Me too," Abigail responded. Her sudden, energetic acknowledgement made Constance believe she'd experienced much more than she was admitting to. This was turning into a harmless but insightful game of tit-for-tat.

"You know, that can all be a natural response to grief. Losing Mama so suddenly makes this harder on us, I think. I guess what I'm trying to say is that there's nothing wrong with us, even though it might feel that way. We're going to have tough times but that's expected."

Constance brought the conversation to a logical place, hoping that it would make the unbelievable parts of their experience feel less intimidating. She pried further.

"Have your daydreams been happy or sad?" She hesitated, then added, "Or scary?"

Abigail looked her in the eyes and took a deep breath before answering. "Happy, I guess but also a little weird because it's always Aunt Lydia or Adeline visiting me and it's hard for me to remember what happened afterward. I haven't seen Mama in my daydreams, only at night. Those dreams are always happy, then sad, when I wake up."

Constance hid her dread behind a stoic face. Abigail's recent behavior had confused her, and she'd been unaware of the cause–Aunt Lydia.

But how could a dead woman do these things? And why Lydia and not Adeline or their mother?

Constance's head spun. She couldn't fathom the thought of their house being haunted, if that's what they call this. After all, they hadn't seen ghosts walking through the house or heard voices in the halls. You know, typical ghost behavior. What these dreams and visions lacked in physical manifestation, they made up for with terrifying psychological visions.

Can a ghost haunt your mind?

"What is it? What's on your mind?" Abigail asked.

"Oh, nothing. I was just thinking about how my daydreams feel more like intense visions sometimes. Do you see them that way?"

Abigail pondered the question. "I guess. They feel *saturated*–like I'm standing where two worlds are being poured together and I can't tell what's real and what's a dream while I'm overwhelmed by the flow."

Constance nodded to show her understanding, but deep down, alarms rang like fire station bells. "Look, I want you to come to me when these daydreams happen, okay? I'm here to help you. You aren't alone."

Abigail smiled and took Constance's hands in hers.

"That sounds good." Abigail giggled, then unfolded her legs to stand.

Constance followed her lead and stood. Abigail's laughter confused her.

"What's so funny?" Constance asked.

Abigail squared her shoulders to Constance and replied, "I'm not sure why you'd want to help *me* when you are the one having the nightmares. My dreams are weird but ... good. Yours seem terrifying."

Abigail turned for the stairs, leaving Constance standing in her room with more questions than answers. *My God, she's so* odd, Constance thought.

Aunt Jenny's voice sailed up the stairs, spurring Constance to follow Abigail. "Constance! Visitor!"

"Who is it?" Constance asked, surprised. She wasn't expecting any visitors today and her friends rarely stopped by unannounced. She reached the top of the stairs and met Aunt Jenny's smiling face on the bottom floor.

"It's Mr. Holcomb," she said.

Mr. Holcomb? Why would he be here today?

Constance galloped down the stairs and crossed the foyer to the open front door. Mr. Holcomb stood on the porch in tan slacks, a white button-up shirt, and a skinny black tie. His smile lifted her spirits.

"Hello, Miss Constance."

"Hello, Mr. Holcomb. I see they let you out early for good behavior."

"Yeah, I snuck out of there before something crazy happened and I got stuck for the rest of the afternoon. This is official business, right?"

"Of course," she smiled and nodded.

"So, last time we spoke, you planned to return to school on Wednesday. Obviously, things change, and I can't imagine how difficult the last few days have been for you. I just want to say it again: you don't have to come back so soon."

Constance couldn't help but marvel at the stark contrast between Roy and Mr. Holcomb. Roy looked worse and worse every time she interacted with a kind, strong, and empathetic man. Her respect for Mr. Holcomb grew.

"I appreciate you checking on me and offering to cover for me a bit longer. But honestly, I think I need to get out of this house and get moving again. I don't necessarily care for that school, but I need the distraction."

"I understand," he said softly. "Well, you know where I'm at; if you need anything at all, don't hesitate to drop by my office. Even if it's just to hide out for a little while. Coming back may sound like a good idea, but you're going to have times where you feel you aren't even on the same planet as the rest of those kids. You may need someone to talk to. I'll be there for you if that happens. Okay?"

Constance smiled up into his caring eyes. "Okay. Thank you, Mr. Holcomb."

"Well, I'll leave you to your day, Miss Constance. See you soon. And if you change your mind about coming back, call me and I'll take care of your attendance record."

"Will do."

Mr. Holcomb tipped an invisible hat to her and made his way back to his car. Constance walked up the front steps and found Aunt Jenny waiting for her at the door.

"He's such a nice man. He looks after you, you know."

"Yeah, I know." Constance smiled. "I didn't like him much at first, but he's grown on me."

"You've always been hard to win over," Aunt Jenny said wryly.

"So, do you think we could run into town for a bit and pick up a few things? I could use a little time away from the house."

Aunt Jenny flashed a relieved smile. "You and me both. Don't get me wrong, I've loved every minute here with you and your sister, but I can only spend so much time in a house before the uncontrollable urge to go shopping pulls me away."

Constance walked through the doorway with her head hung low as the weight of the house settled on her like a lead blanket. She couldn't wait to go into town.

CHAPTER NINETEEN

Constance, Abigail, and Aunt Jenny floated down Route 60 in the Bel Air. Aunt Jenny's contagious smile reflected her happiness about going shopping. It was clear she was happy to get away from the house with the girls for a while. Constance rode in the passenger seat, watching the road's painted lines unroll through the windshield as Abigail watched the world pass from the backseat. The Bel Air's engine hummed as the car overtook the dozen miles of blacktop between their house and the edge of town.

Feeling like a prisoner freed from solitary confinement, she reveled in the cool air and warm sunlight, her eyes exploring the expansive fields, dense woods, and lumbering cars along the way. She loved how the sky seemed taller in the colder weather, the clouds thin and elevated against a brilliant blue sky.

They entered the Toano town limits after a ten-minute drive. Aunt Jenny relaxed her foot and allowed the car to coast as the speed limit dropped from fifty-five to thirty-five miles per hour.

Aunt Jenny steered the car through a gradual left bend in the road as the small town materialized in the windshield. Several three-story buildings, some brick and others painted white wood, crowded the two-lane road dividing the small nexus of town. Constance thought Toano resembled so many other small towns dotting the state between the bigger cities. Toano sat between Richmond, the state capital, and Hampton Roads, a thriving collection of port cities on the coast. She felt like the two metro areas would inevitably swallow this little village whole as they merged into one big, sprawling connection of highways and commuters. For now, the slight, huddled buildings provided a rest point for commuters to Williamsburg and supplies for local farmers at this end of the county.

They rolled through town in the blink of an eye and continued for another fifteen minutes until they reached the edge of Williamsburg. Aunt Jenny pulled the car off Route 60 and into the parking lot of Milton Co.'s Department Store. Abigail bounced with excitement on the back seat like a popcorn kernel on a stovetop.

"I can't wait to see all the Christmas decorations!"

Aunt Jenny laughed. "Girl, it's not even Thanksgiving yet! You're too much."

The damp fall wrapped around Constance as she stepped out of the Bel Air. The cool air mixed with the high humidity chilled her exposed skin, but she felt toasty beneath her rust red sweatshirt and beige polyester pants. Aunt Jenny shivered like an explorer leaning into a blizzard. Constance and Abigail exchanged an eye roll at Aunt Jenny's dramatic response to the chilly breeze. The girls crossed the parking lot and entered Milton Co.'s. Thirty minutes later, they left the store, each carrying a small shopping bag. Constance had found her favorite Clairol Flicker Stick lip gloss and Abigail had picked out a new pair of gloves. Aunt Jenny got ahead of her Christmas shopping and picked up a bottle of Aramis cologne for Uncle Hank.

"I needed this trip," Constance said, eliciting a confirmatory smile from the other two.

"Amen to that," Aunt Jenny replied.

"Where are we off to next?" Abigail asked.

"I need to pick up some groceries for you girls. Do either of you need a new book from the library?"

"Yes!" the girls replied in unison.

"Okay, we'll stop at the library, then we'll go to Harry's in Lightfoot and grab the groceries. Deal?"

"Deal," Abigail said.

They made the brief trip to the library and spent more time than planned, walking the tall aisles of hardback and paperback books in silent awe. The library had a magical air to it. A trip to the library always felt like a silent adventure. A new world waited for them behind each spine and cover. Abigail loved teen mystery novels and had recently discovered the Hardy Boys series. She hit the jackpot when she stumbled on a returned copy of *The Mystery of Cabin Island*. Constance got her hands on a copy of Shirley Jackson's *We Have Always Lived in the Castle*. Constance had discovered Jackson that summer and felt devastated when she learned she had recently passed away.

As they checked out their books, Constance noticed a few kids from her school seated at a table near the librarian's counter. She felt their prying eyes before she saw their dumb faces. She turned her head in their direction as they scrambled to hide behind their lifted books.

Nosy freaks, she thought. She knew returning to school would be awkward, but she hadn't expected kids in town to acknowledge her. She felt foolish for giving them the benefit of the doubt. Anyone with a shred of drama in their lives enamored them. She realized that because of their tragedy, she and Abigail were in the spotlight of an especially ugly element of human nature—the one that drives people to relish the misfortune of others. Constance ignored their curious stares and hushed comments as she, Abigail, and Aunt Jenny left the library for the market.

Constance tried her best to push the experience in the library out of her mind as Aunt Jenny closed the distance to the market. She felt annoyed and on edge. Aunt Jenny must have noticed something amiss with her.

"You good, kiddo?"

"Good to go," Constance said, without diverting her eyes from the windshield.

Abigail piped up from the backseat. "People suck."

Constance whipped her head around to find Abigail's mischievous grin. Abigail must have also noticed the kids in the library. The sisters high-fived each other. Minutes later, they rolled into the paved parking lot in front of Harry's Market.

Harry's was a local staple at their end of the county. The grocery store occupied one of Toano's oldest commercial buildings. They mostly sold dry goods and fresh produce from the surrounding farms. Constance thought the market always had an *old* smell to it. Decades of produce had settled into the walls and floors despite Mr. Harry's steadfast focus on cleanliness.

Aunt Jenny let Abigail pilot the small buggy between the narrow aisles. One wheel sputtered and jumped under the bent frame, threatening to drive Constance crazy with its clatter.

"Why did you pick that buggy? Isn't that driving you nuts?" she barked at Abigail.

Abigail laughed her off. "It makes steering fun."

"Whatever, weirdo," Constance replied, shoving the front of the buggy, driving Abigail further off course.

"You two behave," Aunt Jenny said with a slight smile, curling her mouth up on one side.

They made a trip up every aisle, gathering supplies for the week ahead. Constance led the selection. After all, she was in charge of cooking for the next few days. She filled the cart with oatmeal, a box of Abigail's favorite cereal, a carton of milk, some coffee creamer, a few potatoes, chicken breasts, assorted vegetables, and supplies for lunch sandwiches. That haul would hold them over for a few days until they made their next trip into town.

They migrated to the open cash register at the front of the store. Constance cringed when she saw Betty Chandler, the one girl she despised most in school, standing behind the checkout counter. Betty wore her blonde hair in two pigtails, the left strap of her cashier's apron smeared with makeup from her face. Her eyes lit up and she fidgeted in her spot behind the counter as she recognized Constance.

"Hello, ladies. I hope you found everything you needed." Betty forced a smile.

"We did. Thank you," Aunt Jenny said.

Constance watched Betty while Abigail unloaded the buggy's contents onto the checkout counter. Betty picked each item up and pounded the buttons on the cash register. *You're avoiding eye contact with me just to make me feel uncomfortable*, Constance thought.

Aunt Jenny gasped as Betty rang up the last item.

"Oh! I completely forgot to grab toilet paper. I'll be right back." Aunt Jenny sped away before Abigail or Constance could offer to grab it for her. Betty finally acknowledged Constance.

"I'm sorry about ... whatever happened."

Constance couldn't believe her ears. Her blood pressure climbed unchecked.

Betty continued, ignoring Constance's rising anger. "It's terrible and I wouldn't wish that on my worst enemy. I'm really sorry."

Constance kicked her brain into gear. "What the hell do you mean, '*whatever happened*?' You know *exactly* what happened. I ought to drag you over that counter and beat your face in."

Betty's jaw dropped as Constance got louder.

"The *nerve* of you to say that in front of my little sister," Constance fumed.

Abigail placed a hand on Constance's right arm. "Hey, it's okay. Don't get in trouble over this loser."

Betty's eyes narrowed as she turned her attention to Abigail.

"Who are you calling a loser, twerp? I'm not the one who lost my mother. *You're* the loser."

Constance reached across the counter at lightning-fast speed. Betty barely dodged her hands as the counter inhibited her reach.

Betty, empowered by the minor victory, kept on.

"Your family is cursed, loser. The whole town knows it. First, your cousin, then your aunt, and now your mother? You're *cursed*."

Harry, the store's owner, swooped in from the double door entrance a few paces away. "Hey! What the heck is going on? You can't talk to a customer like that, Betty. Step away from the register. *Now*."

Aunt Jenny hurried up next to Constance, a package of toilet paper in her arms. "What in the world is going on here, girls? Are you okay?"

Constance snatched the first few bags from the counter, Abigail following her lead. "We need to leave before I teach her a lesson in front of this entire store," Constance huffed.

Harry went into damage control mode. "I'm sorry, ladies. I promise to take care of this. It will *never* happen again. Let me take some items off this bill to make it up to you." He burned a hole in Betty with his eyes as he worked the register.

"Well, I most certainly appreciate that," Aunt Jenny said, unsure about what had happened during her brief departure.

Constance's blood simmered as she tried to calm down. "Come on, Abi. Let's wait in the car." She took one last chance to address Betty. "You'd better avoid me like the plague when I get back to school. You hear me?"

Betty only smiled in return. Her silence probably saved her job and her face.

"Again, my apologies," Harry said, handing Aunt Jenny a handful of bills and loose change.

Constance stormed toward the door, her hands full of groceries. She turned to push the door open with her back-side.

Once outside, Constance took several deep breaths of fresh air, trying to calm herself. She wanted to hit something, anything, to take out the frustrations she didn't get to unload on Betty's face. But looking over at her sister, Constance knew she couldn't do that. She had to remain calm. So instead of doing anything rash, she forced a grin onto her face and nodded toward the car.

"Come on, Abi. Let's get out of here."

The girls barely spoke on the ride home. Constance's mind raced through the confrontation with Betty, then jumped to the kids in the library. *This is going to be tougher than I expected.*

Her thoughts burrowed deeper into the events of the past few days. That letter from Uncle Wade to her mother and how the room seemed to come alive in response to her discovery of the letter ... there was something there.

Then, of course, the conversation with Abigail about their experiences and dreams had turned weird at the end. That seemed to happen more frequently with Abigail lately.

I feel like I'm not safe anywhere. I'm not comfortable at home or out in town. School is bound to be a disaster. Maybe leaving would be the best option. Maybe I should have given all of this more thought before I decided to pony up and be a hero. Is it too late to change my mind?

"Hey." Abigail's voice from the backseat interrupted her spiraling thoughts. "We're going to be fine. Okay?"

Constance turned in her seat. She locked eyes with Abigail and couldn't believe what she saw. It may have been a trick of the setting sun's light through the car window, but Abigail's eyes looked …

Not again.

Abigail's solid black pupils appeared just as they were during Constance's vision at the kitchen table days before. Her heart ached deep in her chest, pulling her already dire mood further into darkness. As Constance's emotions bottomed out, her fight-or-flight instincts came alive as adrenaline surged through every fiber of her body.

Please don't do this. Please.

"I'll burn them all," Abigail said, turning her gaze to the window.

"What was that?" Aunt Jenny asked, her face scrunched up.

"She said she'd beat them all," Constance responded before Abigail answered.

"We've got a little fighter on our hands, folks," Aunt Jenny said with a short, sarcastic laugh.

Constance settled back in her seat, her mind racing, her heart pounding in her ears.

For just a moment, she experienced déjà vu. Was sitting in the passenger seat reminding her of the dream she'd had the night her mother passed? That had to be it. She scanned the windows and vents for signs of smoke. She couldn't tell if another vision was ready to pounce on her or not.

Please.

Constance pressed her eyes to the trees whipping by her side window, refusing to look in the car's cab. The trees felt safe. As long as she saw them, she wasn't seeing her sister's blackened eyes, threatening smoke, or the faces of the people she was growing to hate.

CHAPTER TWENTY

The rest of their night and the following day passed without oddity or incident. The girls spent Tuesday preparing for Wednesday's return to school. Aunt Jenny wrote letters to their respective principals explaining the circumstances of their recent absence. Constance thought the letters were unnecessary because everyone in town already knew what had happened, but tradition and procedure required them. In the letter to Abigail's school, Aunt Jenny stated Constance was her legal guardian. Aunt Jenny also added her phone number and address to update their emergency contact information. Seeing the words on the paper made it feel real to Constance.

Life after the accident was quickly progressing. Time was short. She had to step into their new life with confidence in less than twenty-four hours. Constance felt anxious but she accepted responsibility for setting the pace. She'd been the sole decision maker to take custody, run the house, and return to school so soon. This was on her. Despite all the thoughts banging around in her head, she slept well that night and woke rested and ready to take on the world the next day.

Constance left her bedroom motivated and optimistic for the first time in weeks. She stopped by Abigail's bedroom to rouse her before heading downstairs to prepare a quick breakfast. Shortly after, Aunt Jenny met her in the kitchen for a cup of coffee.

"Do you have everything you need for your day?" Aunt Jenny asked.

"Yes, ma'am," Constance replied. "I should be all set. I appreciate you sticking around this morning to see us off to school. Things have been a bit more challenging than I expected."

"It's our pleasure, dear. We can stay longer if you'd like. Otherwise, we'll head back to our place after you two head to school. Uncle Hank will bring the car over later this afternoon. This way, you have something to get around in during the week." Aunt Jenny sipped her coffee, letting the offer hang in the air between them.

"I think we'll be okay. I promise to call you after school and let you know how the day went. And thanks again for loaning me a car."

"Shoot, you're doing me a favor. That old car's just sitting in our driveway, anyway. At least you'll put it to use."

Uncle Hank appeared at the stairs with Abigail following close behind. "Good morning, ladies," he said, tipping an invisible cowboy hat in their direction.

"Good morning. Coffee's ready," Aunt Jenny replied.

Abigail smiled as she took a seat at the table. She poured a glass of orange juice and made an oversized bowl of cereal as Constance watched from over her cup of coffee. Abigail looked content with her situation.

"You still onboard with going to school today?" Constance asked.

Abigail answered with an exaggerated nod as she chewed a rather large mouthful of cereal.

"Alright. Make sure you give Aunt Jenny a big hug before we walk out the door. We won't see her again until the weekend."

Abigail gave a thumbs up with her free hand as she scooped another massive spoonful of cereal into her mouth. Aunt Jenny smiled as Constance stood and left the kitchenette to brush her teeth and grab her things. Twenty minutes later, the girls left the house for their bus stop.

Constance floated through the day in silent compliance. She went from class to class, keeping her head down and her pencil moving to avoid conversation with other students. Each of her teachers pulled her aside after class to express their condolences and offer their help as she caught up on missed assignments. In each instance, she politely accepted their kind words and offers of help before sliding away to the next class and repeating the same routine.

Halfway through her lunch period, Mr. Holcomb appeared at the edge of the lunchroom. He scanned the crowd of boisterous students until he located Constance sitting with Eli at a sparsely populated table.

"Pardon the interruption. Can you come by my office before you head back to class, Constance?"

"Yes, sir. I'll be right there." Constance and Eli exchanged curious glances.

"Great. I'll see you soon." Mr. Holcomb spun on his heels and exited the lunchroom without stopping to talk with any other students.

"Well, I guess I'd better go see what that's all about," she said, taking a huge last bite of her sandwich. She tossed a soiled napkin and a half-eaten apple into her paper lunch bag.

"I like him. He may be the only adult in this building that I can stand for more than five minutes," Eli said.

"You and me, both. Alright, I'll catch up with you later, loser." Constance stood and nudged him on her way by.

A few minutes later, she entered the main office. Mr. Holcomb waved her in as she crossed the small seating area and made her way around the school secretary's desk.

His face lit up as she entered the small beige office. He did a terrible job of hiding his enthusiasm for her return.

"Hello, Miss Constance. It's great to see you back at school. How are your classes going today?"

"Calm down, sir. We're only halfway through the day. Let's not get ahead of ourselves."

"Of course, pardon me." He smiled through her pessimism. "Did you enjoy your lunch with Eli?"

"Yeah, we were just a few minutes away from solving all the world's problems, but this meeting cut our fun short."

"Of course, yet another intrusion on my part." Mr. Holcomb smiled as he apologized again. "All jokes aside, how has it been? Running into any issues with the other kids? Teachers doing their best to help you?"

"No problems so far. The teachers have been very supportive and I've avoided direct contact with the natives."

"Very well." His eyes dropped to his hands and his smile faltered. "Did you drive to school today or did you take the bus?"

"I took the bus. Why? What's up?"

"Well, I got a call from Mrs. Polanski at the middle school. Apparently, there was a minor issue with your sister on the bus this morning."

"Wait. What kind of issue? Is Abigail okay?"

"She's fine. She just got into a small ... scuffle ... with a boy on the bus. Apparently, he said something to her that upset her, and she lashed out at him." He stopped talking and studied her face for a reaction.

"Well, do I need to go get her from school? Should I call Mrs. Whatever-Her-Name-Is?"

"Polanski. She's the vice principal. Normally, they would call a parent at home and explain the situation. In this case, they called here, knowing you were in school. Being that it wasn't an emergency, I recommend calling her back. You can use my office for a few minutes if you'd like. I'm happy to step out and give you some privacy."

Constance needed a moment to think before she responded. She hadn't expected her sister to need her this soon in the transition back to life. Perhaps she'd been foolish to plan their return to school so soon. She certainly felt that way now that an issue had arisen. She'd set her poor sister up for failure. This was all her fault.

Constance shook her head to regain focus. "I appreciate the offer, sir. I'm sorry this is happening. I promise I won't take long."

"It's no problem at all. I'll get Mrs. Polanski on the line, then hand the phone to you."

Mr. Holcomb picked up the phone, dialed the number, and exchanged brief pleasantries with Mrs. Polanski before handing the phone over. He stood and left the room as Constance took the phone receiver.

"Hello, this is Constance, Abigail's sister."

"Hello, Constance. My name is Mrs. Polanski, the vice principal at Toano Middle School. I'd like to start by saying just how terribly sorry I am for your loss. My heart goes out to you girls."

"Thank you, ma'am. I appreciate that. Is my sister okay?"

"Oh, yes. Abigail is fine. Apparently, she got into an argument with a boy, Danny Tillman, on the bus this morning. Danny has a history of being problematic. Allegedly, he said something that your sister didn't appreciate, and the situation escalated to physical confrontation."

Constance didn't know what to say. A million thoughts raced through her mind as Mrs. Polanski recounted the incident on the bus. Should she defend her sister's actions or condemn them? She was proud that Abigail stood up for herself, especially if this Danny Tillman kid was a jerk, but it shocked her that Abigail had become physical. That just wasn't her nature. Mrs. Polanski waited patiently on the other side of the phone line for her response.

"I'm sorry, I'm surprised to hear this. Abigail's never been in trouble in her life. She's never even had a C in a class. What exactly did she do?"

"I know this is a lot to handle. Especially since you are trying to get back on your feet in school as well. I would have called your aunt instead, but her note specifically directed these matters to you."

"I appreciate your concern, but I can handle the situation. Again, what exactly did Abigail do? Did she punch this boy? And did he deserve it?"

"Yes, she punched him in the stomach, and no, he didn't deserve it. No matter what one student says to another, and regardless of what's going on at home, there is no justification for violence. However, I won't suspend her this time."

Constance pinched the bridge of her nose in frustration. "Thank you for that. I understand that it's not okay to hit someone. So, is *she* okay?"

"Yes, I spent some time with her this morning and she's fine. She understands that what she did was wrong, and she showed remorse. I already told her I won't suspend her."

"Okay. I appreciate that."

"With that said, this is her one get-out-of-jail-free card. I am sticking my neck out quite a bit to protect her. Danny's mother isn't thrilled with my decision, but she understands the difficulties of your sister's circumstances. If things escalate, I'll have no choice but to suspend her. You understand, don't you?"

Constance no longer appreciated Mrs. Polanski's tone and the direction the conversation was taking. "Of course I do. Like I said, I appreciate you looking after Abigail. I'll take care of the rest from here. So, I'm curious; did you tell Mrs. Tillman about her kid starting the confrontation? Is she aware that my sister finished what her boy started and that he shouldn't pick on girls who just lost their mothers? I mean, what kind of kid does that?"

Constance sensed Mrs. Polanski's surprise through the phone line.

"I assure you Mrs. Tillman is aware of her son's behavioral issues. But that isn't relevant to this conversation. I'm concerned about your sister. She's been through a lot and I'm worried that–"

"You have nothing to worry about, ma'am. Rest easy knowing that my sister isn't the problem here. The kid with the history of bullying is the problem. He just picked on the wrong person today. Maybe he'll finally learn his lesson."

"Constance, that isn't the appropriate way to approach this situation."

"Well, that may be the case, but I won't condemn my sister for standing up for herself, *especially* now. She's been through enough. She shouldn't have to worry about being bullied on her first day back to school but here we are."

"Are you insinuating that I have some level of culpability here?" Mrs. Polanski asked, clearly agitated.

"I'm not insinuating anything, ma'am. If you want to help us, I'd appreciate you focusing on punishing the repeat offender so my sister doesn't have to defend herself on the bus anymore."

"I won't have you speak to me that way."

"And I won't have you question my ability to care for my sister, Mrs. Polanski. You take care of your responsibilities and I'll take care of mine. If you'll excuse me, I need to turn this line back over to Mr. Holcomb. Have a great day, ma'am, and thank you again for looking after my sister."

With that, Constance hung up the phone. She released a pent-up breath in relief as Mr. Holcomb entered the small office, his eyebrows raised in curiosity.

"So, did it go as well as I suspect it did?" His facial expression told her he'd likely heard her entire half of the conversation.

"It went as well as Mrs. Polanski could have hoped. You know, considering the circumstances."

"Well, I'll let you know if she calls again." Mr. Holcomb dropped into his chair, a knowing smirk on his face.

"Thank you, sir. Have a great day. And thanks for everything."

Constance left the office more frustrated and on-edge than she'd been all day.

On the bus ride home, Constance realized she faced an unforeseen challenge–her bus drove past the location of her mother's accident every day. She struggled to push the memory of that day from her mind as the bus lumbered down past the area at speed.

You need to get over this. You can't relive that day every time you get on the bus or drive past that part of the road.

Constance wondered if Abigail was going through the same thing. Was her sister battling memories of that day? Had the confrontation that morning made things worse for her? Constance felt her natural motivation to protect her sister overpower her concern for herself.

She didn't have to wait long to discuss these things with Abigail. Her sister's bus dropped her off thirty minutes after Constance walked through the front door. She'd dropped her bag in the sitting room, grabbed a cold glass of iced tea, and sat on the porch waiting for the bus to arrive.

Abigail arrived unscathed and unbothered by the day. She climbed off the bus with the same smile and bounce in her step that she always brought home. Constance stood as Abigail reached the front steps. The bus gradually picked up speed, the sound from its loud engine trailing off as it drove out of sight.

"Hey there, Bonnie, did you ditch Clyde on your way home?" Constance asked. "Why am I having phone calls with your vice principal on the very first day back?"

"Clyde couldn't keep up. And that wicked ol' Mrs. Polanski is struggling to keep up, too."

"Ain't that the truth?" Constance tipped her glass of tea toward Abigail like a gangster tipping a cocktail in a movie. "Want to tell me about your incident this morning, or would you prefer to let it be for now?"

"I think you know everything already. It wasn't very involved."

"So I hear. What did this Danny Tillman kid say to you?"

Abigail plopped down on the step and sighed. "Well, he was in the seat behind me, and he started by tossing little pieces of torn paper in my hair. I told him to stop, and he laughed at me. Then he started up again. So, I turned around and warned him one last time. He said something ugly to me, so I popped him for it. I hit him in the stomach instead of the face so I wouldn't hurt him too bad or leave a mark. That's it."

"Sounds like a pretty crappy start to the day."
"Yeah."

"So, do you want to tell me what ugly thing he said, or is that top secret?"

Abigail stalled for a moment, pushing a small pile of leaves around on the step beside her as a distraction.

"He said I needed to chill out. When I told him to stop the second time, I told him his mother didn't love him and that he was lucky she'd kept him after seeing him at birth. He didn't like that and said, 'Well, at least I have a mother.' So, I popped him. That was it."

Constance's anger stirred. How dare that little punk say such an ugly thing to her sister? "Well, it's over now, right?"

"Right," Abigail answered. "You gonna ground me?"

The sisters smiled and poked at each other's ribs with their pointy fingers.

"No way. I'd rather make you my slave instead. Go make us supper."

Abigail laughed and quickly stood. "Okay, but you asked for it. I'm a terrible cook and you know it."

Constance felt relieved to have that conversation behind them. But she also didn't want Abigail to think she'd be soft on her in the future. However, considering the week they'd had and the reason for Abigail's issue that morning, she decided not to bring it up. They had bigger concerns to worry about, they just didn't know how big those concerns would be.

CHAPTER TWENTY ONE

Uncle Hank steered the '56 Plymouth Fury into the driveway as the sun slid farther behind the trees on the west side of the property. Constance loved every aspect of autumn except for the inconvenient early sunsets. She lamented this condition as she crawled over the car in the waning dusk light.

Aunt Jenny had followed him in the Bel Air so they'd have a car to drive home after the drop off. She opted to inspect their supper situation and spend time with Abigail in the house while Constance learned the ropes of the Fury in the driveway.

After going over the layout of the car's driver side controls, Uncle Hank shifted to the passenger seat so Constance could take the car for a spin. She liked how the

Fury felt small yet powerful under her foot. She reflected on how much freedom the car would grant her in their day-to-day lives. If she or Abigail needed something, they could hop in the Fury. If the school bus remained an issue, she could drive Abigail to school. She became overwhelmed with appreciation.

"Thank you so much for lending us the car, Uncle Hank. This changes everything for us."

"No problem. We're happy to help. And we're happy to help more if you ever need us." Uncle Hank flipped through the owner's manual then set it between them on the bench seat.

"Really, thank you. I'm so grateful. Now I just need to figure out how to get gas money. I'm considering 'murder for hire' services, but it seems like a hard business to sustain long term."

"Yeah, you may want to resort to working part-time at Harry's. I hear the cashier job may be open soon."

"Ha! I don't see that happening. What did Aunt Jenny tell you?"

"Not much, just that your best friend works there."

Constance laughed heartily at his sarcasm, sitting taller in her seat to see over the hood as she returned to their driveway.

"Great job. Park next to the Bel Air so we can squeeze by when we leave."

She parked the Fury, admiring the dim lights of the gauge cluster as they idled for a few seconds, then killed the ignition. The engine stuttered as it came to rest under the hood, shaking the car and drawing an entertained laugh from Constance and Uncle Hank.

"Don't worry, she's reliable," he said as they opened their doors and entered the early autumn evening.

"I'm not worried. I'm grateful, as I'll also be for supper. Thanks again," she said as they crossed the driveway, climbed the front steps, and entered the house.

An hour later, Constance was indeed grateful for the baked chicken and potato supper that Aunt Jenny and Abigail had prepared. As the rules dictated, those who don't cook must clean, so Constance had dishwashing duty. She didn't mind the assignment, as it gave her time to think about the strange yet productive day. She tossed her conversation with Mrs. Polanski around in her head while she dried plates in the company of her reflection in the dark window.

You handled your first day as a surrogate mother well. I can't imagine that tomorrow will be harder than today was.

She placed the last dish in the cabinet above the counter and made a cup of coffee before joining Aunt Jenny and Uncle Hank at the kitchen table. Abigail was in her room, catching up on homework before bathing and getting ready for bed.

"Are you sure you're comfortable with us taking off for the night?" Aunt Jenny asked.

"Yes, ma'am. We should be good to go. I appreciate everything you've done for us."

Uncle Hank chimed in. "Look, I'm only going to say this once so you don't hate me forever, but I don't like the thought of you two girls being alone in the house at night. Call me old-fashioned, but I just ... I don't like it."

"I'm sure we'll be okay. We can test it out for a few days and if it's weird or I hate it, I'll tell you guys and we'll reconsider our options."

"Fair enough," Uncle Hank conceded. "You have our number, and I can quickly get here if you need us for anything. We're only twenty minutes away."

Aunt Jenny stood and brought their empty coffee cups to the kitchen sink.

"Don't worry about them, Aunt Jenny. I'll wash them before I go to bed."

"Nonsense. You sit there and enjoy your coffee. We had a head start," Aunt Jenny said as she quickly rinsed and dried the two cups.

"Well, we'll get going so you can finish your homework and get ready for bed." Uncle Hank stood and stretched with his hands placed on his lower back.

"I'll walk you to the door."

Constance stood as Aunt Jenny stowed their cups and met them at the table. They made their way to the front door in a single file line. Uncle Hank stopped at the foot of the stairs and called up to Abigail's room.

"We're taking off, Abigail! Sweet dreams, kid!"

Abigail remained silent.

"Leave that girl alone. She's probably trying to study. Keep it moving," Aunt Jenny huffed, pushing Hank in the back with one hand.

"What's wrong with wanting to say goodbye to my niece?" Hank protested.

Constance followed them to the front door, where they exchanged hugs.

"I mean it. You call if you need anything at all," Uncle Hank said as Constance held the door open for them.

"I will." She yawned.

"Goodnight, dear," Aunt Jenny said, pushing Hank out onto the porch. "Take me home before I change my mind and stay here for the night, Hank."

Constance laughed and called out to them as they reached the Bel Air. "Thanks again for the car. Have a safe ride home!"

She closed the door as the Bel Air roared to life, bathing the driveway and front of the house in harsh headlight beams. Exhaustion tugged at her limbs and begged her to head straight to bed, but she passed the stairs and made her way to the kitchen to lock the back door and turn out the kitchen lights. Her bed called to her from across the house. Finally, she reached the stairs and took them one at a time. A few steps from the top of the staircase her eyes became level with the upstairs floor. A soothing lavender light radiated from the gap at the bottom of Abigail's bedroom door. Through the gap, she saw the balls of Abigail's feet in the glow.

Where is that light coming from? Abigail doesn't have any colored lights in her room, she thought. *She's standing on her tippy toes?*

Abigail's voice permeated the closed door. Familiarity washed over Constance.

She's talking to that imaginary friend of hers again. She must be awake.

Constance approached the door and considered knocking but decided instead to ease the door open and peek inside without announcing her presence. She quietly turned the cool doorknob in the darkness. As she pressed the door inward, she noticed the light shift to white. Abigail stood at the foot of her bed with her arms extended at her sides, hands level with her hips, and her head tipped back. She murmured, her words not quite comprehensible to Constance.

Memories of Abigail seated in her closet before the portrait rushed back to her. *She's in that dream state again.*

She strained to better hear Abigail's quiet utterances. No luck. Constance froze in the open doorway, unsure whether to enter and risk ending Abigail's experience or slowly leave. She was stuck in a paralysis of indecision when Abigail settled onto her heels, raised her head, and dropped her hands. Her eyes remained closed, but her mouth stopped moving. She came out of her dream state, Constance exposed in the doorway.

Say something.

"Hey. Are you okay?"

Abigail turned her head, blinking her eyes as if emerging from sleep. She smiled. Constance thought she looked–relieved.

"Yeah, I feel great. Why do you ask?"

"Well, you were standing with your eyes closed. It sounded like you were talking to someone."

Constance couldn't disguise the concern in her voice. Abigail must have picked up on it because she dropped her eyes, sat on the edge of the bed, and patted the comforter, inviting her to join her. Constance accepted the silent invitation and took a seat beside Abigail.

"What's going on, Abi? Who were you talking to?"

Abigail hesitated before answering. "It's nothing to be worried about. I'm fine."

"That's not what I asked," Constance replied.

"I know. I just don't want you to be concerned. I ..." Abigail paused.

"You what?"

"I was talking with Aunt Lydia."

The earth shifted beneath Constance. She squeezed her eyes shut, trying to make sense of Abigail's words.

"What? Aunt Lydia? I thought maybe you were talking to an imaginary friend. Lydia is ..."

"She's here. She's been here since we moved in."

Constance sat in stunned silence. *This shouldn't surprise you. You knew this was happening. You just didn't want to admit it.*

"Yeah, but I didn't think it was real," she accidentally said out loud.

"You've seen her too?" Abigail asked, her eyes wide with surprise.

"What? No. Well, yes." She stopped and took a deep breath. "Let me start over. Yes, I've felt her here, but no, I haven't seen her here."

That's not entirely true. Tell her the truth.

"I've seen her in my dreams. But not just here. I saw her at school, at the funeral home, and here."

Oh, boy. You just spilled all *the beans, kid.*

Abigail's jaw dropped. "That's why you were acting so weird!"

"Weird? I'm not the one hiding in my closet or meditating or whatever that was."

"I wasn't meditating. I was talking with Aunt Lydia."

Constance leaned back and lowered her gaze to her sister. "Excuse me? Your eyes were closed, and you were muttering to yourself. That is *not* the same thing as us talking right now."

Abigail's face twisted as she grappled with Constance's claim. "I wasn't muttering. And my eyes weren't closed. I'm telling you, Constance, I was talking to her just like we're talking right now."

"Fine. I'll play along. So, what were you two gals talking about? Catching up on the latest episode of *The Monkees*? Or that new *Star Trek* show or whatever?"

Abigail slouched and rolled her eyes. "Don't be ridiculous. And don't act like it's a big deal. It's innocent."

"Fair enough. But you must admit, it's not normal to have casual conversations with our dead aunt. Look, I'm not mad or anything. We have a lot going on. This may be how you're dealing with things."

"Well, you told me you've seen her too, so it's not just me," Abigail said.

"It's not the same, Abi. I've had dreams. You're having active conversations in a meditative state while you're awake."

"Maybe. But my experiences are beautiful and yours sound terrifying, so which is worse?" Abigail asked defensively.

Constance lacked any sensible response. She felt exposed and confused. And her sister asked a good question. Why were their experiences so different?

"I don't know. This is crazy."

Neither sister spoke as they each considered where to take the conversation next.

"Okay, let's just accept that we're both having these ... experiences, or whatever they are. Don't you think it's odd that yours are so pleasant and mine are not? Are you sure you're not sugarcoating them? Nothing disturbing happens in your experiences with her?"

Abigail gave her question some thought before responding. "Well, there is one thing. She calls me Adeline. It's like she sees her instead of me."

Fear plowed through Constance like a runaway train. Tremors shook her hands as nausea pressed the contents of her stomach into her throat. She closed her eyes to regain control, barely refraining from ejecting her supper onto the shag throw rug.

"I feel so bad for her, you know? I think she's looking for her."

CHAPTER TWENTY TWO

Constance struggled to fall asleep between exhaustion and an overactive mind. She craved rest after the day she'd had, yet her persistent thoughts wouldn't allow it. She struggled to discount the small moans and pops of the house as darkness and cold had their way with its wood and glass.

What if that wasn't the house making that noise? Was Abigail up and about? What if whoever left those wet footprints the other night came back?

Maybe Lydia roamed the house at night, searching for Adeline.

She eventually fell asleep as the battle in her head raged on. Dreams, both good and bad, kept her close to the surface, refusing her depth and true rest. At one point, she awoke to wind howling in the eaves of the house as Lydia's voice filled her ears with whispered proclamations of damnation.

"You can't stop me from reaching her."

"I'll burn you all to have her back."

"Give me my child."

Constance's pulse raced as she fought to gain awareness. Was Lydia in the room with her or were her words remnants of the dream? Regardless, her words left Constance confused and contemplative.

It's like she doesn't recognize me. She never spoke an ill word to me while she was alive. Does she see us as we are or do we resemble something more supernatural, like shadow figures from another plane of existence?

She lay in her bed, fighting for more sleep, but lost. After a few hours, she gave in to the rising sun and got to her feet. Her head throbbed with exhaustion as she stretched her arms above her head. The warm sunlight pouring through her window beckoned her to lie down and take another shot at rest, but she couldn't succumb–she had obligations to fulfill, starting with waking Abigail.

She crossed the silent hall to Abigail's room and pushed the door open. Abigail opened her eyes as Constance entered.

"Hey, sis. You look beautiful."

Constance snorted. "Yeah, not quite. I probably look like a train hit me last night. I hardly slept."

Abigail pressed her arms above her head, yawning as she stretched her entire body. "I slept like the dead."

"Now, that's funny," Constance said, dwelling on their conversation the night before. "You won't live to see tomorrow if you make me late for school. Get a move on."

She left Abigail's room and walked downstairs to grab breakfast. She crossed the kitchen to the coffee pot and almost jumped out of her skin when the kitchen phone rang.

Who in the world is calling us this early?

She picked up the phone and cleared her throat to speak. "Hello?"

"Good morning, sunshine." It was Aunt Jenny. "I just wanted to call and check up on you. How did you girls sleep?"

"Abigail slept well, but I struggled."

"I'm sorry to hear that. I'm sure you'll get used to sleeping in the house without us soon. As for Abigail, that girl could sleep through the apocalypse," Aunt Jenny quipped.

"She most definitely could. I'm just starting the coffee pot and getting a quick bowl of cereal before we head to school. Abigail asked if I would give her a ride today instead of taking the bus." Constance had neglected to share the news of Abigail's incident on the bus with Aunt Jenny and Uncle Hank during their visit last night.

"That's very sweet," Aunt Jenny said. "You'll get some good sister time together."

"Hey, thanks again for helping with supper last night. I really appreciated it. I had a lot on my mind with it being our first day back at school."

"Of course, dear. We can come by to help again this evening if you'd like."

Constance brainstormed how to gently decline the offer when she heard Uncle Hank's voice in the background. She couldn't make out his words.

"Never mind," Aunt Jenny said. "It sounds like Hank is dragging me to his parents tonight."

Constance heard Aunt Jenny cup the phone to hide her next statement from Uncle Hank's ears.

"But, hey, if you know of a way to get me out of going over there, I'm all ears."

Constance laughed and replied, "You aren't dragging me into that. Have fun. We'll be fine for supper."

"Okay. Well, you girls have a great day. Call if you need anything. I miss you already."

Constance smiled. "I miss you, too. We'll talk later."

She hung up the phone as Abigail walked into the kitchen.

"You ready for that ride to school?"

"Yes, and thank you," Abigail replied.

As expected, Constance struggled through her morning. They left the house a few minutes later than planned because she forgot to warm up the car before leaving. She started it and tried to leave the driveway, but the car's engine died as soon as she put it in gear. Luckily, the car started again and ran fine after the engine idled for a few more minutes.

They made it to Abigail's school just in time for her to beat the first period bell.

"I'll pick you up at the end of the day, so don't take the bus home, okay?"

"Sounds good to me. See ya later, alligator." Abigail climbed out of the car and merged into the flow of students entering the school.

Gosh, this is such a mom moment, Constance thought as she watched Abigail disappear into the crowd.

Constance arrived at the high school ten minutes later and found a parking spot at the far end of the student lot. Finally able to catch her breath for the first time that day, her mind settled as she walked to the school building. At first, she considered how to better prepare for the next morning. Then, she thought about how proud her mom would be of her and her energy seemed to drain away almost instantly. A lingering depression filled the void and weighed her down.

She thought a lot about her mother. She owed much more time to honoring her memory and felt guilty for being so distracted by the unorthodox events and discussions of the past few days. Her exhaustion compounded the emotional turmoil of her morning by the time she met with Eli in the cafeteria for lunch.

"Hey, loser. Did you bring food today or are you planning to beg for half of my lunch again?" Constance asked, setting her lunch bag on the table.

"Oh, I'm *definitely* begging for your lunch today. My mom thinks a single slice of bologna on stale bread and an undersized apple are sufficient for a strapping young lad."

"Strapping? I'd like to strap you to something heavy and drop you in the bay."

"Wow. Having a rough morning or is that genuine sentiment?" He leaned away from her, exaggerating his attempt to create space between them. When she failed to respond to his joke, he returned to a normal posture and dropped the comedy. "Sorry. I'm sure every day is rough lately."

"Thanks," she said. "I didn't sleep much last night, and I've been thinking about my mom all morning. One minute I feel like I've got everything under control and the next, I realize I have almost no control whatsoever."

She was bringing him down fast. "Sorry, I don't mean to be such a downer."

"No, don't apologize. You've been through so much lately. You have nothing to apologize for. And you are handling things so well. It's quite remarkable."

Constance looked up from the lunch table's grimy surface for the first time since they'd sat down. Their table was the only one in the lunchroom that wasn't mostly occupied. Everyone was avoiding her. Except for Eli. She looked into his face. He was pulling apart his poor excuse for a sandwich, oblivious that she was looking at him. Her aching heart beat a little deeper and harder.

"I appreciate you being so supportive of me. You're a good friend, Eli."

He looked up from his mess. His eyes softened as he realized how she was looking at him. "Hey, don't get upset." He quickly wiped his hands on his napkin and reached for her arm.

A tear ran down her left cheek.

I'm crying? What the heck is wrong with me?

Her tears surprised her.

Great, I'm going to make him think he did something wrong.

"I'm sorry," she said. "I'm just overwhelmed with every-thing." She wiped her cheek dry and turned to hide her face from the monsters of the room.

"Do you need to get out of here?" he asked.

"And where would we go?"

"I don't know. Want me to take you to Mr. Holcomb's office?"

"There's no need for that. I just need a moment to get myself together. I'm okay, thanks."

She drew a big breath and tore her sandwich in half. She handed him one half while shoving the other in her mouth.

He mimicked her and shoved his entire half into his mouth. She considered how ridiculous they must look and fell into a fit of laughter. She did her best to avoid choking on the oversized mouthful of food as tears stung her eyes. He laughed as well and a chunk of food fell out of his mouth, smearing his shirt on its way to the floor.

That made her laugh even harder. He reflexively pushed back from the table and nearly tipped over in his chair. Students at surrounding tables looked over their shoulders before dismissing the two nerds causing all the commotion.

"Man, we need new friends. I can't live like this much longer," he said, wiping the smear from his shirt with his napkin.

"I agree. I'll start the search at once."

"Seriously, we need to get you away from life for a little while," he said. "We should go to the Fall Festival in town tomorrow night. What do you say? Want to go with me?"

"Are you asking me out, Eli?" she asked through the last bit of food lodged in her throat. The disgusted look on his face almost pushed her to laughter again.

"You aren't my type. But I'm happy to take you and cancel my plans with all the desirable women of James City County," he said matter-of-factly.

"Gee, I'm a lucky gal. Sweep me off my feet, why don't ya?"

"So, you'll go?" he asked more seriously.

"Yes. You're right. I need a little normalcy in my life."

"Great. So—can you drive?" he cringed as he waited for her response.

"You're quite the modern man. Sure, I'll drive," she said, rolling her eyes.

"Thanks. I don't have a car this weekend. My parents are taking it to the Fall Festival themselves. If I picked you up, we'd have to ride with them. That's a level of excitement I'm not sure even you can handle."

After a rare minute of silence between them, he shifted the topic of discussion.

"So, you and your sister are doing okay by yourselves? Your aunt and uncle didn't insist on staying?"

"Yeah, we're two single chicks living like college roommates."

"Well, never hesitate to let me know if I can help with anything at the house. Just don't ask me to cut the grass."

She warned him with a narrow glare.

"Okay, I'll cut the grass but only if you promise to hang out with me afterward. I'm cheap labor, but only for friends."

"You've got a deal."

The obnoxious class bells rang, signaling the end of their lunch break and the start of afternoon classes.

"Here. Take this." He slid a slip of paper across the table to her. She looked from his hand to his face before taking it.

He looks nervous, she thought.

"Use it for good in the world." He stood before she could respond. "Gotta run to my science test. Later, nerd!"

She watched him cross the lunchroom and disappear into the mass of bodies pouring into the halls. She unfolded the slip of paper and smiled at the phone number scribbled in pencil above a happy face wearing glasses.

CHAPTER TWENTY THREE

Constance felt a little better by the time she picked Abigail up from school in the afternoon. Her exhaustion clung to the edges of her thoughts and reflexes, but her heart seemed to have reached a point of sustainable aching. She realized that she'd never be pain-free again. Substantial grief was a long-term affliction and over time, she suspected the pain would shift to a subtle, yet constant, burden. The challenge was to get out from under the crushing weight of depression as early as possible in the healing process. At least that's what she told herself as she dug deep to keep her spirits up.

She saw Abigail standing with a group of kids near the curb on the side of the school as she pulled into the pickup zone. Yellow buses filled the lanes in front of the school, kids filing into their doors in an orderly fashion under the supervision of the bus drivers. Abigail and her best friend Sailor stood together engaged in a conversation. As Constance slowed to a stop, she noticed a few of the kids covering their mouths and snickering at Abigail. Apparently, the kids at Abigail's school were just as judgmental and nosy as the kids in her high school.

Oblivious to the other kids, Abigail climbed into the Fury. The sound of the car's deep exhaust bounced off the curb beside them. She shut her door and tossed her book bag onto the floorboard at her feet.

"Nice hair," Constance said, laughing at Abigail's wind-whipped wisps.

"Thanks," Abigail said, relaxing into the passenger seat. Constance thought she looked just as beat as Constance felt.

"Did you have a good day?"

Abigail hesitated for a moment. "I guess. It started well but felt blah."

"Amen," Constance agreed. "Anything you wanna talk about?"

"Nah, I think I'm okay."

They enjoyed an uneventful ride home. Constance felt the emptiness of the house as they ascended the front steps and entered the front door. Just a few weeks ago, Mama would have been there waiting for them to get off the bus. Back then, the distinctive scent of Murphy Oil Soap or Old English furniture polish mixing with the fresh air communicated through open windows often greeted them. But not today. Constance noted the stale, silent atmosphere of the home. The emptiness felt expansive and overbearing.

Now it's my job to provide those comforts. I need to add those touches to our life.

She sighed deeply. So many of the day's elements had reminded her of the void her mother left in their lives. She'd taken all of it for granted for so many years, passing them with little thought. Now, every detail appeared to her as a flashing neon sign to remind her of their loss.

"Want to eat a snack before you do your homework?" she asked.

"That sounds great. I think I'll have some of those new cracker snack things you can wear on your fingers like little hats. What are they called again?"

"Bugles. I think I'll join you for a bowl. Want to sit on the back porch?"

"Sure. I could use the fresh air." Abigail said, still deflated from her day.

The girls tossed their book bags on the floor of the small family room beside the RCA television set that Roy had been so proud of buying a few years before. Of course, he lost it the day he left them. Mama took solace in keeping his prized television.

Constance rummaged through the kitchen cabinet for the Bugles and eventually found them hiding behind a stack of Jiffy Pop. She filled two bowls with Bugles and poured a Coca-Cola into two small drinking glasses. She figured they deserved the sugary treat after the day they'd had.

"There you go, ma'am. One stiff drink and a bowl of sin," she said, filling Abigail's hands with soda and Bugles.

"Just the way I like it," Abigail replied with a devious smile.

They passed through the back door to the screened-in porch and sat in opposing chairs facing the yard. They filled the air with the sounds of crunching Bugles and enjoyed the cool shade.

"So, Eli invited me to the Fall Festival tomorrow evening. Do you want to come with us? I understand if you aren't up to it. You could always stay at Aunt Jenny's, and I could pick you up afterward."

"I'd love to go to the festival," Abigail said without lifting her eyes from the bowl of Bugles. "Can we bring one of my friends? I want to go, but I'm sure you lovebirds want some time alone, too."

Constance laughed through a mouthful of Bugles. "We are *not* lovebirds. And yes, you can bring a friend."

"Cool, I'll ask Sailor if she can go. I'm sure her mom will let her. She loves me. Everyone does." Abigail danced in her seat.

"You wish." Constance tossed a Bugle into Abigail's hair. It was a perfect shot. They erupted in laughter.

The surrounding yard grew dark as a cloud passed before the sun. Constance heard an odd sound in the distance.

Are those birds?

A massive flock of starlings poured from the sky like a river of black-feathered tar until they coated every inch of the yard. The girls gasped in wonder. Constance had never seen so many birds in one place before.

"Those are the birds that fly around the sky in those cool formations," Abigail said with excitement.

"A murmuration," Constance answered in a dreamlike voice. "It's called a murmuration."

The black mass of birds filled the yard with a cacophony of fluttering wings and warbles. The girls stood to take in the full view of the yard.

"Look," Abigail said, pointing to the right side of the yard. Beyond her finger, Constance saw the broad, winding path to the cemetery. The birds had landed everywhere but on the path.

"How do they know?" Constance was at a loss for words. She realized Abigail had walked to the screen door leading to the open deck, her hand poised to unlatch and open the door.

"Don't, Abi. You shouldn't go out there," Constance said.

Abigail never took her eyes off the path. "I'll be fine."

"Abi don't–" Abigail left the porch before she could finish. Constance started after her, but the screen door slammed shut. She flinched and dropped the bowl she'd been holding.

The birds at the base of the porch steps parted before Abigail, revealing a clear route across the lawn to the cemetery path.

Constance grabbed the screen door and yanked as hard as she could. She'd expected resistance from an invisible force trapping her in the screened porch but she found none. The door flew open and hit her hard in the right shoulder. She cried out in surprise.

The birds exploded up from the yard in a massive black tidal wave. Abigail stood on the open porch, shrinking back from the wall of birds whipping past her.

Blackened sky.

Full light.

Constance stood like a statue, bracing for an impact that never came. Sunlight poured into the yard from the unobstructed sky.

"Wow!" Abigail gasped for air. "That was amazing!"

Constance jogged across the open porch, down the stairs, and onto the grass. She craned her head to see the flock shifting in unison over the roof of the house. The murmuration changed directions in sudden, coordinated movements that defied her understanding. Then, the flock disappeared past the roofline in a flash.

She walked in a broad circle, trying to locate the flock in the sky beyond the house without success. Her heart raced with excitement. She couldn't believe what she'd seen.

Something caught her eye as she neared the back corner of the house. Movement in the grass–a lone starling.

The bird laid on its side, fluttering one wing. Constance pulled her hair behind her ears as she approached the frail, wounded creature. Its wings stopped moving as its chest heaved, struggling for air.

"What is it?" Abigail asked from across the yard.

"An injured starling. I think it broke its neck flying into the house."

Constance looked up to her mother's bedroom window above. A shadow moved across the wall beside the window, then out of view.

"Do you see something?" Abigail asked, now standing at her side.

"Nothing," Constance lied.

Constance struggled to keep her eyes open as the girls finished their homework in the family room after a spaghetti supper. The rhythmic ticking of the hanging clock was the only breach in the silence.

"I think I'll head up to bed early," she said.

"Me too. I'll take a bath first and then I'm going straight to bed."

"I'll take mine in the morning," Constance said.

"You're gross, but I get it," Abigail said.

Closing her history textbook, Constance dropped it on the floor next to her book bag and stood. She regained her balance and helped Abigail out of her chair. She checked the doors and windows one last time before they made their way upstairs for the night.

Constance fell asleep within minutes of laying down.

She stood in a sea of small black birds in the backyard. The trees behind the home stirred in a light breeze as the stars lit the dome above. She must have been there awhile. The sun had been relieved of its station in the sky by the brilliant, oversized full moon. The gentle breeze kissed her bare arms, face, and neck.

My God, I feel so light.

She'd somehow shed the emotional burden she'd carried throughout the day. The weight had miraculously lifted from her shoulders and chest. She no longer struggled to breathe.

Abigail, clothed in a white cotton nightgown, stood on the porch a few yards ahead of her. She raised her right arm and pointed past Constance to the path parting the woods.

Constance turned toward the path and came face to face with Aunt Lydia. Constance braced for a collision as Aunt Lydia walked through her. In the moment of their merging, Constance's body temperature plummeted, and her throat closed, choking back a terrified scream. A second later, her body went slack as Aunt Lydia separated from her and continued to the house. Constance drew a desperate breath.

"Lydia!" she screamed, stopping her aunt in her tracks. She'd panicked. She didn't know what to do, but she knew she didn't want Aunt Lydia reaching Abigail on the porch.

"Is someone there?" Lydia asked in a doubtful, worried tone.

"Yes, it's your niece, Constance. Can you see me?"

Lydia scanned the yard. Apparently, she couldn't see Constance.

"I need to find Adeline." Lydia turned and resumed her passage to the porch.

"She's not here, Aunt Lydia. She's ..."

"Yes?"

"She's in the family cemetery."

The truth shall set you free, *she thought.*

"No, she's not. She's in the house. I need to find her," Lydia said, continuing to the bottom step. Abigail no longer stood on the porch. Constance was unsure where she'd gone.

"What makes you think she's in the house?" she asked.

Lydia stopped and turned toward her. This time, Constance saw her differently. Her eyes glowed in the moonlight, her pale, translucent skin hanging loose on her aging corpse.

"I see her upstairs every night, sometimes in her room and other times in the hall bathroom. But she won't follow me. Something's wrong; I need to get her out."

Hearing Lydia say those words broke Constance's heart. She was a loving mother, desperately seeking her child. She needed help and couldn't get it.

"Aunt Lydia, I'm sorry, but she's not up there. She's in the cemetery—with you."

Lydia's facial expression contorted with confusion.

"You're wrong. I see her in the house every night. How do you think I got here? She came for me. We sit together and talk each night. But she won't follow me home. I need to go now."

Out of options, Constance reached for Lydia's shoulder. A bright, blinding light tore through her mind the moment she gripped Lydia's shoulder. Her knees buckled, dropping her to the starlings under the cartoonish moon.

"I'll stop at nothing to get her back. Do you hear me? That's my baby.*" Lydia turned and resumed her walk across the porch to the back door. She walked into the house and out of sight a moment later.*

Constance couldn't move in the sea of starlings, their black bodies and empty eyes watching over her.

The back door opened.

Adeline appeared. She walked alone across the porch, leaving small, wet footprints as she went. Constance trembled on her hands and knees, vulnerable and terrified.

Frozen in shock, Constance watched in fear as her nine-year-old cousin's wet, bare corpse descended the porch steps and entered the yard. Her skin had lost its youthful thickness. Golden rings set deep in her pupils. The starlings parted to grant her passage to Constance.

"I can't believe it's you," Constance said.

"I need you to see."

Adeline stopped, raised her hand, and pointed past Constance to the path parting the woods.

Do not turn your head, *her mind demanded.*

Despite this request, Constance slowly turned her head. There, at the path's edge, across the undulating sea of starlings, stood Aunt Lydia and Abigail. They turned, hand in hand, and started down the cemetery path. A desperate groan seeped from Constance's constricting throat.

"No!" she spat, shaking her head in protest. "You've got the wrong girl! She's not your daughter! Give me my sister!"

The sea of starlings erupted up from the ground in a blinding constellation of pounding wings and deafening cries. Constance dropped to her side and covered her head with her arms, screaming as loud as she could into the maddening night.

CHAPTER TWENTY FOUR

Constance fell to the floor beside her bed in a panicked, hyperventilating heap. Fresh pain bloomed in her head and left arm from the fall. She winced, rolling onto her back, searching the darkness for her bearings.

Abigail.

She jumped to her feet, despite her foggy mind and aching body. Her head swam as her blood pressure dipped. She bounced off the partially open door and stumbled into the pitch-black hall. Constance jogged to Abigail's bedroom, steadying herself with one hand on the wall as she went. The world swam into focus by the time she reached the room.

She slowly opened the door, anxious about what she'd find on the other side.

Abigail's bed sat empty, the covers tossed aside.

Downstairs.

Constance moved to the stairs. Her feet barely touched the steps as she flew down them with both hands on the handrails.

Go left to the sitting room or right to the backyard?

She turned to the right as her feet landed on the bottom floor. Darkness disguised the angles and edges of the sleeping house. She slowed as she entered the kitchen, dodging the table to reach the back door.

The door's still locked, so she's probably still inside.

A reflection in the door's glass pane caught her attention. Light poured into the hall from the sitting room behind her.

Constance crept to the short hall, slowing as she neared the sitting room's arched entrance. She peered through the opening and saw Abigail laying under a blanket on the couch. Breathing a sigh of relief, she entered the room. Abigail looked up at her, clear sadness and exhaustion deepening the dark rings under her young eyes.

"What are you doing up?" Constance asked.

"I had a crazy dream."

"Me too." Constance patted Abigail's leg and took a seat beside her on the couch.

"Can I ask you a weird question?" Abigail asked in a timid voice.

"I promise you that your question won't be as weird as my dream, so go for it."

Abigail pulled her legs in and sat up, tucking her feet further under the blanket. "Where did I fall asleep?"

The question surprised Constance. "In your room. You know that."

"I guess. But I woke up on the couch, and I don't remember coming downstairs. I'm confused."

"You don't remember waking up and walking down here?"

"No."

Constance looked around the room as she struggled to think of a response. "Do you remember your dream?"

Abigail closed her eyes as she strained to recall the details of her dream. "I remember talking to Mama in my room. Then I was on the path to the cemetery. You were there, in the yard."

Constance tried to swallow, but her dry tongue stuck to the roof of her mouth and wouldn't budge. She closed her eyes, the details of her dream rushing back to her in excruciating, vivid detail.

"I think you were asleep, but I couldn't tell," Abigail continued. "You were laying in the grass, covered in those birds from today."

Constance leaned over Abigail's legs, demanding her attention. "Abi, are you sure you saw Mama in your dream and not Aunt Lydia?"

Abigail rolled over, hiding her face from Constance. "I don't know. I'm so confused."

"Hey, it's okay. We don't need to do this right now. Let's get you back upstairs. You can sleep with me in my room if you want."

Abigail nodded and stood without saying another word. Constance followed her lead. As they filed out of the room, she glanced over her shoulder at the portrait of Aunt Lydia and Abigail and thought, *you need to stop whatever you're up to.*

She left the lamp on as they exited the room. The thought of walking out of that room in complete darkness unsettled her. Besides, they needed to see where they were going in the hall and on the stairs and the small lamp spilled enough light into the hall to satisfy their needs.

Abigail stopped on the stairs. "I'm sorry if I'm making things more difficult for you. I know you're doing your best to take care of us."

All of Constance's worries fell away as she looked up at Abigail standing on the stairs, wrapped in a blanket. She looked so small at that moment.

"You aren't making things difficult. We're going through a lot. I love you, too."

Abigail smiled and continued up the dark stairs. Constance focused on the steps so she wouldn't trip and take them both down. Her bare foot pressed into something gritty and wet.

She stopped dead in her tracks, straining to see what she'd stepped on.

Bits of grass and wet soil sullied the steps behind Abigail.

Dread seeped into Constance as her mind reeled at the discovery. Abigail stopped at the top step and looked back at her.

"You coming?"

Constance couldn't speak. She looked down at the soiled stairs, imploring Abigail to do the same. Abigail flipped the light switch at the top of the stairs. Harsh yellow light bathed the stairwell between them.

Constance watched the color drain from Abigail's face as she saw the organic remnants on the stairs. Her eyes grew wider when she opened the blanket and saw the traces of dirt and grass clinging to her bare feet.

Abigail's mouth moved in silence before she found her words. "Oh boy."

They ate their cereal in contemplative silence as the world outside the kitchenette window came to life in the rising morning sun. Constance had struggled all morning to understand her dream—*their* dream—and how relevant their dreams and visions were to their reality.

"You really don't remember leaving the house?" Constance asked between spoonfuls.

"I really don't."

"I checked the back door before I found you in the sitting room. It was still locked so you must have unlocked it, left, returned, and locked it again. How could you not remember doing all that?"

"I don't know. I told you that."

More chewing. More thinking. More questions.

"And we had the same dream, from different perspectives. That's insane. I'm not sure how to explain that."

"I don't know," Abigail said. "But I know it's super freaky. This is like something out of an Alfred Hitchcock movie."

"When did you see a Hitchcock movie?"

"I saw *The Birds* at the drive-in theater last year with Sailor's family." Abigail boasted.

"Don't tell me how it ends. I'd hate for it to come true for us or something wild like that."

Abigail chuckled and crossed the kitchen to wash her bowl.

"I'm so tired. Can't we just skip school and sleep all day?" Abigail asked.

"I wish. We're going to the Fall Festival tonight and half the town will be there. My luck, Mrs. Polanski would see us there after you were absent, and she'd skewer me for being the most neglectful adult on earth."

Abigail came back to the table and took Constance's empty bowl to the sink.

"Thanks, Abi."

"No problem."

Constance watched Abigail peer out of the kitchen sink window as she washed the dishes. Abigail turned to her.

"Can we visit Mama before we leave for school?"

"Of course. We have time for a quick visit. It's a benefit of being up so early. Maybe it'll help us make some sense of what happened last night."

"Thanks." Abigail flashed an appreciative smile.

They left the house for the cemetery a few minutes later. Constance scanned the yard for traces of Abigail's night trip as they approached the path.

"Is this stirring any memories from last night?" she asked.

"Nothing new."

Constance enjoyed the silence and fresh air as they moved between the still trees. She loved how the sun kissed the frosted vegetation bordering the path.

Abigail stopped ahead of her and whispered, "Look."

A doe stood where the path met the cemetery. Two small deer huddled beside her like statues. Constance stopped one step behind Abigail, placing her hands on her sister's shoulders. Her movement motivated the doe to jog off the path and into the quiet morning woods. Her babies followed her, dodging in and out of the trees until they disappeared. Constance heard their hooves in the fallen leaves for another minute as they moved out of earshot.

They reached the cemetery a moment later. Constance passed Aunt Lydia's grave with heightened senses. Her eyes darted amongst the headstones, waiting for something extraordinary to surprise them. Nothing of the sort happened.

A few steps later, they reached Mama's gravesite. The recently disturbed ground remained void of growth and piled higher than the surrounding soil. Constance stood with her hands in her jacket pockets, her throat tight with emotion. Abigail stood at her side.

"How long do you think it'll take for us to get used to this?" Abigail asked. "Do you think we ever will?"

"No. I don't think we'll ever get used to this."

Constance wiped a solitary tear from the corner of one eye. She looked up at the sky, repressing a potential stream of tears.

"We can't stay long. I don't want to get too upset," Constance said.

"That's fine," Abigail replied. "Do you think she's still here?"

"You mean like a ghost?"

"I guess. Can we just call her a spirit instead? Ghosts sound so spooky. She was never spooky." Abigail said, wrapping her arms tight across her chest.

"I don't know if she's still here. But if she is, she's definitely a spirit." Constance nudged Abigail.

"She was so pretty in my dream last night," Abigail said softly.

Constance cringed, thinking about how Aunt Lydia and Adeline looked in her dream. Death clearly held them.

"Look, Abi; I think we need to be careful. There's too much happening that I can't explain, and it's got me worried. I would never forgive myself if something happened to you. Promise me you won't leave the house at night again."

Abigail looked down at her feet. "I wish I could, but I don't know how I can promise when I don't remember doing it."

"I understand," Constance said. "Let's just be careful."

"Maybe Mama can keep an eye on us."

"Maybe," Constance agreed.

CHAPTER TWENTY FIVE

Constance changed clothes, ready to get her Friday night started. She and Abigail had finished their first week back at school, and she was ready to put that behind her and spend time with friends.

She raced downstairs while still buttoning up her shirt. Abigail waited for her at the bottom of the stairs.

"I'm ready to go," Abigail said.

"Let's rock and roll."

They picked Sailor up first, spending a few minutes speaking with her parents in the driveway before heading down the road to Eli's house. Eli lived in one of the county's upscale neighborhoods in a new home, reminiscent of the original settlements in the area. Constance adored the gray-blue paint and steep roofline. The house had a welcoming, artistic look which, in her mind, contrasted with the plain white, boxy look of the area's older farm homes.

Eli ran out of the front door to the Fury as his mother waved to them from the porch.

"Have fun! I love you!" she yelled.

"Okay," Eli answered flatly.

Constance saw disappointment settle on his mother's face at his reply. She chastised him as he plopped into the passenger seat, rocking the car.

"Tell her you love her, dufus. That's your mother."

He tried to counter her direction but stopped abruptly, rolling his window down to comply with her order.

"Love you," he said half-heartedly, rolling his window up before they could hear his mother's reply.

"You're such a terrible son," Constance said, putting the car in reverse to back out of the driveway. Abigail and Sailor laughed at her insult, while Eli shrugged it off.

The car buzzed with teenager energy as they made the quick trip to the Toano open air market. Constance struggled to concentrate over the singing in the backseat as she squeezed the Fury into a tight parking spot across the street from the market.

"Okay, everybody out!" she hollered. The car's doors opened, and they spilled out into the dirt-and-gravel parking lot, bringing their energy with them.

The Toano Fall Festival was an annual event full of music, food, games, and vendors peddling every assortment of wares. A bouquet of fresh-baked goods, grilled meats, popcorn stands, and candy apples filled the air. The upbeat sounds of Jumpin' Sam Slim, a local cover band, filled their ears with the top forty hits from the '40s and '50s.

As they entered the inner circle of vendors, Constance cut Abigail and Sailor loose.

"Here's some cash for game tickets and food. Stay together and try not to cause any trouble."

"Aye-aye, Captain," Abigail replied with a sloppy salute.

Constance grabbed Eli by the arm. "Come on, loser. I want popcorn on the double."

"Yes, ma'am," Eli huffed.

They strolled along the aisle, taking in the sights and sounds of successful sales, old friends recalling old memories, and children begging parents for game tickets and snacks. The sun provided a last gift of light as the day transitioned to night behind the trees surrounding them. Constance felt an odd and unjustified sense of foreboding at the peaceful transition. Eli must have seen her unease in the shadows of her face.

"You okay?"

"Yeah, I'm just tired." She realized how dire that last sentence sounded. "I'm sorry, I don't mean to be a downer. All I need is that popcorn. Feed me or else ..."

He laughed at her insignificant threat. Ten minutes later, she had her popcorn, and all was right with the world. That's when she saw her.

Adeline stood in the center of the festival grounds, her hair matted and pressed to her decomposing scalp. Dirt stained the hem of her burial dress. The color of moist Virginia clay stained her knees, feet, and hands, as if she had crawled from her grave before walking into town.

Don't panic. Say nothing. She can't be real.

Constance closed her eyes and willed her racing heart to a slower pace. Her mind sprinted ahead.

She looks worse than she did in your dream last night. Where is Abigail? You need to find her.

Constance opened her eyes. Adeline remained, standing under a great oak tree strung with hanging lights. Adeline raised one arm and pointed. Constance followed her hand and saw Abigail and Sailor petting a baby goat in a small chicken wire pen several yards away.

Move now.

"What's up? Where are you going?" Eli called from behind her as she closed the distance to her sister in a frenzied jog. She looked to her side at Adeline's apparition, still standing with her arm raised and her too-straight pointer finger extended. Constance's head whipped from side to side, searching for Aunt Lydia while she moved. Her abrupt arrival at the makeshift petting zoo startled the distracted girls.

"What are you doing? What's wrong?" Abigail asked rapid, panicked questions.

She leaned into Abigail's ear and pulled her close by her jacket.

"Adeline's here."

The color drained from Abigail's face. "What? Where?"

"Behind me, near the big oak."

Abigail leaned to look around Constance. "I don't see her." She quieted her voice and asked through clenched teeth, "Are you sure you saw her?"

Frustrated and terrified, Constance barked, "Yes, I'm sure. We *have* to go."

"There's no one there. I don't want to go. We just got here!"

Constance looked over her shoulder. Adeline remained, her arm extended. She took one large step toward them, her eyes glowing rings.

Constance turned to implore Abigail again. "Abi, we have–"

The world around them ground to a halt, each soul frozen in an inanimate world. Abigail stared in Adeline's direction, her eyes fully blackened and her mouth agape. The aroma of food disappeared.

Adeline took another step toward them.

"Stop!" Constance screamed, terrified and helpless to stop her dead cousin's advance.

Adeline's fiery eyes appeared larger than before. Her slight frame shuttered as she rotated in place, her decaying joints struggling to support the weight of her limbs. Constance's eyes followed her pointing hand toward the opposite side of the festival grounds. Uncle Wade stood in line in front of the candy apple tent.

"Uncle Wade?" Constance exhaled his name.

Adeline looked back at Constance and corrected her. "Daddy."

CHAPTER TWENTY SIX

Wade startled as Constance approached him with wild eyes.

"Can we talk?" she asked.

"Hi, Connie."

She realized she'd skipped all formalities in her haste. "I'm sorry. Hi. Can we talk?"

His eyebrows drew closer with concern. "Of course. Do you or Abigail want a candy apple?"

Constance glanced at Abigail, Sailor, and Eli standing a few feet behind her. Eli and Sailor did little to hide their confusion.

"No, thank you. I need to get back to my friends, but I need to talk to you first. Please."

He looked back at the candy apples lined up on the table. "Let's step over there where we can talk in private." He nodded toward an empty place behind the row of vendors and abandoned his place in line.

"We're going to grab a candy apple and hang out near the band," Eli said as Constance and Uncle Wade walked to the edge of the tent.

Constance directly addressed Abigail. "Grab me immediately if anything happens."

Eli raised his eyebrows in disbelief and turned to the line. "Come on, girls."

She thought he'd had enough of her odd behavior but, being a gentleman, he kept it to himself. Uncle Wade brought them far enough to prevent being heard by passersby.

"I'm sorry for interrupting your time here, but things aren't good, and I need to know that I'm not crazy."

His face went slack as he nodded in agreement. She read the understanding in his eyes.

"I found your note to my mom about the house. And I believe things are happening. Not the same things, but ... I'm ... seeing things."

"What sort of things?" he asked in a hushed tone.

"I'm having extremely vivid dreams. Sometimes they're daydreams and ..."

"Do you see my ... do you see Lydia?"

Constance exhaled in relief. "Yes but–"

He grabbed her arms, a new intensity in his eyes. "Wait. Have you seen Adeline?"

Adeline stood behind him, her eyes glowing gold rings in the dark shadows of the trees.

"Yes, I have."

His chest buckled with relief. He released his grip on her. "I'm sorry about that. I just had to know. I never heard or saw Adeline despite hearing from Lydia every night." Darkness filled his eyes again. Wade scanned the surrounding area to make sure they were still out of earshot of others. He looked right past Adeline.

He still can't see her. She decided not to mention Adeline being there. She wasn't sure how he'd respond, and this conversation needed to happen.

"So, you said you *see* things? You don't just hear them?" he asked.

"That's right. I see them in dreamlike visions."

"Okay. Do you hear the hall bath every night?"

Constance paused. "No."

"Not yet, anyway," he said presumptively, giving her a cautionary look. "Look, Constance. Everything I told your mother in that letter is real. Everything. I wasn't sure if anyone else would experience the ... whatever it is. Haunting? That sounds so ridiculous when I say it out loud. I'd hoped moving would prove whether it was the house or Lydia haunting me each night. If I left and she came with me, that would eliminate the house. But she didn't follow me."

He stopped to gather his thoughts. The pause also allowed her a moment to let the words sink in.

"After I moved, everything stopped. I panicked at first. I needed to get away from her but once I was free, I feared I'd made a mistake." Tears built in his eyes. "Now I'm afraid I'll never hear from her again. Sometimes, the thought of never hearing from her again seems worse than being haunted."

He wiped his tears and gave Constance time to reply. "I'm not sure we can put all the blame on the house. I had several visions away from the house. They've come to me at school, the hospital, here–"

He interrupted her. "What do you mean 'here'? Did you see something tonight?"

Constance's mind swam as she considered backing away from her last comment. However, she realized the truth was necessary if this conversation was going to help them.

"Yes."

"What did you see?" he asked, leaning closer.

God, I hope I don't regret this, she thought, taking a deep breath to prepare for his response.

"I saw Adeline. I-I *see* Adeline."

"Right now?"

"Yes. She's behind you, under those trees."

Wade closed his eyes, then turned toward the trees. Adeline stood in the shadows, gold-ringed eyes glowing like fog lamps. Nothing in his expression indicated he could see her.

"I can't see her," he said with heavy disappointment.

"I know. I don't know why I'm the only one who can see her. Abigail can't see her either." She placed a consolatory hand on his shoulder, and he shrugged it away.

"I'll never see her again," he said. Constance felt his heart break across the air between them. "Does she speak to you?" he asked.

"Not yet, but I'm not sure how this works. Maybe she can. I don't know."

Wade scanned the trees with more intensity. Disappointment pulled his face tight.

"Adeline, baby. If you can hear me, know that I love you ..." he trailed off, his last words shaky and riddled with emotional instability. He dropped his head. "I'll never stop loving you. I'm nothing without you."

Constance almost lost it. Watching a father's heart break for his dead daughter was too much to bear, but Adeline's deadpan face and glowing eyes helped suppress her tears. Constance saw Wade's grief as a mirror reflection of her anguish for her dead mother.

Adeline raised one hand to her heart.

"She said that she loves you, too," Constance said softly.

She gave him another minute of silence to process his emotions. When he was ready to speak, he turned to Constance.

"You've got to get out of that house. Sell it. Do whatever you have to do, just don't stay. It's dangerous."

"We aren't leaving. That house meant so much to Mama. Our family, our girls, are there. What if they're trapped? I need to help them."

Wade's eyebrows drew together as his voice deepened. "That house is powerful. You read the letter. You know it trapped me. Lydia was still alive when the house acted against me. I wondered for a while if perhaps Adeline used the house to trap me so she could get Lydia back. But that's crazy."

Constance heard doubt in that last sentence. She wasn't sure he'd convinced himself that Adeline hadn't used the house to reunite with Lydia.

"I wish I knew. What I *do* know is that I feel Lydia in the house. And I fear that she's communicating with Abigail more than I see or hear. I can't let anything happen to her. What should I do? I'm not giving up the house and I'm not letting something happen to my sister."

Wade stared at Constance for what felt like an eternity. Finally, he spoke.

"Take me to the house."

CHAPTER TWENTY SEVEN

"Are you going to tell me what's going on?" Eli asked, low enough to keep his words from reaching Abigail and Sailor, who chatted happily in the backseat.

"You wouldn't believe me if I did," Constance said.

Part of the issue with their situation was how unbelievable it was. She didn't think anyone would understand what she and Abigail were experiencing without seeing the visions for themselves. Wade was the only other person she knew who had experienced the hauntings in the house.

"Try me," he said in defiance. "You have so much going on. Maybe talking with me about some of it would help."

She pulled her eyes from the windshield for a second to make eye contact with him. "Trust me, okay. Talking won't stop the visions and nightmares I'm having."

She'd been truthful but withheld details which could cause him more concern for her. She also didn't want to scare him away by making him think she was crazy.

"I can't imagine what you're going through. Just promise me you'll talk to someone if things become too much to handle." He reached across the bench seat and placed his hand on hers.

She nodded. "I promise."

They dropped Eli off first, then Sailor. The mood in the Fury changed once the girls were alone. Constance started the conversation as their wheels gained speed beneath them.

"I need you to be very honest with me, okay?"

"Okay," Abigail said.

"Are you good with being in the house tonight?"

"Yes. I'm fine with being home. Is Uncle Wade coming over?"

"He is. You don't know this yet but, he experienced things in the house before he left. Kind of like we do, but different."

"I know," Abigail said.

"You do?" Constance didn't tell her about the letter. How could she know anything about Wade's experiences?

"Aunt Lydia told me they used to talk every night before we got there. She also told me she protected him the night she died. She didn't tell me how, but I'm pretty sure that's what she said."

Protected him? That's not what it sounded like to me. It sounded like she trapped him against his will so he couldn't stop her from reuniting with Adeline.

Constance played it cool. "Why didn't you share that with me before?"

Abigail shrugged. "I don't know. I guess I forgot."

"Well, is there anything else you've forgotten to tell me?"

"She misses him."

A shiver surged through Constance. There was an ominous aftertaste trailing that innocent statement.

Constance followed the dips and bends in the last mile of their drive. She kept a sharp eye for deer as they cut through the pitch-black night, the woods stretching out along both sides of the road. She eased the gas and let the Fury coast to their driveway. The house came into view among the trees. Light from an upstairs window shone into the darkness like a lighthouse safely guiding her sailors home.

Lighthouses also warned sailors of hazards, she thought. *How did Uncle Wade access the house? He shouldn't have a key anymore.*

Constance swallowed hard when she saw Uncle Wade's truck idling in the driveway beside the house, its brake lights casting angular light against the stark white siding of the home's exterior.

He's not in the house. Did he go in and come back out?

Constance parked the Fury beside Wade's truck. Uncle Wade killed the truck's engine and lights as the girls climbed out of the car.

She couldn't hide her concern when she made eye contact with him over the car's trunk.

"Are you sure you're comfortable with me being here?" he asked her.

"Yes. I'm just curious who turned that upstairs light on while we were gone. Do you have a key?"

He looked up at the house, then back at Constance. "No. You didn't leave that light on?"

"I don't think so," she said. "We may have left it on and didn't realize it. I'm sure it's no big deal. Come on."

"Maybe I should go in first. Just in case," he said.

"In case of what?"

"I don't know. In case someone broke in?" he said as the trio traversed the front walkway to the porch. Constance tested the doorknob–still locked. She put her key in the door and the light illuminating the yard from the upstairs died, casting the front yard into impenetrable darkness. They exchanged an incredulous look.

"Let me check the back door before we go in. Just to be safe," Uncle Wade said. Constance nodded in agreement.

She watched him inspect the windows around the house as he made his way across the front and side yards to the back porch. A few minutes later, he materialized from the dark like an apparition.

"The back door and windows are fine," he said, rejoining them on the front porch.

Abigail shrugged her shoulders, and they turned their attention to the door.

Constance turned the key, then the knob. She pushed the door into the shadowed foyer, leading Wade and Abigail into the house. Still shadows and cold air filled the house.

"Wow, it's pretty chilly in here," Wade remarked. "Did you turn the heat down before you left?"

"No, it should be good." Constance flipped the hall light switch and walked to the thermostat. "It's set at sixty-eight degrees, but the temperature in the house is reading sixty-four degrees."

"Something must be up with the heater or this thermo-stat because it shouldn't be this cold in here," Wade said from over her shoulder. "I'll look at the furnace for you. Let me take a quick look around upstairs first. Just to be safe."

"Thanks. That would be great."

Constance appreciated his willingness to help. The situation with the light upstairs made her uneasy. If someone had broken in, she'd prefer he handle it. However, she knew he'd find the upstairs empty and she suspected he knew the same. Also, she knew nothing about home-heating systems.

"What should I do?" Abigail asked. "Should I lead the way so I can beat up whoever we find?"

Constance smiled and lightly shoved Abigail. "Calm down, tough guy. Why don't you hang out with me downstairs for a few minutes? We can go upstairs and get ready for bed once Uncle Wade comes back."

The girls made a quick round of the downstairs. By the time they were done, Uncle Wade had checked the upstairs.

"Come on up, girls."

They trudged up the stairs, their exhausted legs protesting every step. Abigail went to her room to change into pajamas and Constance continued to the primary bedroom. From the dark hall, she saw Wade's silhouette in the open doorway, his shoulders sunken, his head moving as he scanned his former bedroom.

"Everything's just as you left it," she said, stepping into the room.

"I see that. It feels smaller than I remember. It's funny how time distorts our memories of places."

She saw sorrow in his eyes, despite the tight-lipped smile on his face. He spoke before she could pry.

"I checked the other rooms first. There were no signs of anyone prowling around."

"Same downstairs. Everything was in order," she said. "I appreciate you sticking around." She paused before continuing. "You asked to come over before we left the festival. Did you see what you wanted to see?"

He dropped his eyes to the floor and the smile from his face. "I suppose not. I guess I got my hopes up when you said you'd seen Adeline there. I thought she may finally be here."

He looked away, hiding his face from her.

"I'm sorry, Uncle Wade."

He sighed. "It's okay. I'm just a victim of wishful thinking, that's all."

The defeat she heard in his voice increased her own sense of exhaustion and defeat. Her dreams and visions were a product of her hyperactive imagination spurred on by severe trauma. They weren't actual events with actual spirits. She was just too damaged to know the difference and you couldn't trust the judgment of damaged minds like hers.

He turned to her. "I need to come clean about something. I lied to you at the festival. Lydia still haunts me every night." The desperation deepened in his wet eyes. "She talks to me every night. I never see her, but I hear her *every night*. I thought leaving here would end her visits, or whatever they are, but it didn't."

Tears collected in his eyes, his bottom lip quivering with emotion.

"That's terrible. I'm so sorry," she said. The tension in her chest wound a little tighter as he continued.

"Despite her visits, I'm glad I left. I had to go. I couldn't take the sounds in that hall at night anymore." He pointed one limp hand at the bedroom doorway beside them. "*Every night*, I lived through the worst night of my life again. The sound of her drowning in that tub–I had to go."

Pieces of the puzzle collided in Constance's mind. The wet footprints, the thrashing sounds in the tub, it was all consistent with what he'd experienced.

"You heard noise in the hall bathroom every night?"

He nodded.

"And you never saw anything?"

"Well–I saw light. And wet footprints in the hall."

Constance closed her eyes for a moment, steadying her spinning mind. She opened her eyes and drew a deep breath. "I've seen the footprints."

In the hall beyond the door, the sound of small feet on hardwood planks raced toward them.

Constance flinched at the sight of Abigail emerging from the darkness.

"My God," Constance said, placing one hand over her racing heart. Uncle Wade crossed the room to the window and wiped tears from his face out of sight of Abigail.

"Are you guys ready to go downstairs? I don't want to go alone. I'm a big scaredy cat."

"I need to check the furnace," Uncle Wade said. He crossed the room in a hurry and turned his body to squeeze between them on his way through the doorway. Constance watched him disappear down the hall.

"It's hard for him to be back here, huh?" Abigail asked.

"Yeah, he'll be okay, though. Come on, let's give him a hand."

Constance turned the bedroom light off and felt the room's dark presence bloom behind her. She couldn't get into the unlit hall fast enough. She stayed close to Abigail as they moved down the hallway to the stairs. Looking over her shoulder, Constance started down the staircase. She swore she saw the bedroom door closing in the depth of the black hall, but her rational mind refused to believe it.

"Well, I found the problem. Your furnace pump isn't kicking on."

"Can you fix it?" Abigail asked from beside Constance.

"Not until tomorrow when I can make a trip into town."

Constance pressed her temple into the door frame in frustration. "I thought we'd make it through at least a week before the curse of homeownership bit."

Uncle Wade chuckled. "That would be a record, my dear. Looks like we're starting a fire. I'll pull some logs off the stack of firewood in the backyard." He stood, favoring one leg as he grunted.

The girls helped him stack logs outside the back porch under the starry night sky. Constance carried an armful of logs into the house and filled the basket beside the fireplace. Uncle Wade kneeled on the hearth and opened the flu damper. Constance felt cold air pour from the fireplace onto the floor around her feet. A few minutes later, Uncle

Wade stacked two more logs on the small fire he'd started with assorted kindling.

Constance stood a foot away from the fireplace, eagerly awaiting the warmth from the growing fire. She struggled to keep her eyes open as she watched the dancing flames.

Uncle Wade brushed his hands into the fireplace and smiled at his work.

Abigail tugged at Constance's sleeve and leaned into her ear. "Is it okay if he stays the night? I would feel better if he stayed while we used the fireplace. That and the whole thing with the upstairs lights earlier."

Constance nodded. "He can stay on the couch. It'll be like a sleepover."

Abigail's face lit up with excitement. She turned to Uncle Wade.

"Yes! Uncle Wade, would you like to have a sleepover with us? You can sleep on the couch. Constance said it's okay."

"I would enjoy that," he said. "I prefer to not leave you girls alone with a lit fire. No offense, Constance. I know you've got this under control, but I can't help my dad tendencies."

"No offense taken. I appreciate the help. As tired as I am, I'm not sure I could manage a fire during the night."

She was relieved to have him stay with them, but she also felt nervous. What if Wade's previous experiences in the house came back to haunt *them*?

Constance looked at the portrait of Lydia and Adeline sitting above the fireplace. Anxiety buzzed in her head and chest like a nest of hornets. She saw the image of Adeline at the Fall Festival in her mind, her dead eyes and slack face contrasting with the youthful beauty in the portrait. The memory of Adeline's extended dead hand pointing at Wade played in her mind.

CHAPTER TWENTY EIGHT

Constance woke in the middle of the night to heart-stopping screams in the hall. Sitting straight up in bed, she pulled in a panicked, desperate breath, trying to figure out what was happening. She struggled to see in the complete darkness of her room.

What was that! What time is it?

"No! Nooo!"

Amidst the screaming, Constance heard wet bodies crash to the floor in the hall bath. The sound of moist flesh colliding with porcelain tiles rang down the hall.

I'm dreaming. I must be dreaming.

Constance jumped blindly out of bed, stumbled across her room into the hall, and struggled to make sense of her surroundings.

The cries in the bathroom morphed into helpless sobs. Constance heard what she thought was the sound of a fist pounding on the floor. She felt the reverberations in her feet as she neared the end of the hall.

Light streamed from Abigail's open bedroom door.

Oh, God, oh, God, oh, God.

But that's not Abigail's voice.

She tried to stop her momentum and slid on wet floorboards as she rounded the corner to the bathroom. Constance barely caught herself and prevented falling down the stairs. To her left, Abigail's bedroom door stood open, her light on and bedding spilled onto the floor. To her right, the closed bathroom door withheld the horrific screaming.

Where's Uncle Wade? There's no way he's sleeping through that screaming.

"Constance!" his voice boomed from the sitting room downstairs. His feet pounded across the floors as he ran toward her.

She didn't have time to wait. She threw the door open.

No light. All dark.

A body writhed on the floor, indistinguishable in the utter darkness. Constance reached for the light switch, hesitated, then pressed it upward, preparing her eyes for the blinding transition.

Time morphed as light chased the dark from the room in slow motion. In the split second of transition from utter darkness to full illumination, she saw *everything*.

Lydia sat against the wall, her face racked with shock and terror, her legs in a crisscrossed, tangled mess. She'd soaked her nightclothes through. Her bloodshot eyes pierced Constance's mind like twin blades.

Lydia cradled Abigail in her arms. Water poured from Abigail's mouth down her cheeks in steady streams. Her eyes were empty spheres, glassy and void of life.

Constance opened her mouth to scream. Lydia's mouth opened in unison with hers. Their voices collided in the space between them.

Abigail's eyes opened wide, and a column of water shot from her mouth, chased by a violent torrent of screams.

As the light peaked, the darkness pressed from the room. Lydia's body turned to liquid and crashed to the floor in a surge of water, leaving Abigail floundering unsupported on the bathroom floor.

Constance dove on her. Behind her, she heard Uncle Wade tumble down the stairs in a raucous, thundering crash.

She pulled Abigail into her arms in a frenzied, grabbing motion. Her eyes jumped from Abigail's eyes to her mouth, to her chest, and back to her eyes.

"Breathe, Abigail, please. My God, how did this happen?"

Abigail's eyes looked alive, so incredibly *aware*.

"I saw her. I saw her for real! She was beautiful, Constance," she stuttered.

"Don't talk, Abi. She tried to kill you."

"No, she saved me. Mama saved me."

"What? That was not Mama, Abi. That was Aunt Lydia. I saw her, then she was gone. But it was her, not Mama."

Abigail's face twisted in confusion. "No, it was Mama. I woke up and followed her out of my room. Then I was under water in the tub and she pulled me out. She *saved* me," she said with undeniable conviction.

"Okay, okay. I believe you. Let's get you out of here."

Constance stood and tried to lift Abigail but failed. The girl was too heavy.

"Uncle Wade! I need help!" Constance hollered through the open door.

"I fell down the stairs! I think I broke my ankle!" Uncle Wade yelled to them.

Constance turned back to Abigail in time to see her pulling herself up on the edge of the tub. She grabbed Abigail under the arms and pulled her to her feet. The girls swayed in opposing directions as they steadied themselves.

"Abi, this is real. Until now, I thought they were just visions and dreams, but this is *real*. We need to get out of here. You almost died."

Abigail looked away. Constance thought she looked conflicted about leaving. The girls began shivering as their adrenaline dropped.

"Can you walk? We need to get you warm and dry. I'm cold, you must be freezing."

"Yes, I'm okay to walk. I'll grab some dry clothes from my room."

"No, you sit down. I'll get your clothes and we can go downstairs, help Uncle Wade, and warm up in front of the fire."

Abigail shivered and nodded as she left the bathroom and clumsily sat in the hall. Constance grabbed a dry towel from the linen closet. She helped Abigail shed her wet pajamas and wrapped her in the oversized towel.

She ran into Abigail's room and fished a dry set of pajamas from the top dresser drawer. Back in the hall, she helped Abigail stand and slip on her new pajamas. Arms interlocked, they walked to the stairs and saw Uncle Wade braced against the wall below.

"Are you girls okay? Watch your step. There's water all over the stairs." His lips and chin trembled.

"We're fine. You don't look so good," she said as they navigated the drier points on the stairs.

"I woke up and heard"—he paused and looked around—"someone was screaming, so I ran to you. I didn't see the water. I slipped and my ankle folded under me. There was a loud snap and the next thing I knew I was falling down the stairs on my back."

They reached him without incident, Abigail taking hold of the banister to relieve Constance of her load. Constance turned her attention to helping Wade. "Let me help you up."

They locked hands, and she grunted as she pulled him up. He grimaced and groaned as he came to his good left foot. He looked as white as a bedsheet. Wade's eyes met hers and spoke a thousand volumes. He'd recognized that scream, and it frightened him more than he'd shared.

"I know it was her," Constance said. "It was Lydia. I saw her."

Wade exhaled and nodded his head. "I'll never forget that scream. That was the night Adeline ..." he looked away, swallowing hard.

"I understand. Let's talk in the sitting room. We need to get her somewhere warm, and I can take a good look at your ankle," Constance said, relieving him of his obligation to continue. She draped his arm over her shoulder and helped him down the hall.

Abigail walked ahead of them, weaving on her feet like a drunkard as she coughed up remnants of tub water lingering in her lungs.

"Help her. I'm okay," Uncle Wade said.

"I don't need help," Abigail insisted, stumbling into the wall leading to the foyer.

Constance reached out with her one free hand and steadied Abigail by the shoulder. She felt overextended. She wanted to help them both but couldn't. Her frustration mounted.

"Really, it's okay. Just help her," Uncle Wade said, lifting his arm from her shoulder and finding the wall to support his weight with his hand as he limped. Constance went to Abigail.

"Give me your arm," she said.

Abigail pulled her arm away from Constance. "I'm fine. I don't need your help." She stumbled again, her eyes spinning wildly in her head.

"You'll hurt yourself if you fall. Let me help you."

"Leave me alone!" Abigail snapped.

Constance froze, stunned by her sister's unjustified aggression. Abigail stumbled into the sitting room, perilously careening toward the open fireplace. She reared up halfway into the room, like a puppet pulled by its strings. Then her body relaxed, and she collapsed to the floor, landing hard on her bottom. Constance stood in the sitting room doorway, Uncle Wade posted up beside her against the framed opening. They exchanged concerned glances.

Abigail collapsed backward, her head landing hard on the wood floor. She arched her back, her face red in the fire's light. Abigail strained her head toward Constance, the veins standing out in her neck. Constance nearly screamed as she watched Abigail's eyes cloud over with black liquid. Deep in the onyx orbs, small flames rose, mirroring the growing flames in the fireplace.

"What the ..." Uncle Wade's jaw dropped.

He sees her eyes. It's not just me this time.

Constance ran to her sister.

Abigail writhed on the floor, her muscles taut as her limbs contorted. Constance dropped to her side, grabbing Abigail by the arms.

"Abi, wake up!" Constance didn't know how to break through to her. Abigail coughed and gasped. She tried to sit up and fell backward. "What do we do?" Constance pleaded with him.

Uncle Wade limped to them. "Get her to the couch. She's going to hurt herself on the floor."

He lifted Abigail by one arm like a doll. Constance grabbed an arm and leg and helped him drag her to the couch. Stepping back, her mind spun as Wade tried to situate Abigail.

"What do we do?"

"We need to get her out of here," he said.

"I think she's in her. I think Lydia's *inside* Abigail."

"That's crazy, Constance." He looked at her with wild eyes. "Right?"

"I know, but what else could it be?" She walked in a frustrated circle. "You weren't there in the bathroom. I saw her holding Abigail and then she just turned into water and now she's inside her."

Abigail tried to sit up and Uncle Wade gently resisted, keeping her on the couch.

"What the hell is wrong with her eyes?" he asked.

"It's not her!" Constance yelled.

"I'm sorry! I don't know what's happening," he said.

Constance forced her way onto the couch beside Abigail. Seated nearly on top of her, she leaned into Abigail's face. "Open your eyes, Abi. Look at me."

Abigail opened her solid black eyes. One ashen gray tear trailed down her wet cheek. Constance gripped Abigail's wrists and spoke into her face.

"You need to leave us alone, Lydia. Get out of my sister. Adeline isn't here. She's moved on. We're here and we're moving on as well."

Abigail's hands shot up with unnatural speed, grabbing Constance firmly by the head. Uncle Wade tried to reach into the tangle of arms to separate them, but Constance refused him.

"Don't! Let us talk."

Abigail leaned forward, planting her face alongside Constance's left cheek. She spoke in a low, raspy voice.

"I'm not going anywhere without my daughter. I've unlocked your mind. You can't hide from this. Step aside. This is your final warning."

Abigail's wretched breath turned Constance's gut sour. It smelled like decomposing flesh. Constance squeezed her eyes tight and willed her stomach's contents to stay down. Behind her closed eyes, she sensed Abigail's hands sinking into her skull, her fingers probing the coiled channels of her brain.

They slipped into the violent dark together.

Constance opened her eyes to the passenger seat of her mother's burning car. Outside, an impenetrable wall of dense smoke reflected the orange flames consuming the vehicle and filled the cab with noxious fumes.

She recalled the details of her last dream about the car. Lydia had taken Abigail and Adeline and they'd burst into flames.

Not this time, Lydia.

She looked at the empty driver's seat.

Where is Mama?

She whipped her head to the right and came face to face with Delilah. Constance screamed in surprise. Her mother pressed her face and hands to the passenger window. Her desperate, heavy eyes implored Constance to move.

Delilah pleaded through the glass pane, "Go after them, Constance. It's not too late. Run!"

An unseen force yanked Delilah backward into the billowing smoke. Her fingernails screeched across the window as she flew into the veiled wasteland beyond the car.

Gone.

Constance yanked the door handle as hard as she could and sprang from the fiery car. This time it worked. She ran into the featureless expanse.

"Mama! Lydia! Abigail! Show yourself!"

She sprinted further into the toxic cloud.

"Lyd—!"

The word ripped from her throat as she suddenly plummeted into a gaping hole in the earth. She pitched violently forward, out of the smoke, and into darkness.

Falling.

Her arms flailed in the cold, damp emptiness. The smell of freshly turned earth overwhelmed her.

A shape emerged from the dark. An open casket. Fear flooded her defenseless body.

"Mama!" she braced for impact as she crashed into the waiting coffin. The collision blasted the wind from her lungs and shocked every nerve in her body. Her vision spun as she wheezed through lax lips. The metallic taste of blood coated her tongue and throat.

She's killing me.

Delilah's voice came to her in a whisper. "Fight."

Constance cried in frustration, rolling onto her back in the tight box. The coffin's lid sat open above her. The walls of a newly dug grave rose around her.

I've got to get out of here.

She reached one hand up toward the twinkling stars beyond the grave. She drew her first full breath since the fall. Cold air flooded her lungs and flexed her broken rib cage. Pain bloomed across her body as her arm fell back to her chest.

A face peered into the grave from above.

"Mama."

Delilah's mouth moved light years away. Her voice flooded Constance's ears.

"True love is deeper than any grave. I'll see you on the other side, baby."

Constance lost all hope. A deep fissure tore through her spirit, severing her faith from her will.

Her head rocked side to side in the moonlight. One final anguished cry left her.

"Mama, please!"

Lydia emerged beside Delilah. She shoved Delilah into the open grave. Constance watched her mother descend toward her as Lydia raised one hand and the casket lid slammed shut.

Total darkness.

Delilah's body crashed into the closed lid above her. The sound of soil falling onto them from above began.

She's burying us together.

Constance flopped to her side in the claustrophobic confines of the closed coffin. She searched in the utter darkness. Her fingers landed on a gloved hand in the dark. Her knees struck legs beside her.

Two golden rings appeared in the dark.

No. No. No.

The golden rings intensified, filling the tight casket with low, warm light.

Adeline lay beside her, eyes aglow. She clutched a dead starling in one arm like a stuffed animal. Her lips parted and the scent of formaldehyde seeped into the confined space.

Shovel loads of dirt continued to rain down on the casket as Constance struck the lid in a panic. She kept her eyes locked with Adeline's radiant eyes while she fought to escape.

Adeline spoke. "My mother will never stop looking for me. She sees me in Abigail. You are an interference."

"She doesn't know that you've moved on, Adeline. She doesn't know that she's searching for someone who isn't here." Constance hammered the lid. "I'll never stop fighting for my sister."

"You can't escape. Accept your death." Adeline's voice faltered.

"I know it's you in there, Aunt Lydia. My cousin was a sweet girl, not some puppet with glowing eyes."

She struck the lid with her full strength.

"And I'll fight for my sister as long as I live."

"Very well then." Adeline stretched her mouth wide, and water flowed from her open maw in a stream. Foil smelling water poured into the seams between the lid and base.

Constance's panic short-circuited her thinking. She punched and scraped and pressed the lid with all her might.

Beside her, Adeline's skin turned into black liquid and ran from her body as it contacted the rising water. The glowing gold rings in her eyes extinguished as they melted and ran into the water.

Constance had mere seconds to breathe before the water reached the top of the space and Adeline completely dissolved into the rotten emulsion.

She pressed her face to the lid's surface and drew her last breath. In an ultimate act of defiance, she proclaimed, "I'll fight for her for as long as I live!"

Total immersion.

Constance tipped into complete hysteria. She fought hard, but eventually, her mouth opened, and she inhaled the liquid death. Her lungs burned like wildfire as she accepted her inevitable end.

The world rolled on its side.

Constance and the coffin's liquid load spilled to the sitting room floor. Water poured from her nose and mouth while she collapsed on her side in an exhausted, soaked heap.

I'm alive. Jesus, I can't believe I'm alive.

She lifted her head to the cold, lightless room. Her mother's casket sat under the front window as it had during her viewing. However, now it sat askew and rolled to its side with black water running from its lower edges. The very casket which had ferried her mother to eternal rest beneath the cemetery had birthed her to the sitting room.

Behind her, before the frigid, empty fireplace hearth, sat Lydia and Abigail. They posed for their portrait while Constance returned to life on the chilled wooden floor.

"Where is Adeline? My sister doesn't belong here, Lydia," she said.

Constance planted her hands on the floor, pressed her body weight up, and paused on her hands and knees. She lifted her head. "You hear me, Lydia? I know none of this is real. It's just in my head. I'll never let you take her."

Lydia looked down at Constance with intense eyes. Abigail sat frozen and immovable. She resembled a wax figure in an oddities museum.

"This is your last warning. Get out of my way or you will burn," Lydia said sternly.

Anger surged through Constance's shattered body. She screamed so loud her vocal cords threatened to fail. "I'll fight for her for as long as I live!"

A rumble from deep in the walls shook the room. Constance braced herself as a torrent of starlings burst from the fireplace in a thundering symphony of beating wings. They whipped past Lydia and Abigail and overwhelmed the room in a flash. Constance howled and collapsed onto her side under the descending sea of starlings.

Constance's screams fell away as Uncle Wade pried the girls apart. Abigail collapsed back onto the couch. Her eyelids fluttered as Constance rose to her feet on shaky legs.

"What was that? What were you doing?" Uncle Wade asked in a stupor.

She steadied herself, drew a deep breath, and turned to him. "She'll haunt me until she takes my sister. I won't let it happen. This ends now."

Constance ran to the portrait above the fireplace mantle where Lydia and Adeline sat tall and pretty for their picture. Anger overwhelmed her, and she ripped the portrait from the wall. She screamed into Lydia's face.

"You've ruined everything! Everything! Why are you doing this to us? She's not your daughter!" Constance threw the portrait to the hard floor, knocking the frame ajar.

"She's my sister!"

Constance stomped on the portrait, then picked it up again in a fit of rage.

Wade jumped from the couch. "Give it to me, Constance!"

She could see the pain and anger rising in him.

"Give me the portrait."

"She's tormented me since the day my mom died. She's ruining my life. I can't take it anymore!" Constance pounded her fist against her head with every word spat through gritted teeth.

Wade lunged for the portrait, but she dodged him as he planted his bad foot and sprawled across the floor. Abigail screamed on the couch, sitting straight up, her arms bent backward at unnatural angles. She rolled off the couch and collided with the coffee table, an ashtray and several coasters spilling onto the floor.

Abigail came to her hands and knees, her face shaking and twisting with pain.

"Leave her alone!" Constance screamed.

She turned and threw the portrait into the dying fire. Flames erupted from the fireplace. Constance went rigid and tipped straight back like a high diver. She crashed into the floor, her arms pinned to her sides and her knees locked straight like a soldier standing at attention. The impact of the fall disoriented her. The ceiling spun above her, and she heard Uncle Wade screaming somewhere in the room. A heat wave washed over her.

A massive weight settled on her chest. She lifted her head and lost any remaining shred of sanity.

Lydia stood above her, one foot planted on Constance's chest and the other on her legs. Flames rolled across every inch of Lydia's sleeveless dress. Her eyes blazed hotter than any fire, her porcelain skin reflecting the light of the hungry flames. She extended one hand and pointed into Constance's face.

"Don't you dare get between me and my daughter."

CHAPTER TWENTY NINE

Uncle Wade stopped screaming and crawled across the floor toward them. Lydia raised her extended arm and balled her hand into a fist in his direction. Constance looked up and across the floor as Uncle Wade collapsed to the floor under his deceased wife's power.

Abigail. She's completely exposed.

Constance felt another thread of sanity break in her mind. She was helpless to defend her sister or herself.

"Lydia, listen to me. She's not your daughter! She's my sister!"

Lydia's eyes narrowed and her knees bent as she pressed her weight into Constance.

Constance felt a rib give way in her chest, snapping like a twig as Lydia's weight dramatically increased. Her mouth opened in excruciating pain, the air pressed from her collapsing lungs.

Abigail screamed from across the room. "Mama, please! Save her!"

Constance twisted her head toward Abigail's voice. She couldn't believe her eyes. Her mother draped herself over Abigail, protecting her from Lydia's flames.

"Protect ... her." Constance breathed the words. Tears streamed down Delilah's face. Constance saw the heartbreak in her mother's eyes. She'd chosen to protect Abigail at the expense of her firstborn child.

Lydia snapped her fingers and Constance's head snapped forward. Lydia looked toward Delilah and said, "Give me my daughter or she dies." Flames rose from her Lydia's open hand.

Abigail screamed, "Do something!"

Delilah spoke, "I cannot give you my living child. It's not her time. They live. We died. Follow me beyond the home. I'll help you find Adeline."

Abigail protested, "She's already here! I've seen her."

Lydia insisted, "Give her to me now!"

Constance mustered her strength and spoke, "Your daughter is dead."

Lydia shook, vibrations radiating down through her legs into Constance's body. She closed her eyes, lifted her arm, and tipped her hand. Liquid fire poured from her hand to Constance's paralyzed body below.

Constance burst into flames, the ultimate agents of give and take.

Pain spread across her exposed arms, neck, and face. The flames chased down the inside of her legs to her bare feet. Her toes burned like lit candles. Every nerve in her body came alive under the heat of the expanding fire. She cried out as the growing blaze consumed her.

She'd reached the pinnacle of ultimate sacrifice through extreme suffering. The flames ignited her fears and doubts, consumed her strengths, devoured her past, and turned her future to ash before its birth.

As her sister's screams reached her crackling ears, Constance learned what it meant to truly serve and sacrifice for another human——at all costs. The flames took everything. They turned her potential to ash. She'd never experience motherhood. She'd never know a lover. She'd never run against the wind again. She'd never leave this hell. The flames took all.

Abigail's voice cut through the blaze.

"Adeline! Please!"

Constance felt something pass through her, numbing her pain and stilling her heart. Adeline rose from Constance's burning body in a slow ascension. She took her fire on, sharing in Constance's pain and anguish as she entered their world once again.

Lydia shuddered at the sight of her daughter emerging in flames. She cried out, "No, no, no!"

Constance thought she saw instant and jarring awareness in Lydia's eyes. Had she recognized what she'd done and what she'd taken from Constance? Her anger now infected the one person she loved the most–her sweet child burned as well.

Lydia muttered, "I'm so sorry."

Delilah wailed, "Save them, Lydia!"

As Adeline reached her full height, Lydia dove into her, embracing her daughter as they fell toward Constance's burning body. As mother and daughter collapsed downward, they burst into a cloud of expanding ash, extinguishing Constance's flames.

She lost consciousness to the sound of Abigail and Wade sobbing in the dark.

CHAPTER THIRTY

"Lift in three, two, one, lift!"

Constance felt a sudden rise, then jostled back and forth in darkness. She forced her eyes open to obscure, foggy vision. She passed through waves of light but couldn't make out her surroundings.

"Her airway appears clear, but ready the oxygen. I want frequent inspections of her airway for swelling and obstruction during the transit. I'll look for an unburned area to start an IV. We're going straight to Richmond. Let's go!"

Is this an ambulance?

"Want me to remove her burned clothes first?" a female voice asked.

"Yes, but only if it doesn't compromise the skin. If it's stuck, leave it. They'll get it at the hospital."

They must have begun their trip because she felt the sensation of rolling wheels over pitching blacktop. She felt every contour of the road beneath them. Her pain defied understanding, pulling her out of her body and into a realm of indescribable agony. Nausea and overwhelming disorientation washed over her, pulling her far below the light again.

Constance woke to the sound of Abigail's voice.

"Hey, can you hear me? I think she's coming out of it!" Abigail exclaimed.

Aunt Jenny's voice reached her. "Oh, thank God. Connie, baby. Can you hear us? We're here for you."

Constance opened her eyes. Her head swam as her eyes adjusted to the light. She tried to move her arms and legs but couldn't. Fresh pain shot from her limbs, forcing a groan from her sore throat.

"Try not to move. You're all wrapped up in a hospital bed," Abigail said, trying to help.

Constance felt cold although she couldn't sense air on her skin. She looked down the length of her body, searching for familiar forms but finding only layers of blankets. She couldn't move her arms to inspect her body beneath the covers. Panic welled up within her.

"Constance, you're in the University Hospital burn ward. I need you to stay still, okay? I know this is scary, but you're safe."

That must be a nurse.

Hunger built in her gut. She felt like she hadn't eaten in days. She tried to move her mouth, but bandages restricted her jaw. Her tongue sat in her mouth like a dry slug of sandstone. Her mind skipped, trying to piece together words, to communicate her thirst and hunger.

My God, what is this? Is this me?

For the rest of her awful existence, she'd remember this as the moment her life in hell began.

She broke–again.

Constance wept in pain under a pile of blankets and sterile dressings. Blurred forms of Abigail, Aunt Jenny, and her uncles joined in her tears as they circled her bed.

The family united with her. In a way, they worshiped her sacrifice through their mourning. She carried the mantle of their suffering. She bore their curse. And they all knew it.

She'd been the sacrificial lamb.

Abigail and Aunt Jenny visited her in the hospital every day. Constance couldn't communicate well, but she managed a few words between bouts of coughing.

On the third day of visitation, Abigail finally had a moment alone with Constance. Aunt Jenny had gone to the nurse's station for a private conversation with the attending nurse. Abigail took advantage of her opportunity and pulled a small wooden chair close to Constance's bed.

"I hope you slept well last night. I'm staying with Aunt Jenny and Uncle Hank. They've set up the back bedroom for me.

"We can't wait to get you home. They've got a room for you too. I think you'll like it. You have your own small television and everything.

"Aunt Jenny is talking with the doctors about when they'll send you home. No one seems to know when that'll happen, but they say you're getting closer every day."

Constance had been awake for two hours, but exhaustion settled on her again. She was amazed how much energy thinking consumed after her injury. She tried her best to keep her eyelids open as Abigail continued.

"I had to talk with the police and the fire department. I told them everything that had happened, but they didn't believe me. One detective said I'm either crazy or full of crap. The other cops all agreed that I'm full of crap."

Abigail laughed.

"They gave poor Uncle Wade a hard time. They questioned him more times than Lee Harvey Oswald. They won't tell me what he said, but I wouldn't be surprised if he had to hide some of the truth so they wouldn't lock him up. It's one thing for a kid to tell the truth and sound crazy, but they throw adults in Eastern State for things like this."

Abigail adjusted Constance's top blanket to cover her shoulders.

"I don't think we're going back to the house anytime soon. Uncle Hank has been packing our things and bringing them to their house. He promised to keep all of Mama's things in storage for us."

Aunt Jenny walked into the room, the sound of her heels echoing through the small room.

"Come on, kiddo. Constance needs her rest. We'll come back in the morning and you two can catch up on all the gossip."

"Thank you. Love you," Constance mustered for the first time since coming out of her medically induced coma days before.

Abigail leaned over the bed rail and kissed Constance's wrapped right hand.

Constance lived on a sine wave of horrific nightmares and painful realities. As the days rolled on, it became more difficult to differentiate reality from unreality.

Day and night, she relived the terrors of Lydia standing over her while she burned, unable to move, just like now, losing everything, gaining hell in exchange.

On her last night in the burn ward, she dreamed of her last day as a healthy young woman. She'd cared for her sister, spent the day with a boy she cared for, and tried her best to enjoy time with them in town. None of it ended well. It never would.

In her dream, life passed her by. Eli married a nice girl after leaving for college. Her classmates graduated and started families and careers. The adults in her life aged, losing their freedoms as time pressed them toward an inevitable death. Her aunts and uncles, Mr. Holcomb—everyone—aged and became infirm creatures dependent upon their children to care for them. Roles reversed, time imposed its cruel toll on all.

Through it all, the house remained. In her last dream of the night, Constance stood in the front yard, watching Abigail, now an adult, climb the front steps. Lydia,

Delilah, and Adeline stood on the porch above her, a welcoming committee assembled through generations of pain and dire fate. They parted as Abigail approached, allowing her uninhibited passage to the home. Abigail walked through the front door, her welcoming committee slowly filing into the home behind her as every window in the home came alive with pulsing light.

Through it all, no one heard Constance screaming.

WHAT'S NEXT?

*B*urn the Girls is the first novel in The Haunting of the Whispering House series. The next book, *Bless the Mother,* becomes available in the spring of 2024.

Join Lucas's newsletter for the latest updates, membership benefits, and early access to books before the rest of the world gets them!

https://www.lucasmarinowrites.com/

QUICK FAVOR

Thank you so much for dedicating your time to reading this book! May I ask a quick favor?

Will you please take a moment to leave a review on Amazon, Goodreads, or wherever you purchased the book? Your words have power. Your review can help this book serve more people. I appreciate you!

THOUGHTS AND THANKS

All thanks start with my wife, Tammie. Tammie, you are the most wonderful human in my life. Thank you for enduring daily conversations about these characters and events as this story came together. I love you!

Caleb, Gabriel, and Madelyn – every word I ever write comes from a heart that beats for you. I love you so much. You complete me. Caleb, Constance's motivation, desire, and edge is inspired by your heart and my teenage years. Keep that edge, brother. I love you.

I hope this book honors the memory of Nancy Clements, the inspiration for Nurse Nancy. You're finally home with your babies.

The list of professionals who supported this novel starts with my friend, book coach, and editor, Zach Bohannon.

That makes two books, Zach! My body count remains low thanks to your careful oversight.

Clarrisa Yeo created this amazing book cover. Clarrisa, you knocked it out of the park! Thank you so much for making another book of mine stand out in the best of ways.

Stephanie Ellis, thank you for proofreading the book! It's an honor to have your name listed on this novel.

To my mentor and dear friend, Honorée Corder, thank you for the continued support and guidance. I hope every writer finds a mentor like you and never lets them go. #fulla$$

Finally, I extend my sincere thanks to the early-release serial readers on Vella, Ream, and Substack. I look forward to sharing the next novel with you starting—now!

MUSICAL INSPIRATION

Hey there! I hope you'll check out these artists. Their music moved me during the writing of this novel.

- Christen Lien – Elpis (album)

- Tesseract – War of Being (album)

- Mastodon – Hushed and Grim (album)

- Swallow the Sun – Moonflowers (Deluxe edition album)

- Leprous – The Sky is Red (song)

- Persefone – Metonia (album)

- Persona – All for You (song)

- Tori Amos

- Veil of Maya

- The Fixx

- Tears for Fears

- Make Them Suffer

- Times of Grace

Have you read *Bury the Child*, the suspenseful prequel to The Haunting of the Whispering House series?

Available in paperback, eBook, and audiobook.

About the Author

 Lucas writes thriller, suspense, and horror fiction. If he's not writing, he's reading, playing guitar, or enjoying time with his family. Lucas is also the host of *The Suspense is Killing Me* podcast.

A military engineer by experience, he spent twenty-one years in the United States Coast Guard. He earned his Doctor of Engineering and Master of Science degrees in Engineering Management and Systems Engineering at The George Washington University.

He now lives in a pile of trees in Virginia.